The Year of Chasing Dreams

You'll want to read these inspiring titles by

Lurlene McDaniel

ANGELS IN PINK
Kathleen's Story • Raina's Story • Holly's Story

ONE LAST WISH NOVELS
Mourning Song • A Time to Die • Mother, Help Me Live
Someone Dies, Someone Lives • Sixteen and Dying
Let Him Live • The Legacy: Making Wishes Come True
Please Don't Die • She Died Too Young
All the Days of Her Life • A Season for Goodbye
Reach for Tomorrow

OTHER OMNIBUS EDITIONS
Keep Me in Your Heart: Three Novels
True Love: Three Novels
The End of Forever • Always and Forever
The Angels Trilogy
As Long As We Both Shall Live • Journey of Hope
One Last Wish: Three Novels

OTHER FICTION
The Year of Luminous Love • "Wishes and Dreams" (a Year of Luminous Love
digital original short story) • Red Heart Tattoo • Reaching Through Time
Heart to Heart • Breathless • Hit and Run • Prey
Briana's Gift • Letting Go of Lisa • The Time Capsule
Garden of Angels • A Rose for Melinda • Telling Christina Goodbye
How Do I Love Thee: Three Stories • To Live Again
Angel of Mercy • Angel of Hope
Starry, Starry Night: Three Holiday Stories • The Girl Death Left Behind
Angels Watching Over Me • Lifted Up by Angels
For Better, For Worse, Forever • Until Angels Close My Eyes
Till Death Do Us Part • I'll Be Seeing You • Saving Jessica
Don't Die, My Love • Too Young to Die
Goodbye Doesn't Mean Forever • Somewhere Between Life and Death
Time to Let Go • Now I Lay Me Down to Sleep
When Happily Ever After Ends • Baby Alicia Is Dying

From every ending comes a new beginning. . . .

Lurlene McDaniel

The Year of Chasing Dreams

EMBER

Text copyright © 2014 by Lurlene McDaniel
Cover art copyright © 2014 by Trevillion

Visit us on the Web! randomhouseteens.com

Educators and librarians, for a variety of teaching tools, visit us at RHTeachersLibrarians.com

The Library of Congress has cataloged the hardcover edition of this work as follows:
McDaniel, Lurlene, author.
The year of chasing dreams / by Lurlene McDaniel. — First edition.
pages cm
Summary: In the time since their friend Arie died, new problems have surfaced for Ciana Beauchamp and Eden McLauren of Tennessee—Eden is heading to Australia to rekindle her romance with Garret, Ciana is being pressured to sell her family's land to a developer, and a long buried family secret is threatening to end her relationship with Jon, the man she wants to marry.
ISBN 978-0-385-74173-6 (trade hc) — ISBN 978-0-375-98676-5 (ebook)
1. Man-woman relationships—Juvenile fiction. 2. Best friends—Juvenile fiction. 3. Family secrets—Juvenile fiction. 4. Bildungsromans. 5. Tennessee—Juvenile fiction. 6. Australia—Juvenile fiction. [1. Love—Fiction. 2. Best friends—Fiction. 3. Friendship—Fiction. 4. Secrets—Fiction. 5. Coming of age—Fiction. 6. Tennessee—Fiction. 7. Australia—Fiction.] I. Title.
PZ7.M4784172Yd 2014
813.54—dc23
2013034052

ISBN 978-0-385-74174-3 (tr. pbk.)

Printed in the United States of America

10 9 8 7 6 5 4 3 2 1
First Ember Edition 2015

*This book is dedicated to my friend Tom Chapman,
who lost his battle with cancer. I'll miss you, Tom.*

*"To everything there is a season,
and a time to every purpose under the heaven: . . .
a time to plant, and a time to pluck up that which is planted."*
—ECCLESIASTES 3:1–2 (KING JAMES)

1

Alone horse and rider stood at the top of Bellmeade's long tree-lined driveway. Ciana Beauchamp had noticed the duo as she passed a window inside her house but hadn't paid them much mind. Horseback riders often passed her property on the road fronting her land. Yet this pair had been motionless at the entrance for a while.

She couldn't see them clearly. Gloom from the darkening sky had gathered from the west, promising autumn rain. Plus she'd been in a funk all day. It was October twenty-fourth. It would have been Arie Winslow's twentieth birthday. If she had lived.

Her friend, Eden McLauren, had gone into town, and her mother, Alice Faye, was banging around in the kitchen. The final harvest was completed, and Ciana should have felt peaceful satisfaction, but she didn't. She was sad, on edge, with the horse and rider adding to her tension.

She'd thought about Arie all day, remembering the trip to Italy with Arie and Eden the summer before, remembering the good times, glossing over the hurts. She missed Arie sometimes as much now as she had on the day she fled her earthly life. What she wouldn't give to see her, talk to her one more time.

Through the window, Ciana saw the horse stamp, growing restless. She squinted, trying to see the rider more clearly. Exasperated, she stepped out onto the wraparound veranda of the old Victorian house. The rider urged his mount forward and the horse came up the drive under tight rein, almost as if it knew where it was going. The rider, a man, sat tall in the saddle, and as he drew nearer, she saw that the horse was a buckskin, toffee tan with a black mane and tail. Ciana's heartbeat quickened, and her breath pressed like a weight inside her breast.

At the front steps, the cowboy removed his hat and hung it on the horn of the saddle. He slid off the horse, grabbed a leather bag, and laid it on the top step. Ripe red apples rolled from the pouch, stopping at her feet. "Here's a gift," Jon Mercer said.

Ciana's chin trembled. She was almost overwhelmed by the sight of him and the gesture, but she kept her composure, squared her shoulders, and asked, "Who told you about the apples?"

"Arie. It was one of her favorite stories about your grandparents. She said it was how Charles came to court Olivia. Fresh apples were all he had to offer."

Ciana saw instantly that Arie had shared the story in a final act of kindness, when she had realized the truth about Ciana and Jon. "Arie died in April," Ciana said stoically, feeling old resentments toward Jon rise.

"Abbie let me know. I had asked her to call when . . . after it was over."

2

Ciana felt slighted that Jon had asked Eric's wife and Arie's brother. "She was my best friend. I would have let you know if you'd asked me."

"I know. But I asked her instead. Thought we needed the space." His horse, Caramel, once Arie's horse, wandered to the grassy lawn and began to graze. "How's Eden?"

Ciana needed space, all right. "She lives here now with me and Mom. Some changes around here too. I've taken in horses to board for their owners. I don't have an empty stall for Caramel." She added the last to let him know he couldn't just walk back into her life or her heart without explanations, and certainly not without permission.

"I talked to Bill on my way from Texas. He'll let me crash at his bunkhouse and board Caramel."

Ciana glanced up at the sky and the gathering rain-filled clouds. "Well, you might want to head back before the rains come. They look to be gully-washers."

Jon propped his boot against the bottom porch step. "Not until you tell me if you meant it."

"Meant what?"

"That last kiss you gave me. Did you mean it? Did it matter?"

She blinked, conjuring up the heat from that cold March day when he'd loaded his horse and driven away. "Why now? Suddenly you have to know?"

His jaw muscle tightened. "Yes. I need to know. Why did you kiss me like that when I was walking away and leaving this place? I don't get it."

She felt a ripple of irritation. "And I don't get you. Seven months and not one word from you."

His expression tightened. "I didn't know what to say."

His answer annoyed her further. "How about a phone call

saying, 'Hi. I'm fine. How are you? I miss you.' What's wrong with saying that?"

He swept her face with his green eyes, recited, "'Hi. I'm fine. How are you? I miss you' . . . every minute of every day and night," he added softly.

She purposefully steeled herself from the effect he was having on her. "Why have you come back?"

"Because everything I want in my life is right here."

Just then the screen door opened and Alice Faye stepped out. "Eden's on her way and supper is—" She stared. Her face broke into a smile. "Why, Jon Mercer! You've come back to us!"

"Yes, ma'am."

Alice Faye beamed at him. "A sight for sore eyes, you are. How's your daddy?"

"Settled in at the county facility. Safe."

"Any recovery from his stroke?"

"Not much progress. Doctors say this is the best he'll ever be."

Alice Faye shook her head, perked up, and said, "Stay for supper."

His gaze found Ciana's. "I couldn't—"

"Tie your horse up in the barn before the rain starts." She glanced at Ciana, and the older woman's expression was challenging. "You're invited. I'll go set another place." The door slammed behind her.

"Mother's flexing her muscle," Ciana said, with a note of bitterness. Jon's look was questioning, but she wouldn't elaborate. Why had he intruded into her life now, when she'd almost put him behind her? She had missed him, but she had no idea what lay ahead for her . . . the fate of Bellmeade, perhaps the fight of her life to keep it from financial ruin, a possible

4

permanent riff between herself and her mother about selling the land. And what of the things he'd said he wanted, a spread of his own to breed and train horses? How would they fit into the picture?

"What do we do now?" she asked.

"I don't know. I was hoping we could figure it out together."

On the lawn, Caramel grew restless, sensing the approaching bad weather. "You'd better tend to your horse," Ciana said.

Jon searched her face, nodded brusquely. "This isn't over between us, Ciana."

She wasn't sure if he meant the discussion or the relationship. She folded her arms, the past returning in a flood of painful memories. "Today was Arie's . . . would have been . . . Arie's birthday."

Jon's eyes saddened. "I didn't forget. Is there a statute of limitations on your forgiveness?"

Ciana winced. His question hit her psyche hard and she was ashamed. Her simple words were packed with emotional dynamite, and it was unkind of her to have reminded him of what had almost torn them apart. "Eat with us," she said, offering an olive branch.

He nodded again, turned, and walked to Caramel, then picked up her reins, and led her toward the barn.

"Sorry," Ciana whispered, knowing he couldn't hear her but knowing she needed to say it. She fidgeted, waiting for him to return to the house, watched the rolling clouds, heard the low rumble of distant thunder. The smell of dampness lay heavy in the air, and dead leaves danced in eddies of swirling wind. The day, once bright and calm, had turned darker, cooler. The winds of change were blowing. An omen? Ciana shivered.

A storm was coming. . . .

5

2

"Ciana? This is Pat Winslow. How have you been?"
Ciana's throat tightened with Arie's mother's voice on her cell phone. Swallowing down emotion, she said, "All right, Pat. How about you?"

"Oh . . . you know, some days are better than others."

Since Arie's funeral, Ciana had talked to Patricia twice and run into her once in town. Patricia had looked wan and too thin. "How's Mr. Winslow?" she asked. Swede, Arie's father, was in the cabinetry business in town. "How's he doing?"

"Busy. He's buried in work, but it's seeing him through his worst days."

"That's good," Ciana said, knowing that hard work had helped her through her first few grief-filled months after Arie's death. "What can I do for you?"

"Could you and Eden come by the house this week?"

Ciana's heart squeezed. She hadn't been to Arie's home since the night Arie had said her final goodbye to her and

Eden. The memory was almost too much to bear. "I—we'll come," she said. "Any special time?"

"How about Saturday around one?"

"We'll be there," Ciana promised, confident Eden would drop everything to accompany her. Death could not bury the lifelong friendship among the former threesome. What mattered now was homage to the living.

Pat opened the front door before Ciana took her finger off the doorbell. She smiled, pulling Ciana and Eden into the foyer. "Oh my, you two look beautiful! Eden, country life really agrees with you!" Ciana almost unraveled seeing Pat's eyes tear up. "You were way too skinny. I'm glad to see some meat on your bones."

"All this fresh air and country cooking." Eden thrust out the large basket she held. "From our garden. Plus Alice Faye's fresh-baked bread."

Pat raised the dish towel covering the top and peeked at the contents. "Looks luscious."

"Well, this time of year only the squash is fresh picked, and I canned the beans and tomatoes in the summer," she said proudly. Her eyes darted to Ciana. "With Alice Faye's help, of course. She a pro. I'm a wannabe cook."

It wasn't a secret that Eden had become the helping hands Ciana had never been to her mother. The outdoors suited her, the hard work and farm chores. Ciana didn't begrudge Eden one minute of time she spent with Alice Faye after the neglect Eden had faced from Gwen, her bipolar mother. The added benefit was that it kept Ciana and her mom from fighting about Bellmeade's future.

Pat linked her arms with Ciana's and Eden's. "Come into the living room. Sit. Let me take good long looks at you."

The formal room where Arie had spent her last days had been cleared of the hospital bed and sickroom equipment and returned to its visitors-only status, but Ciana felt Arie's ghostly presence everywhere. She eased onto the sofa beside Eden, and Patricia took the chair across from the coffee table where Arie had sat the night she'd told her friends she was quitting chemo treatments.

Pat asked, "Want some sweet tea?" Both girls declined. "Relax," Pat said with a smile. "I asked you here to tell you good news." Her eyes glowed. "Eric and Abbie are having a baby."

"Awesome!" Eden blurted out.

Ciana whooped. "That's wonderful! When?"

"Next spring. In early May, her doctor says, but babies come when they feel like it. Eric came two weeks early, and Arie was so late, I thought I'd be pregnant until Christmas." Her expression softened as she talked about Arie, then clouded. "Oh, I'm babbling. Forgive me."

"No, no. It's fine. Really," Eden said.

Pat stood abruptly. "Follow me. I'll show you what I'm doing with her old bedroom." She led them down the hall of the ranch-style house, paused at the closed door that had once been Arie's room. When she'd turned twelve, when she'd been told her cancer had returned and that she'd have to go back onto chemo, she'd wanted her whole room painted bright pink to help her feel happy during the expected difficult weeks ahead of her.

"We're changing it into a nursery for the baby." Pat opened the freshly painted white door and led Ciana and Eden into the room. "I could hardly come in here for a long time after . . . well, afterward. But when Eric and Abbie told us about the baby, I knew it was time to make changes. I think Arie would have loved it."

The now empty room under renovation smelled of paint and new lumber. Three walls were the color of rich vanilla ice cream, the fourth wall a sizzling lime green, and Arie's pink carpet was replaced by smooth, dark, wood plank flooring. "We donated all her furniture to charity," Pat said, as if apologizing. "I realized after a time that the room was turning into a shrine and it wasn't right. It wasn't what Arie would have wanted. I've already picked out a crib and a Nana rocking chair." Pat embraced her new status with a smile. "And Swede's built cabinetry to grow with the baby." A bank of white cabinets, bookshelves, and a desk surface lined one wall. "He's building a toy box at his shop."

"The room looks great," Ciana said, relieved that it was true.

"We worked on a lot of class projects in here," Eden said, glancing around fondly. "Any idea if it'll be a boy or girl?"

"Not yet. But the kids will find out on a sonogram visit. Do you want me to tell you when we know?"

"Yes," Ciana and Eden said in unison.

They followed Pat out of the room. "Which brings me to another reason for asking the two of you over." She paused at a small hall table. "Cleaning out Arie's dresser and desk and all her drawers was hard. But I did it."

"We would have helped," Eden offered.

Pat shook her head. "It was a project only I could do. I created a memory box. I figure someday her little niece or nephew might want to know more about Aunt Arie." Pat's gaze drifted to an imagined future, then snapped back to the present. "Anyway, in her bedside table she left letters addressed to each of you. Still sealed," she said, handing each a long white envelope.

Immediately, tears stung Ciana's eyes.

"I'm sorry I didn't do the clean-out project sooner. If I had, you'd have gotten these sooner. Not sure when she wrote the letters, but it's on me that they're arriving so late."

Eden pressed the letter to her breast. "I'm just happy to have mine, and believe me, I'll treasure it."

Ciana nodded, not trusting her voice. She'd read it when she was alone and able to wallow in a good cry.

Eden sat on the bed in Olivia's former bedroom, a room she'd begun to think of as her own, even though it wasn't, even though it never would be. In truth she had no home. She held Arie's letter in her lap, already twice read, and considered what her deceased friend had written.

March, Before I Sleep Forever!

Dearest Eden,

Guilt is a cruel taskmaster, and my guilty feelings are yelling at me. I know what you're thinking . . . "Why do you feel guilty, Arie?" Think about it. If not for me getting sick in Italy, you'd be on a walkabout with Garret, or at the very least somewhere on planet earth with him. Don't shake your head! You know I'm right. That guy's crazy about you. I know because he told me so, and how could I doubt an Aussie with a smile like his?

So now that it's established (Garret wants Eden), I'm betting you're crazy about him too. It might not be LOVE just yet, but it is love waiting to happen. . . . I see the

10

signs. Trust me. After what you went through with Tony, don't shy away from love. Garret is in a whole different category from dirtbag Tony.

But I'm wandering off purpose. With guilt weighing on me and with nothing but time on my hands between drug-naps, plus a computer and the Internet, I decided to try and find Garret for you! I know—MYOB. But I can't. So humor me. Let me tell you what I found.

Except for his magazine articles, he's invisible. No social websites, no links to his name in Australia. Surprising, but I guess the world's full of people with no Internet profile. So, I confess, I haven't found him. (I'll bet your heart sank to your knees when you read that sentence!) BUT don't despair. I have found the next best thing: Colleen Galen, the Irish girl in Garret's group. Who can forget her? Her email address is at the bottom of this letter in red ink, ensuring that you can't miss it. I would have emailed her myself and pretended to be you, but thought I'd best leave it to you to chase your own dreams. So, dear friend, contact her ASAP. You owe it to yourself to find happiness. Never a guarantee when you catch up with it, but always an adventure looking for it. Be happy!

I love you, Eden!

Arie (BFF)

Of course, Arie had called it correctly. She wanted to see Garret, wanted to know what they might have together. She herself had searched for him, but admittedly, less and less, half-heartedly, and for just one reason: Fear of finding him and having her hopes crushed. She'd been so wrong about loving Tony. She didn't want to be wrong again. Garret had been amazing, but now so much time had passed since she'd left Italy and Garret without a word of goodbye. Where was he now? Did he even remember her, ever think of her?

Inertia about what to do won out. Eden folded the letter carefully and tucked it away, left the room without so much as a glance at her laptop computer.

3

Ciana stared out her window watching rainwater gush off the edge of the veranda from a broken gutter. "Farms need rain," she mumbled, without an ounce of gratitude. After two days of nonstop November rain, she was restless, anxious to ride her horse, longing to be outside in fresh air. She could hear her mother and Eden knocking around in the kitchen and knew that soon something delicious would emerge. Big whoop. What was *she* going to do on this cold, wet day?

An answer came in a flash. The attic! She'd been wanting to clean it out for months but had steadily put it off. Why not now? She changed into her grubbiest jeans, gathered up a space heater, an industrial strength extension cord, and a few cleaning supplies. In the days when the house had been built, the attic space was accessible through a door in a back bedroom and up a short flight of stairs. She quickly climbed and entered the attic that smelled musky with age, found a light switch that controlled a single bare bulb hanging from the ceiling and flipped it. The lightbulb barely penetrated the gloom. Cobwebs looped liked forgotten threads over pieces of forgotten furniture that lay like an obstacle course around stacks of boxes, suitcases, and trunks. She shivered in the poorly insulated attic, managed to find an outlet, and plugged in the heater.

"You in here, Ciana?" she heard Eden call from below.

"Unfortunately, yes. Place needs work." She had to shout above the roar of the rain pounding on the roof above. She glanced up, hoping there were no leaks.

"Want some help?"

Ciana didn't care about the help, but she'd love Eden's company. "It's pretty nasty. You may need a hazmat suit."

"I know nasty," Eden called. "Remember I cleaned out Mom's old house before I sold it. Let me change and I'll be back in a jiff."

By the time Eden returned, the heater had knocked the worst of the chill off the air. "Whoa," Eden said, seeing the clutter. "When was the last time this place was cleared out?"

"No telling, but from its looks, not for a really long time."

"Any bats? 'Cause I'm scared of bats."

"Hope not."

They set to work, first clearing a path to the back where the roof sloped low to the eaves. Ciana said, "I thought you were baking."

"Everything's in the oven . . . bread, rolls, corn bread . . . your mom's fixing to stick in a ham when the breads are done."

"Who're we feeding?"

"No one except us, and yes, we're overdoing it."

Ciana pulled a sheet off an oddly shaped structure. "Look! It's my old dollhouse. Daddy and Grandpa Charles made it for me for my fifth birthday. I used to play with it all the time, but after they died in the plane crash, it made me sad to be around it. Olivia trucked it up here ages ago."

Eden ducked down to peek into every room of the house. She'd not known her father, or any of her relatives for that matter, so Ciana's family history always interested her. "Looks like a time capsule."

"Daddy loved the fifties." Ciana bent, shuffled around a few of the pieces of furniture. "If Abbie has a girl, I'll give it to her."

"What if you marry and have a girl someday? Don't you want to keep it in your family?"

Ciana bristled at the suggestion, knowing that the institution of marriage was often an onerous burden to Beauchamp women. Over the two hundred years since the land was originally settled, as a point of pride, most of the female descendants had chosen to keep their maiden name, even when they married. Olivia had been happily married to Charles Samuels, but had kept her Beauchamp name. And when she was just a child, Ciana had promised her grandmother she'd do the same. A child's oath, but as she grew, it had become easy to ignore involvement with Windemere boys in school, and then its men, and steer her own life course. The only bump was Jon Mercer, who had unexpectedly come along and made her feel things that sent her into a tailspin and out of control. "Not every female wants to marry, you know," she said testily.

"Why are you sounding down on men? Jon do something to set you off?"

"No." Ciana dragged out the word reluctantly, knowing it was just the opposite. All Jon did was make her want *more* of him. "I'm just honked about this town meeting. Gerald Hastings has no right coming here trying to change things up."

15

"Don't you want Windemere to grow?"

"Now, that's my mother talking," Ciana said, shaking her finger. "It's all about the money and leaving here."

"My plan too," Eden reminded her.

"But you're still here."

Eden felt her back go up. "That a problem?"

Ciana flushed. "No way. I'd have cracked up if you'd left after Arie died."

Mollified, Eden said, "But now Jon's returned, and you have to make some choices about what you want."

Eden had hit the mark exactly. What did she want with Jon? He had once *said* he wanted land to raise and train horses for ranch work, but she knew he also had a gypsy spirit that liked chasing after rodeos and sleeping under the stars. He had *said* he wanted her, but would giving in to the simmering passion between them be enough for her? "You should talk," Ciana said, deflecting Eden's attempt to pin her down. "What have you done about finding Garret?"

Eden had shared Arie's letter with Ciana. "Nothing yet. Still thinking of what I'll say to him—if Colleen even knows where to find him."

"You won't know until you ask," Ciana countered.

Eden shrugged. "In the meantime, I guess the two of us are stuck cleaning out your attic."

Ciana smiled ruefully. "All right. Personal lives off the table for now." She shoved several boxes out of the way, exposing an old steamer trunk tied shut with rope. "Here's a real antique. Wonder why it's tied up?"

Eden hovered over the trunk with her. "Open it."

Ciana undid the knot, lifted the lid, and saw that it was filled with books and stacks of paper bound with string. She picked up a paper pile. "Looks like old stuff from school." She

16

dug deeper, extracted a packet of small books and skimmed several. Her face lit up. "This is my grandmother's stuff— lesson books from when she was in school. Look at her penmanship. Awesome."

Eden rooted through the contents and came up with a slim hardcover book. "Look at this! A yearbook from Windemere High School dated 1945. Is that the year she graduated?"

Ciana computed backward. "I think so . . . it was right before World War II ended in Europe." She looked over Eden's shoulder as she thumbed through the pages. The hairstyles and clothing were definitely from the forties. In every picture, girls wore skirts or dresses, boys long pants. Jeans seemed to be earmarked for the poor and the field hands.

"Things sure have changed," Eden said, not just talking about fashion. Their yearbook had been digital, available for downloading, although she never had done so. Too many bad memories of her times with Tony.

Ciana tossed the lesson books and yearbook back into the trunk and closed it. "Come on, help me drag this down to my room. I want to go through the whole thing."

"What about the attic clean-out?"

Ciana rolled her eyes. "Get real. Reading through Grandmother's stuff is far more interesting."

Together the two of them wrestled the heavy trunk out of the attic and into Ciana's room on the ground floor.

Once inside Ciana's bedroom, and winded from exertion, Eden said, "Bet it's full of secrets."

"Hope so," Ciana said with a sly grin. "I always thought she was perfect. Maybe I'm in for a few surprises from prim and proper Olivia Beauchamp and the list of life rules she used to throw out at me. I've always wished I knew more about her. Now maybe I will."

4

"What's this?" Alice Faye asked, coming into Ciana's room later that afternoon.

"Grandmother's old stuff." Ciana sat on the floor, sorting through the trunk and organizing the books, letters, old newspaper articles, and diaries into piles.

Her mother watched silently. Finally Ciana looked up. "Want to help?"

"No. Not interested."

"But it's full of history, a first-person report of her life and times. Wouldn't you like to read it?"

"Honey, I don't care about history."

Ciana hunched up her knees. Her mother's attitude about Bellmeade and in particular about Olivia had always baffled her. "Maybe I'll find something really interesting. Wouldn't you want to read the best parts if I mark them for you?"

Alice Faye pinched the bridge of her nose, sighed. "Ciana, I know you and your grandmother had a special connection when she was alive, but for reasons I never understood,

Mother never really took to me. Growing up with her was hard on me. Giving birth to you was the only thing I ever did that truly pleased her."

Ciana had heard the lament off and on all her life. And during her own childhood, she had certainly heard Olivia frequently crab out Alice Faye over the smallest thing. As she grew, though, she wondered if her mother had taken to alcohol—sweet tea and gin, her drink of choice—because Olivia picked on her, or if her drinking had irritated Olivia into constant fault-finding. Ciana could make a case for either. Too bad Olivia wasn't around to see Alice Faye now, all sober and attending AA meetings regularly.

"Well, I plan to read every word," Ciana announced. "I want to know what her life was like. I want to know about her and Grandpa Charles. I miss her, and this stuff"—she gestured at the heaps—"will help me be with her again."

Alice Faye crossed her arms, leaned against the doorjamb. "I hope it does. But that's not why I'm here to talk to you. I want to know if you're ready for the downtown meeting tonight."

"I guess." Ciana stretched out her long legs. She was unsure what to expect, and defiantly not looking forward to it.

"Mr. Hastings will have numbers, statistics . . . everything he needs to make his case," Alice Faye said patiently.

"And I have nothing except my determination to say no."

"You don't have to say no. You can hold out this house, the barn, and the surrounding pastures and let him buy the rest of the land."

Anger stirred inside Ciana. Yet she knew she held the upper hand, because the way Olivia's will was written, neither she nor her mother could sell the land without the consent of the other. In short, it took both of them to say yes, only one of them to say no. "This is the best farmland in the county, probably in half the state. Why turn it into a housing tract?"

"And what are you growing on it except alfalfa hay for a few horses? Most of the tillable land is fallow."

"That isn't a reason to sell it! And it would be planted if Olivia hadn't died and the leases hadn't tanked with the economy. I'm going to get it up and running again, just like Grandpa Charles and Daddy and Olivia had it."

"And that takes money," Alice Faye fired back. "Selling the property to Hastings—"

"Would give us money and precious little land to farm."

Alice Faye held up her hands. "I don't want to fight with you about this. I was only asking if you were ready for tonight."

"I'm ready," Ciana growled, hands fisted at her sides.

Her mother turned but paused at the doorway and over her shoulder said, "I'm not your enemy, Ciana. But I want things too. And one of the things I want is not to be saddled with this place for the rest of my life. Selling is a way out for me. For both of us, even though you don't realize it now. Why, you could own a place in Italy and split your time between here and there if you sell. You had a good time in Italy, didn't you?"

The almost three months she'd spent in Italy with Arie and Eden had been a dream, and she'd spent most of her college money to fund the trip without regrets. Italy had been wonderful, a sabbatical. But that was all it was. Reality and Bellmeade were here. This is what she wanted. "Yes, we had a great time in Italy. You should go someday."

Alice Faye turned. "On what? My butter and egg money?"

Ciana ignored the sarcasm. "Tell you what, Mom. With the first profits I make from farming again, I'll send you to Italy on vacation."

Alice Faye shook her head in disgust and walked out of the room.

Eden circled her bedroom like a cat in a cage. She'd emailed Colleen but as yet hadn't heard anything. Eden had no way of knowing where the walkabout group would be, or even if they were still together. Only the fact that her email hadn't returned to her with a "failure to deliver" notice gave Eden any hope that it might have landed in Colleen's in-box. She told herself to remain calm.

She still had a good bit of money in the bank from the house sale and plenty of squirreled-away cash from what had been Tony's drug cache, but not much else to call her own. Unlike Ciana, she had no roots. Her mother, Gwen, was somewhere in Florida, probably off her bipolar meds and living who knew where. Eden shied away from thinking about Gwen. Too painful. However, she was feeling the pressure of needing to do something with the rest of her life. She couldn't live in Ciana's house forever. She needed to make plans for her future. Problem was she had no direction, and until she settled with her past and her feelings for Garret, she wouldn't have any. She longed to know how, or even *if*, they fit into each other's lives.

"You ready? My truck's warming in front of the porch."

Ciana's shout from the bottom of the stairs snapped Eden out of her thoughts. Despite being at loose ends about her own future, she was dressed and ready to go with Ciana to the town meeting, intent on supporting her friend. "Putting on lipstick," Eden called, grabbing the tube from her dresser and hastily sweeping it over her mouth. She clattered down the stairs to the foyer, where Ciana was prowling restlessly. "Your mom coming with us?"

"She wants to take the Lincoln. Probably her way of showing people we have different ideas about Bellmeade's fate."

Ciana's face was as dark as the sky outside. "Don't be too hard on her for wanting something different," Eden said before Ciana bolted out the front door.

"She can do whatever she wants. I'm keeping our land," Ciana snapped, and shut off further discussion.

Eden followed her friend outside, deciding that having nothing meant never having anything to fight over. Or for that matter, anything to fight *for*.

Ciana couldn't believe her eyes. People were packed in the old courtroom in city hall used for public meetings. All eyes turned to her and Eden when they came into the room. Why had so many people shown up? Hastings's project didn't even involve most of the attendees. Her stomach did somersaults, but she squared her shoulders and walked to the front of the room. She sat in the first row directly in front of Hastings's presentation table as Gerald Hastings and two of his staff hovered around a large covered board propped up on an easel.

Eden slid into a chair beside her. "You sure you want to sit here?"

"Positive. I want to make sure he sees me." After returning from Italy, Ciana had seen his plans for her property. She'd told him then she wasn't interested in selling, but the man had ignored her as if she were a small child incapable of understanding his great plan.

Eden said, "Well, he can't miss you, girlfriend."

Ciana casually glanced over her shoulder at the crowd behind her. She recognized neighbors, business owners, farmers, teachers—a cross section of Windemere residents. Her gaze stopped sweeping when she saw Jon standing against the wall at the back of the room. His green eyes only on her. He offered a slight nod while keeping his expression neutral. Gratitude flooded her, knowing he'd come for her sake. She saw Bill Pickins, too, and Eric Winslow, who'd arrived without Abbie. Arie's parents had not shown up.

The mayor interrupted the buzz of chatter by calling the meeting to order. He did some talking about the great turnout of citizens and how this new venture could help the town, then turned the mike over to Hastings.

Under her breath, Eden said, "He's good-looking. See how some of the women are staring at him? They're almost panting."

Ciana was forced to agree. Hastings looked casually polished in khaki slacks and a blue golf shirt. His salt-and-pepper hair was precisely cut. She thought his blue eyes looked cold behind wire-rim glasses. "He's the enemy," Ciana fired back softly.

"I'm just saying," Eden said.

Hastings introduced himself and his staff, offered up his professional background while his staff passed out paperwork to any who wanted it, and most people did. Finally he walked to the easel, pulled the cover off, and discussed his drawings for Bellmeade Estates. People listened. Rumors had swarmed about the project for months, but now as it was being laid out publicly, Ciana felt more threatened than ever. Hastings talked about the economic impact for the town, causing murmurs to ripple through the crowd. He told of how he had built such communities in other states, of how he had persuaded both the Federal Transportation Authority and the Tennessee state legislature to okay a new exit off the existing expressway to accommodate traffic, and of how such an exit would impact the town for the better. He alluded to how much his company had already invested because "that's how much he believed in the project."

Ciana curled internally. Of course, the new subdivision sounded like a windfall for the town, economically depressed for years. The new housing and golf course would attract buyers from Nashville and Murfreesboro who would bring money and jobs into Windemere. The only catch was that hundreds of acres of fertile farmland would be sacrificed, changing the face and the purpose of the countryside forever. For Ciana the sacrifice was too great, but when Hastings opened the floor to questions, she clearly saw that for many from the area, it wasn't. Several of the smaller farms bordering hers were owned by elderly folks with no family interested in or even available to take over their properties, so Hastings's buyout offer was a path to financial security.

And yet there were townspeople who liked the small-town atmosphere of Windemere and didn't want unchecked growth that might bring in urban sprawl and worse, crime. Ciana wasn't alone, but she was clearly in the minority.

Once Hastings finished his presentation, an excited buzz filled the room. Ciana felt tensions rising until she could take no more. Her heart thudded, her palms sweat, but she stood, and looking Gerald Hastings in the eye, she said, "You may build whatever you want. Just not on my land."

She marched down the aisle, head high, hearing shocked whispers, with Eden scrambling after her.

5

"Want to talk about it?" Eden asked as Ciana drove them home.

"Looks like farming is a lost cause," Ciana said bitterly.

Eden felt Ciana's despair. "Not everybody feels that way. Some seemed to like the town the way it is."

"You don't."

"Not true," Eden defended herself. "I actually like the gardening and the canning and cooking."

"But you want to blow this town."

"Not for the same reasons I once wanted. Think back to when we were in high school. There was nothing to do in our dead little burg."

"I had plenty to do."

"And so long as you and Arie were hanging with me, I did too. But when we were fourteen and you both left for the summer, well, that's when I met Tony, and we both know how awful that turned out."

Ciana knew. "It was a bad time for you."

"If Italy hadn't happened . . ." Eden let the sentence trail off, remembering how Tony had terrorized their families until a drug deal went bad for him in Memphis.

"We're both survivors, Eden. And I'll survive this crisis with Bellmeade. Bet on it." She turned into her driveway, saw Jon's pickup truck parked by the barn. Light glowed through the side window.

"Looks like you have company," Eden said.

Ciana's heartbeat quickened. "Seems so." She parked and Eden scurried through the rain into the house. Ciana ran into the barn, found Jon sitting on a beat-up chair and whittling a lump of wood. He immediately stood, folded his pocketknife, and shoved it into the pocket of his well-worn jeans.

He opened his arms and she walked into his embrace, longing to be comforted. "Hey, cowboy."

His arms tightened. "Hey, pretty lady. You okay?"

"Not really. I—I didn't expect so many people to be in favor of the project. I thought the land meant more to all of us. Some of those people sounded like they'd won the lottery. Why, they'd sell their heritages without blinking."

"The dude's offering folks a lot of money. Human nature being what it is . . . well, it's hard to resist the sweet smell of money."

"Not for me," she said around emotions stuck in her throat. "Is the whole town against me?"

"Bill's on your side."

Bill's ranch and cattle were on the other side of the freeway, south and west of Windemere and in no danger of being gobbled up by Hastings's project. "Good to know," she said with a sigh, and pushed away.

Jon looked into her eyes fiercely. "*I'm* on your side too."

Tears threatened to spill out as she tried to shake them

away. Beauchamp women were supposed to be tough. Hadn't Olivia taught her to stand and fight against all odds? *"The land is everything, child. You fight for what's ours. You fight to win."* The words rang in Ciana's ears. "You don't have a dog in this fight, Jon Mercer."

He lifted her chin. "I have something more important at stake. I have a girl I want to keep."

His words were comforting and well meant, but Bellmeade was her problem, not his. "I won't change my mind about selling."

"I didn't expect you would, but—" He paused. "You could be in for trouble."

"What kind of trouble?"

"Money changes people. I was at the meeting too. Hastings is throwing this town a lifeline to most folk's way of thinking. I heard them talking. To a lot of them, you're the enemy, not Hastings."

She was struck dumb by his words. Her? An enemy? Impossible. She realized people were disgruntled, but they should understand where she was coming from. Bellmeade was a legend, and the Beauchamps were not just its owners but its protectors and guardians. "I just want to keep my land. It's *my* land!" She was angry now, not at Jon, but that he'd dug up ugly things and dared to flash them at her.

"I'd like to move in again, Ciana. I can help protect you and Bellmeade."

She stared at him in disbelief. *"Protect* me? Jon, nothing's going to happen to me. People will get over it and once Hastings sees I'm serious, he'll go back to Chicago and forget all about us."

Jon's green eyes studied her, his face shadowed by concern. "Don't fool yourself. The man's already invested a lot of money in this project. He won't walk away. Plus the people around here—"

"Are my neighbors," she interrupted. "I've known these people all my life. They aren't going to come after me." The idea was so ludicrous that she turned and walked to the stalls where horses stirred because of the raised voices.

"And you can't move in again," she added stubbornly. Jon had lived in the barn's tack room and helped with chores before having to take his father home to Texas in March. "Barn's full, except for my two freeloaders, Firecracker and Sonata. My four boarders will bring in enough extra money to get us through this winter. Come spring, I'll plant more crops, begin to make this farm productive again. And as you can see, I took out some storage space and built extra stalls. I only wish I had room for more."

Firecracker's head pitched over the stall door and Jon obliged her with a scratch on her forelock. Ciana rubbed the aged, whitened muzzle of her grandmother's former saddle horse in the adjoining stall.

Jon must have realized she'd closed off the discussion, because he walked to one of the new stalls and studied the new horses. "Tell me about your boarders."

Ciana calmed down, switched gears from the meeting. "This one is owned by a tech guy. A kind of weekend cowboy living in Murfreesboro. Fred doesn't ride much, says he's too busy. Just likes owning a horse, I think."

Jon appraised the dark brown horse. "Hope he didn't pay much. Animal has poor confirmation."

Ciana would never challenge Jon's expertise. One thing the man knew, it was horses. He trained wild mustangs for ranch work, rode broncs for fun. She moved on. "This little bay belongs to a fourteen-year-old girl in town. She's a sweet-heart and practically lived here this last summer."

"Not too bad." Jon's gaze swept the horse head to tail. "Better stock than the first guy's."

"And the two others, named Mr. and Mrs. Smith, belong to a nice retired couple in town who just love horses and riding together."

"Look to have some Tennessee walking horse blood in both of them."

By now they were standing in the dark, far back in the barn in stillness and shadows. The sound of the animals moving quietly in the stalls, the steady drumming of November rain on the roof, offered a sense of aloneness in the world . . . just the two of them and no others. Ciana felt time slow. Jon's nearness ignited memories of how his kiss, the touch of his hands, had once lit fires on her skin. That fire had been between them since the first time they'd kissed on a long-ago summer night. He reached for her. "Don't walk away from me, Ciana. Please . . . I want more with you. Why won't you let me in?"

She had no answer. It would be easy, so easy, to give in, and give herself to him in every way. And she might have—if tiny pricks from their tumultuous past and the unseen future had not surfaced in her head and heart. The warnings stretched like the barbed wire over the fences on her property. *Caution. Danger. Be careful.* Unable to put into words what she felt, or why she felt the way she did, she stepped away. She had no answer, no way to explain what she herself did not understand. So she turned and hurried outside, leaving him alone in the dark.

6

Eden was sitting cross-legged in the center of Ciana's bed when Ciana came into her bedroom. "I heard from Colleen."

With nerve endings still afire, Ciana dropped onto the bed beside her friend, glad for a distraction. "Tell me."

"She's back in Ireland." Eden twisted a tissue wrapped through her fingers. "They had to quit the walkabout." She took a shuddering breath. "You see . . . Garret—"

"Hey, hey," Ciana interrupted, suddenly anxious for her friend. "Take it easy. Don't pass out on me."

Eden sucked in air and willed her thudding heart to slow down. "Garret got sick in Sweden. Double pneumonia. One of his lungs collapsed."

Ciana put her arms around Eden, frightened over what she might hear next. "Go on. I won't let go of you."

Eden nodded, wiped her eyes with the wadded tissue. "Tom and Lorna took him back to Australia. They got him home, but Colleen hasn't heard anything from them. It's been

30

over a month. She doesn't know if he . . . if he . . ." Eden broke down once more.

Ciana went cold through and through, the pain of Arie's April death knifing her heart. Neither she nor Eden could face such loss again. She reached beyond the hurt for Eden's sake. "Garret's young and strong. Pneumonia's curable. If he's home, he must have family around him to help care for him. Did Colleen have any way to reach him?"

"She—she gave me an email address. It's Tom's, but he hasn't responded to any mail from Colleen. Why wouldn't he? Unless . . . unless—"

"Don't even think bad thoughts," Ciana insisted. "Let's email Tom right now."

Eden held Ciana's arm in a death grip. "I'm so scared."

"Where's the address? I'll write it for you."

Eden picked up her electronic tablet beside her on the bed with shaking hands. "I'll write it," she said. "I owe Garret that much." She looked into Ciana's eyes. "But please stay with me while I do."

"I'm not going anywhere."

It took Eden a while to compose a message because her fingers kept slipping on the virtual keys, but when it was finally finished, she let Ciana read it, and then pushed send. As it whooshed off into cyberspace, she felt as if her heart and soul had gone with it. "Maybe it won't get there. Maybe Tom won't answer me either."

"Doubtful. Let's write Colleen right now and let her know just in case she hears from Tom before we do. That way she can tell him you're trying to reach Garret. Two messengers are better than one."

Eden clung to the logic. "You're right. I haven't answered her. I just bolted down here when I got her message. I should

31

let her know what happened to us in Italy, and why I didn't show up that day to go with them. She doesn't know about Arie." Fresh tears welled in her eyes.

"We'll compose a message together. I'd like to say hello too." Ciana eased the tablet from Eden's hands, certain Eden's fingers couldn't manage a second message just now. "Let me."

Eden flopped onto the bed, cradled a small pillow against her chest, stared up at the ceiling. "Read it back to me when you're finished, okay? And . . . and would you mind if I stayed here a while? I don't want to be alone upstairs."

"No problem. Stay all night if you want. I don't think I can sleep tonight myself." She glanced at the paper stacks on the floor. "I want to go exploring."

Sunlight woke Ciana where she lay curled up on the floor of her room, covered by a quilt and clutching one of her grand-mother's old diaries. Eden was sound asleep on the bed. Ciana sat up, stretched sore muscles, rubbed her stiff neck. She had no idea when she'd fallen asleep, but it had to be late morning now because sunlight puddled across her lap. The horses! She struggled up, one leg all pins and needles, hobbled into her bathroom, and splashed cold water on her face.

She got to the barn quickly and discovered that someone had already fed the horses and released them to pasture. The rain had left the ground muddy, and the red clay clung to her work boots. The November air was chilly, but weak sunlight spread across the sky.

Back in the house, she went to the kitchen for coffee.

"Eden all right?" Alice Faye asked.

Ciana eased into a kitchen table chair. "I think so." She told her mother what had happened.

"Poor girl. Hope this man she likes is well by now. You want some breakfast?"

"Just toast." She watched Alice Faye slice freshly baked bread and slide two pieces into the toaster. "Thanks for letting the horses out."

"I put fresh water into the pasture trough for them, but didn't muck the stalls."

"I'll do it." As the hot coffee warmed her, Ciana relaxed. When Alice Faye placed the toast in front of her along with butter and a bowl of strawberry jam, she asked, "Do you remember a family named Soder? They used to have a farm next to ours on the north end."

Alice Faye poured herself coffee and sat across from Ciana. "Name's a little familiar. Why do you ask?"

"Now, don't get crabby. I know what you think about Olivia's diaries—which so far have been pretty dull—but that name keeps coming up." Alice Faye looked uninterested but didn't interrupt, so Ciana took it as a sign to continue. "She talks about the Soders adopting a boy, some pathetic kid the sheriff found digging through garbage cans in an alley."

"Awful. But I don't recall the family or the boy."

"I found a newspaper article about it tucked into one of her earliest diaries—1936. Olivia was eight. Seems the boy only gave his first name, said he had no parents. Reporter called him a 'throwaway child.' Guess the Depression broke up a lot of families." Ciana sipped her coffee, ate a bite of toast. "Anyway, they guessed him to be about nine or ten and the sheriff was set to take him off to the county orphanage when the Soders stepped up and said they'd take him. The article quoted Mrs. Soder to say, 'Lord didn't see fit to give us no kids of our own, so it seems like good Christian charity to take in this one. Like Pharaoh's daughter bringing that Moses out of the bulrushes.' Quaint, huh?" Ciana slathered jam onto the second slice of toast.

Her mother said, "Grandpa Jacob often spoke about the Depression. Hard times. Lots of people lost everything. Tennessee was spared the worse of the dust storms, but we had a bad drought."

"I think it's interesting that Olivia wrote about the boy. She was so young, so he must have made an impression."

"Small-town life means *anything* that happens is interesting. When I was growing up, my friend, Suzie Lawson, and I used to pilfer movie magazines from the drugstore, read every word, then sneak them back on the racks."

"You *stole* magazines?"

Her mother's face reddened over what she'd confessed. "We put them back! Life was dull here. Hollywood was exciting. People were beautiful out there, so far from farm pastures and cow dung."

Ciana grinned. "Bad girls."

Just then, Eden stumbled into the kitchen wrapped in the quilt Ciana had left on the floor. "Sorry about confiscating your bed," she mumbled on her way to the coffeepot.

"No problem. Any emails?"

"Just spam." She had the tablet with her and placed it on the table along with her coffee cup.

"Huge time difference," Ciana said, to encourage Eden.

"Breakfast?" Alice Faye asked.

"Not hungry."

In unison, Ciana and Alice Faye said, "Toast!"

Alice Faye rose, went to work on the loaf of bread. Eden stared glumly into her coffee cup.

Changing the subject, Alice Faye said, "We should talk about Thanksgiving. Only two weeks away. I was thinking of inviting Arie's parents and Eric and Abbie over. What do you think? We can plan a menu—"

The ding from Eden's tablet stopped the conversation cold. Eden peered down at the glowing screen announcing the arrival of email. "It—it's from *Garret*," she said breathlessly.

"That must mean he's all right," Ciana said with an encouraging smile.

Eden sat immobile, frozen in place by fear of the unknown. Once she opened the email, her world would change one way or the other. Not reading the words meant maintaining the status quo in which her life was predictable, safe.

"You going to open it?" Ciana sounded impatient. "Want me to do it for you?"

Eden shook her head, picked up the tablet, and with shaking fingers, tapped the surface. For a long minute, she simply stared while Ciana squirmed. Finally she turned the tablet so that Ciana could read the message. It was short:

> I will send you up to half the airfare if you will come to Australia ASAP. Come to me, Eden. Please come.
>
> Garret

7

Thirteen hours of flying on a jumbo jet sandwiched between a teenager playing video games and a woman juggling a baby made Eden feel like a white rat in a too small cage. Especially after her long layover in Dallas/Fort Worth from Nashville before boarding the longer flight to Sydney. She was bleary-eyed from lack of sleep, but hadn't been able to turn off her thoughts. All her restless mind did was churn with memories, or make up scenarios about Garret. How would they feel about one another after so much time?

Eden had waited until after the holidays to make the trip to the southern hemisphere, where it was already summer. She wouldn't miss Tennessee's winter, would miss Ciana and Alice Faye and yes, the routine of the new life she had at Bellmeade. Garret seemed so eager for her to come, and true to his word, he'd wired money to her to help with the long and costly trip, while she had dipped into her bank account for the visit. He'd called once, and hearing his voice had given her goose bumps: that broad Aussie accent, the quick laughter, friendly and charming words.

Yes, he was almost well from his bout with sickness . . . living at home, still rebuilding his strength. And yes, she wanted to wait to tell him the details about her rush to leave Italy. And he was really sorry about Arie's death, news he'd learned through Colleen. And Eden felt bad that she had lost touch until now.

When the plane touched down on the runway in Sydney, it was midmorning of the day after she'd left Nashville. Hard to get her head around that she was almost a day ahead and ten thousand miles away from home. She slogged through customs, passport, and visa checkpoints, picked up her luggage, and headed toward signs that read WAY OUT. Tired as she was, her nerves were tight as a bowstring. Apprehension had turned her hands icy cold.

Garret was the first person she saw when she exited into the public space of the airport. His bushy blond hair was closely shorn and he looked thin, almost gaunt in the face, but he was still broad-shouldered, and wearing a smile that could thaw Arctic ice.

He pulled her into his arms, kissed her forehead. "You're a sight for my eyes. A feast," he said. "Let me take a good long look at ya." His eyes swept over her while he smoothed her cheek with the palm of his hand, his touch like a balm. Her long-held tension let go of her.

"Are you all well?" she asked.

"I am now that you're here," he said with a disarming smile. He took her bags. "Let's get you out of here. Me mum is waiting in the parkin' garage. She insisted on driving, and it's her car, and how's a bloke supposed to grab the keys from his own mum?"

In the parking garage, he walked her to a small blue car, where a woman hopped out and extended her hand. "I'm Garret's mum, Margaret Locklin, but my friends call me Maggie. So glad to meet you, Eden." Her voice was bubbly, almost jovial. Her hair was a mass of curls, just like Garret's when Eden had first met him.

"Thank you for having me," Eden said, hoping her manners were intact after the mind-numbing journey.

Maggie laughed. "Garret said you spoke Southern. I *like* the sound of it."

It hit Eden then that she was as much a foreigner here as in Italy. She was the person with the funny accent, not Garret. "Thank you," she said again.

Once the luggage was in the trunk and passengers settled in the backseat, Maggie got behind the wheel and caught Eden's eye. "Glad you're here, and now that I see you, I understand why my lad's been so keen for you to come," she said, followed by Garret's embarrassed mumble, "Oh Mum . . ." Eden listened to Maggie's travelogue as she drove along the busy Sydney roads. She noted that in Australia cars drove on the opposite side of the road from cars in the States. "Always look left before stepping off a curb," Maggie told her. "Or we'll be visiting you in hospital."

"I won't let go of her, Mum," Garret said, slipping Eden's hand into his for the rest of the drive. Eventually the car entered a residential street lined with houses of many different architectural designs before turning up a driveway on a hill. The terraced yard was green with shrubs and flowering trees. The cream-colored house was ultramodern in design, with banks of windows and a red tile roof.

The inside of the house was just as lovely as the outside. Furniture was low and sleek, with glass-top tables amid a cluster of seating areas. The house was spacious and multilevel, with short, wide stairs branching off from the foyer. "Sleeping wing this way," Garret said, leading Eden up to the right and down a carpeted hall to a bedroom with a private bath. A large, long window across from the bed looked out over a pool and a view of the city below.

"Wow," she said. "Beautiful place."

He caught her around the waist and drew her against himself. "A beautiful girl. I want to hold you proper, Eden." He lifted her chin and kissed her.

She snuggled into his embrace. Her heart filled with peace. She was once more in Garret's arms, and all her doubts were swept away. Coming halfway round the world had been the right thing for her to do. Exactly the right thing.

That evening, Garret invited Tom and Lorna over for supper with his parents and Eden, and it took no time for her to feel comfortable with all of them. Trevor Locklin, Garret's father, was a cheerful man, quick to smile and with a wicked sense of humor. And Tom and Lorna made her feel as if no time at all had passed since that last night together in Italy. Tom and Lorna had an apartment together, which was no surprise. They'd been inseparable in Italy. Both worked in the city and said their traveling days were behind them. "Time to settle down," Lorna said. "Saving to get married."

"A ways to go," Tom said.

Lorna rolled her eyes at him, turned to Eden. "We'll have you and Garret over for grilling on the barbie."

"I grill a mean piece of crocodile," Tom said with a wink. "Tastes better than chicken."

Eden's eyes widened and everyone laughed, making her blush.

"He means to say burgers," Lorna said.

"One Aussie morsel at a time, and I'm first," Garret said.

Later, after Garret shut the door on the company, he led Eden out to the patio and pool area carrying a bottle of wine and two wineglasses. The night air was cool and full of scents from perfumed flowers and eucalyptus trees. He pulled out chairs for them both, a lounge chair for Eden, a deck chair for himself. "I know you're tired. The trip here is always a bugger. I'll take you up to bed soon, but I just want to be alone with you for a little while. Do you mind?"

She was tired but still wound up from the trip. She wanted to be alone with him too. "Not ready for bed yet," she said.

"Good. I've got a whole city to show you." He poured them each a glass of wine.

On the trip she'd rehearsed many speeches to give him, but now that she was here, she wasn't sure where to begin. "I owe you an explanation about not showing up that day at the fountain."

"It can wait."

"No. I want to tell you now." She took a mouthful of the rich red wine, savored and swallowed it, let its warmth spread through her blood. "Arie got so sick in the middle of the night. We had to get her to a hospital right away. It was awful. All we had time to do was react."

"I was disappointed when you didn't show, but I wasn't going to let you back out of coming along. I hopped on my scooter and zipped out to the villa to check on you."

"You did?"

"Course I did. I'm not a bloke who gives up easy. I knew something bad had happened. I walked into that villa and

40

upstairs and saw all the blood. My heart about stopped. But I knew it wasn't your blood because I knew which room was yours. I used to stand outside and look up at your window after you would kiss me goodnight, then bolt inside like a rabbit."

"I didn't bolt," she said, knowing what he'd said was indeed true. She hadn't wanted to get in over her head in a relationship coming on the heels of her ill-fated one with Tony. She'd tried to tell Garret about Tony, but he had always brushed aside talk of her past, saying it didn't matter, so she'd dropped it. "I exited gracefully," she added, raising her glass to him.

He grinned. "Point is, you left me outside cooling off and tied in knots, so I learned by watching window lights which room was yours. When I went to the villa that day, I knew there had been serious trouble."

"Sometime in the night, Arie began vomiting blood. She had cancer—first when she was a child. It kept reoccurring. But after we graduated it was supposed to be in complete remission. The Italy trip was supposed to be a celebration."

"Cancer! Bloody awful." Garret shook his head. "She hid it well. None of us ever suspected she could have been ill."

"She never told me or Ciana that she was out of remission when we began the trip. She wanted to go so much. I can't blame her." Remembering Arie's excitement, her breakout joy, Eden felt tears arise. "We got home, but there was nothing her doctors could do for her. In truth, there probably never was."

The night sounds gentled around the patio. The water lapping the sides of the pool, soft music coming from somewhere inside the house, reminded Eden of their evenings in Italy beside the fountain of Cortona. "Arie felt bad about me having to go home so suddenly without telling you. I had no way to reach you, Garret. I tried. The magazine you wrote for was defunct—"

"A shock to me too," he interjected, refilling his glass.

"You weren't on any of the social media sites I checked either."

"Dad's a Queen's counselor, an attorney, works with the government. Never wanted me on such sites because of his job. Never wants the family too high-profile. How did you find me?"

"Arie. She had Colleen's email address, but I didn't know about it until months after she had died, until her mother found a letter she'd addressed to me. Colleen told me how you'd taken sick and come home. Scared me."

"No fun time for me either. Had to give up my travel plans. But I'm better now. Specially now that you're here." He laced his fingers through hers. "I've missed you, Eden. Had no way to reach you either. A sorry oversight never to be repeated."

The wine had done its work and sleepiness stole over her. She yawned. "I think I'm ready for bed now."

"Pity I have to let you go to bed by yourself," he said, standing and pulling her to her feet. He wrapped her in his arms, rested his chin on top of her head.

"You trying to seduce me, Aussie-man?"

"Of course I am. But for now I'll just tuck you in."

He walked her into her bedroom, where a small table lamp glowed on a bedside table. Garret touched the first button of Eden's blouse. She gently pushed his hand away, smiled up at him. "I'll take it from here."

"I was afraid you'd say that." His eyes twinkled impishly in the lamp's light. "I'm glad you're here. I want you to stay as long as you can. I want all of you, Eden. . . . I want what we couldn't have in Italy."

When she was alone, she turned off the lamp and snuggled under the clean and scented sheets. She wanted all of him too. But she reminded herself to go slow.

Eden awoke to sunlight and the smell of fresh coffee. She stretched luxuriously, felt a bit guilty for having slept in. She shook off the bedcovers, washed her face in the adjoining bathroom, and quickly dressed. She followed the scent of coffee down the hall, across the living room to the far side of the house, where she found Maggie working at the sink and Garret sitting at a white café-style table, surfing on a laptop. "G'day," Eden said, using the familiar Australian greeting she'd heard from Garret many times in Italy.

"There she is," Maggie said with a beaming smile. "Sleep well?"

Garret leaped up and pulled out a chair. "Was thinking you'd sleep away the day."

"Oh posh," his mother chided. "It's barely nine in the morning. Get the girl some coffee. I've peeled some nice mangoes and I can whip up some eggs and bacon for you."

"Just coffee for now."

Garret poured Eden's coffee and seated himself across from her. "Mum will stuff you like a calf if you let her."

Eden took a sip, warmed her hands on the cup. "Ciana's mother is the same way."

"It's in a mum's DNA—" He was interrupted by a rap on the back door.

"Who in the world—?" Maggie started.

The door swung open and a very tall, pretty blond girl stepped inside with the confident air of one familiar with both the kitchen and the people. She quickly crossed to the table, bent down and kissed Garret on the cheek, straightened and looked directly into Eden's face. "Hello there. You must be Garret's American friend." She held out her hand. "I'm Alyssa Bainbridge, Garret's girlfriend."

8

Eden's heart dropped. Her gaze flew to Garret, and saw that his face had turned beet red.

"Bit of a cheeky thing to say, Alyssa," Maggie said frostily. She dried her hands on a dish towel and came to hover beside Eden's chair.

Alyssa ignored Maggie and with a toss of her honey-colored hair, moved behind Garret. She placed both hands on his shoulders. Garret shrugged her hands away. "Thought you had a catalogue shoot all day."

"Conflict in the photographer's schedule. Found myself with nothing to do, so I thought I'd come meet your new friend." The girl's voice was silky smooth, her eyes cool and appraising.

Determined not to let this girl know she was rattled, Eden offered one of her best smiles and turned on her best Southern drawl. "So nice of you to drop by and introduce yourself. I'm Eden McLauren, from Tennessee, USA. Garret and I met in Italy. He made my coffee most every morning." She knew full well that any coffee Garret made for her had been at his job in the espresso bar in Cortona, but she let the implication of intimacy hang in the air.

Bright spots of color dotted Alyssa's cheekbones. Garret's face regained its natural color, and he suppressed a grin. "I've made plans for me and Eden for the day."

"Always best to call ahead," Maggie chimed in with practiced cheer. "Good manners too."

From the dialogue, Eden realized that Alyssa wasn't exactly welcome at the house. And yet the way she'd opened the door and swept into the kitchen with her "girlfriend" announcement was troubling. How did this girl fit into Garret's life?

Alyssa turned wide and innocent-looking blue eyes toward Garret. "I didn't mean to presume. I just so rarely get to meet Americans."

Maggie snorted but left the kitchen to Garret and the two girls.

"No time for a visit," Garret said, rising and going to Eden.

"Well then, maybe later," Alyssa said with a smile that never made it to her eyes. "Depending on how long your friend is staying."

"I have a three-month visa," Eden said. "Too long a trip for a short visit."

The look on Alyssa's face told Eden she didn't like what she'd heard, but her mood turned artificially cheery and she said, "Then you'll have to come to our beach party, before our mates head back to university." She turned to Garret. "You haven't forgotten your promise in the hospital, have you? When you told us we'd have a big beach fest to celebrate your recovery."

Garret's face reddened. "I haven't forgotten, but—"

"I'd love to come," Eden interrupted, smiling but gritting her teeth.

"Good!" Alyssa said in a tone that didn't sound one bit inviting. "I'll call with details." She went to the door, waggled her fingers at Eden, and left, leaving behind an awkward silence.

Garret said, "It's not what it looks like, Eden. I can explain."

"And I want to hear your explanation." Eden scrambled to gather herself. The encounter had left her shaken, but he deserved to have a say. "Can we sit by the pool? I need the fresh air."

Garret gave her a grateful look, grabbed their cups off the table, and ushered her poolside where they took up chairs and positions from the night before. Eden thought how different things looked and felt mere hours later in the clear light of day.

"Alyssa was my mate all through secondary school—"

"Your *girlfriend*," Eden interjected, wanting to be certain she understood the true definition of his term. In Aussie talk a mate could be anyone from a lifelong friend to someone very special. Alyssa gave the impression she'd been more than a pal.

Garret nodded. "Yes, we were together."

"Like Tom and Lorna are together."

His blue eyes held hers. "Yes. That kind of together."

Her stomach twisted and she swallowed her angst with a big gulp of coffee. "Go on."

"We became friends at school. Then more. After we graduated and I got the chance to go on walkabout, I asked her to come with me. She wouldn't do it. Said she had other plans and for me to have a good time."

By the set of his jaw and look in his eyes, Eden saw that Alyssa's rejection had hurt him deeply. "But you went anyway."

"Like I told you back in Italy, my wish is to see the world. Every mile of it if I can. Plus, I had the writing job. Tom and Lorna were game to come along for a spell. So, yes, I went."

The sun had climbed higher and Eden watched a bird flitter to the edge of the pool, then skitter away. She felt pummeled emotionally, telling herself that naturally he'd had a life before meeting her, just as she'd had one before meeting him. Still, coming face to face with a girl from his past, a girl he'd cared for, and who didn't appear to be letting go, unsettled Eden. "What other plans kept her from going with you?"

"She's a model. Successful too. That was all the catalogue talk in the kitchen. A walkabout didn't fit in with her life's plan."

The implication was that neither had he. "But you're home now," Eden said.

He shrugged, offered a smile. "Couldn't be helped. I was a sick bloke. Doctor popped me in hospital the minute I landed. For days I had tubes sticking out every which way. Mum and Dad were right upset. Word got around, and lots of my mates came to visit. Alyssa came every day, and when I came home, she brought me movies, video games, milk shakes. She canceled jobs and photo shoots to stay with me. She was good company, and it helped pass the time. I couldn't hold a grudge."

Eden read between the lines. Alyssa had wormed her way back into his life now that he was home. "And so now she's your girlfriend again?" The words stuck in Eden's throat, but she wanted the whole truth. If he was with Alyssa, Eden wasn't going to hang around.

Garret reached over and took both her hands in his. "That

might have happened if I'd never met you." Again she met his eyes, wanting to believe he was being honest. "But I *did* meet you, Eden, and it changed everything. The way I feel inside. The things I want. All changed. I was a happy bloke in Italy when you said you'd come along with us."

"We didn't have much time together, Garret. I thought I'd never see you again when I left Italy."

"That's true. But once I met you, it woke me up. It made me see I didn't love Alyssa. I understand her now in ways I never could before. And I've told her as much."

"News flash: I'm not sure she heard you."

Garret leaned back in his chair. "She heard me. She just doesn't believe me."

Tony hadn't believed Eden when she'd wanted to leave him either. What Garret didn't know about her past nibbled at her conscience. She wanted him to know, but the timing wasn't right. She changed the subject instead. "A beach party. Hard to keep remembering that it's summer here."

"School term ends in November and starts in February. We'll hit the beach before fall term. I'll teach you how to ride a surfboard."

She'd only seen videos of professional surfers and massive waves devouring them. "I don't know. . . ."

He laughed. "You'll start small with a boogie board. We'll practice over at Manly Beach first."

She liked the idea of a party, and she wanted to meet his friends. She wanted to be a part of his world. She would ignore Alyssa. "Guess I shouldn't miss this one."

Garret relaxed, and his face softened into a smile. "We'll have a blast. Lots of beer and food."

"And your Aussie charm."

His grin widened. "Never to be underestimated."

She picked up her cup, but the coffee had grown cold and stale. Garret took the cup, set it down, stood, and pulled her up to face him. "Thank you for believing me. And for not heading off to the airport because of Alyssa."

"Not my style. I didn't come halfway round the world to be shooed away by an old girlfriend."

He kissed her until her knees went weak, then said, "Come on. It's almost lunchtime. Throw on some walking shoes and I'll take you out for some bangers and mash."

"Some *what?*"

He laughed. "Sausage and mashed potatoes. A real treat."

She wasn't sure about that, but she was determined to go wherever he would lead her. Discovering Garret, all of him, was the reason she'd come so far from the world she knew.

9

Ciana missed Eden. Eden had become the sister she'd never had, and although she heard from her friend via email, it did nothing to lessen her case of wintertime blues. Eden's chatty stories of Garret and sunny Australia only reminded Ciana of their carefree days in Italy, long gone in the snow flurries and sleet storms of January. On top of that, with Jon going off to Texas to visit his family for a few weeks, Ciana found herself cold, lonely, and at loose ends. She kept caring for the horses and projects in the old house, repainting the parlor, moving furniture, and cleaning out the attic. Because the shorter days meant longer nights, she spent most evenings in her room reading through her grandmother's diaries.

For the most part, they were full of schoolgirl drama and day-to-day minutiae. Ciana saw that her life at Bellmeade might hold hard work, but without modern conveniences, farm life had been tough and uncompromising. Water for washing dishes and taking baths had to be pumped by hand and heated on a wood stove. There had been no electricity at the house until the 1930s. Cows had to be milked rain or shine, hot or cold, in sickness and health. Hogs needed slopping—which made Ciana glad she only had horses and chickens to tend—and history from the forties and fifties wasn't nearly as interesting as she'd thought it would be. She quickly grew weary of reading about penny candy and ribbon buys at the general store—in those days the store and church were the centers of Windemere's social activity. The church still stood, but the store had been replaced by a supermarket in the seventies.

The one thing that did hold Ciana's interest was the thread of Roy Soder that Olivia wove throughout the pages from book to book and year to year. As they both grew up, she continued to be fascinated with him. And since Olivia had a habit of pouring her heart along with every detail of her life into the diaries, Ciana's fascination with him grew too. From the earliest entries, he was in constant trouble, branded a loner and a troublemaker by teachers and neighbors alike. He'd even been kicked out of Sunday school when he'd said he didn't believe in God. At age eleven Olivia had been mortified, but as time passed, she wrote of him with an interest that Ciana recognized as a crush.

However, it had been Eden who'd discovered the first entry about Roy that had sent Ciana on the hunt for others about him. Before she'd left for Australia, she and Eden skimmed the diaries together. One evening Eden had sat up straight and said, "Whoa. You need to read this one."

"Read it to me." They were sitting on the floor, books and papers written in longhand stacked neatly, ordered by dates as much as possible.

Eden grinned, waggled her eyebrows. "It's naughty. Sure you want to hear it?"

"I don't think Grandmother's idea of naughty translates to our idea of naughty. Read it."

"Dated August 7, 1942," Eden said. "She was what? Fourteen?"

"Sounds right."

Eden cleared her throat. "'I sneaked off to the swimming hole in Johnson Creek this afternoon. Hot day, school was out and I wanted a cool dip before I had to go home and face chores. No bathing suit—I hate them anyway, and so I stripped down to my undies and jumped right in. If Grandpa Jacob saw me like that he'd tan my hide with a willow switch. Don't care. Heard yesterday that Joel Bufford got killed in the war, in the Pacific, far away from home. Miz Bufford's put the gold star decal from the government in her window that tells everyone Joel's gone. Really sad. Just goes to show you life can be real short, so swimming in my undies didn't seem too awful.

"'I was having a fine time in the water when Roy showed up. He announced himself and sat down on the water's edge and said all kinds of suggestive things to me. (Grandpa calls Roy white trash.) I ignored him best I could, but then he started saying he'd like to come in for a cool dip too.

"'Then, with no mind or manners to move on, he took my dry clothes, which I'd left on the banks, and said, "If you want them, you have to come take them from me." I was scared, but I was mad too. Roy knew I couldn't go home wearing only my panties, so I did the only thing I could do. I crawled right out of that swimming hole and walked right up to him. His eyes were all over me and I bet I turned a hundred shades of red. But . . . I will only admit this to you, dear diary. Even though I hate him, it excited me to see this look that I can only call *hungry* on his face. It was like he wanted to lay me down right there on the ground. I felt this queer fire flare up inside me;

52

scary, but it made me feel alive and strong, like I held some power over him. But I grabbed my clothes and covered myself as best I could and told him to go away! And then he said, "Next time," and walked off whistling.

"'Soon as he was gone, I dressed and hightailed it out of there. I got to our barn and dried off with horse blankets. That night at supper, Mama told me I smelled like a horse and to wash up good before bed. I scrubbed every spot Roy's eyes had traveled on me with lye soap that burned my skin raw. I hate Roy Soder!'"

Eden leaned into the side of the bed after reading the entry. "I don't think she hated him at all. I think she was all hot and turned on for him."

"Farm kids grow up watching animals doing the deed. Sooner or later, it occurs to you that people must do it the same way," Ciana said.

Eden grinned. "Did it make you want to try it?"

"Not for a long time. First time I saw horses doing it, I was traumatized! Got over it, though," she added with a sly look.

"You do it with Jon yet?"

"No! Not that I don't want to," Ciana confessed. "But timing's never been right for us. Not yet, anyway."

They both must have thought of Arie at the same time, because Eden quickly switched gears. "Do you know what I think?" she asked. "I think Olivia really liked Roy. You know that bad-boy attraction thingy we girls get over guys who don't deserve us." She spoke from experience having faced up to her almost fatal attraction to Tony.

"Well, now I'm curious. Was raised to believe she only loved Grandpa Charles. Who knew such a villain was lurking in her past?" Ciana dragged a hank of hair across her upper lip to imitate a mustache. "Yes, this bad boy needs to be investigated further. Détective Ciana on the job!" And so began her research for any mention of bad boy Roy Soder in the diaries.

Ciana woke one night to the sound of engines revving and racing in the distance. Sleepily, she got up, wrapped a quilt around her shoulders, slipped on wool boot slippers, and went out onto the veranda. The sound was louder, with a consistent whine, but not close. She could see nothing unusual on the lawn or at the barn. The night was cold, and she shivered. Yet she didn't sleep well the rest of the night, and very early the next morning she saddled up her horse and rode out across her pastures toward where she'd heard the noise.

Just as night darkness faded to morning gray, she came up to her best alfalfa pastures and reined in Firecracker. The horse stamped and snorted away ice crystals forming on her nose. Ciana stared at her fields, dumbfounded. The fences lay broken in several places, and the earth had been gouged full of wide grooves. ATVs. Her best acreage had been vandalized, run over every which way by all-terrain vehicles. Ciana urged her horse forward over the downed fence and rode onto the scarred ground to survey the damage, which looked extensive. She shook angrily, cursed the riders, rode home, and called the police.

"What did the sheriff say?" Alice Faye poured Ciana another cup of coffee and set the pot on the table.

The sun was high now, but Ciana had spent the whole morning with Sheriff Frazier, walking her land and filing a report. "He says it's just bored kids. Not much he can do unless I catch them red-handed. Like that's going to happen." She fumed. "What am I supposed to do? Sit out by my fields all night with my shotgun?"

"Look, the ground can be plowed out once it thaws. As

for the fences, you'll have to repair them. When's Jon coming back? He'll help."

"I don't need Jon to fix a fence," Ciana growled. "I'm not some helpless twit!"

"My, my. Testy, aren't you? Frankly, I like having Jon around. Don't you?"

Ciana grabbed her coat from the back of her kitchen chair, refusing to engage in her mother's baited question. "I'll get started. Need to go into town for materials, though. If Willis will sell the stuff, what with me being a mere girl and all."

"No need to be crabby. You know I'll lend a hand if you need it. And, Ciana, there's no shame in taking help."

Ciana felt a twinge of guilt. She didn't really want Alice Faye outside in the cold stringing fence line and handling barbed wire. "You want anything while I'm in town?" she asked, her tone subdued.

"Not today. But thanks for asking."

Ciana stomped outside and into the brittle cold, muttering under her breath all the way to her old truck.

From the moment she stepped inside Willis's Lumber and Feed Store on Main Street, Ciana felt as if she were on display. It wasn't her imagination either. She heard people whisper, noticed them avoiding eye contact with her. Ciana set about gathering the wire and new metal posts she'd need to repair her fences, working quickly in order to get away from the glances and stares. At the cash register, as the clerk rang her up, Ted Sawyer Jr. came up alongside her. He was a few years older than her, but everyone called him Junior. One advantage of living in a small town was that everybody knew everybody and their business, and what she knew about Junior was that he was lazy and a bully.

"Howdy, Miz Beauchamp."

His greeting surprised her. He'd always called her Ciana. When had she turned into Miz Beauchamp?

"'Lo, Junior."

"Heard you had a bit of trouble with them ATV machines."

"You heard right." News traveled fast. Especially bad news. She paid the cashier, turned toward Junior. "Know anything about who might have done it?"

"Not a thing," Junior said, rocking back on his heels. "Real shame, though."

She simmered inside. Everything about him announced that he knew who'd done it. Ciana told the clerk she'd drive around to the loading dock for her purchases and load it up. "If you hear anything, you let me know. All right, now?"

"I'll tell you," Junior Sawyer said with a smirk. "Problem is once those things start happening to a place, they can happen again. Don't know why worse luck follows bad. But it does."

She leveled a cold stare at him. "Who you working for these days?"

"Oh, I just hire on with anybody who needs me."

Like Gerald Hastings? she thought. "I'm not going to be selling my land, Junior. Might want to pass that around to anyone who asks." She turned toward the door.

"Disappointing a lot of people," he said more loudly than necessary. "Some folks want to move on, and the town needs to grow."

She knew someone else had put the words into Junior's mouth. He hadn't had an original thought since grade school. "And some folks need to mind their own business. Person can get shot trespassing." Ciana left the store feeling Junior's steely stare stabbing into her back.

10

Ciana faced the difficult chore of resetting broken and damaged fence posts into frozen ground, then stringing wire fencing. She was angry about the vandalism, but resolute. No one was going to drive her off Bellmeade. She started the job on hands and knees with a spade to chip away the crust of ice and dig below the freeze mark. Next she switched to a post hole digger to go down roughly three more feet to set the pole securely. The work was tedious and strenuous, and that night she soaked in a tub of warm water laced heavily with Epsom salts to soothe her sore muscles.

Jon returned three days after the ATV incident. He came into the kitchen, where Ciana was standing by the coffee-pot and Alice Faye was baking bread. "Heard you had some trouble."

Alice Faye welcomed him warmly, while Ciana stiffened and refused to meet Jon's gaze, remembering his warnings about possible trouble that she'd brushed off.

"We called the sheriff," Alice Faye said.

"You have any thoughts about who might have done this?" He looked at Ciana.

"No good to speculate. It happened. Best to just fix things and move on. I'm working on it."

The air went thick with silence. He was angry and it showed. "I'll finish up."

Ciana's recent display of self-sufficiency was greatly impaired by both the slow pace of her repair work and Jon's thunderous expression daring her to object. "I'll help you," she said, granting him permission without saying so.

"Suit yourself, but I'd prefer to work alone."

Ciana's temper went hot, but she held her tongue.

"I'll have a meal on the table for you every day," Alice Faye said cheerily, her tone meant to ease the tension in the air between Ciana and Jon.

"That will be nice," Jon told her, and pulling on his heavy work gloves, he stomped out of the kitchen.

Recent snowfall had kept the boarding horses' owners from coming to care for them until the country roads were plowed; Ciana used that as an excuse to keep to the barn for the next few days and work with the horses while Jon finished the fencing. Each evening the three of them ate together with little conversation before Jon returned to Bill Pickins's bunkhouse. The fence was intact less than a week after the ATV incident.

Days later, Ciana saw Fred Brewster, the techie from Murfreesboro, talking to Jon out by the barn. The next day she was in the front parlor, scraping off what was left of old wallpaper around the front windows, when she saw Fred pull up with a horse trailer behind his truck and proceed to load his horse. She dropped the scraper, grabbed a jacket, and ran out the front door calling, "Fred! What are you doing?"

The man looked nervous as she skidded to a stop in front of him. "Oh, hi, Ciana. Didn't expect to see you."

"Where you going? Why are you taking your horse away?"

"Moving him to a place in Murfreesboro." His horse balked at the foot of the trailer.

She didn't like the news. Losing Fred meant losing a paying boarder. "I had no idea you were considering this. Are you unhappy here?"

"No, no. Your place has been great. You're great." Fred's gaze darted side to side. "I'm thinking of selling him. I mean, owning a horse is a lot of work and expense, more than I can give right now. Plus the man said the horse needs more attention than—"

"What man?"

"That Jon fellow. Your helper."

Shock, then anger twisted inside Ciana. "Well, he was wrong. It's winter. I give your horse plenty of attention."

"I know, Ciana, and you've been really good, but Jon . . . well, seemed like he really wanted me to go, and after thinking it over, I decided he's right. I never was a real horse person."

She was so angry she was afraid to open her mouth, certain that flames would shoot out. She took the horse's lead line and urged him into the trailer, where she tied him off, settled him, then exited and shut the gate behind her. Taking a deep, steadying breath, she said, "Well, you've paid for the month and it's only half gone, so I'll refund the difference."

"No need," Fred said, climbing into his truck. "Really. Just keep the money."

She stepped aside and watched Fred pull away with his horse, along with his steady payments.

Ciana seethed all day waiting for Jon to show up. When he finally did, in the late afternoon, she flew out of the house coatless in a fine driving sleet, and into the barn after him. "Why did you tell Fred Brewster to take his horse and leave?"

Jon removed his hat, shook off the wetness, then shook his coat and hung it on a post nail. "It was a *suggestion*," he said in his slow drawl, infuriating her even more. He took a moment to glance toward the stalls. "I guess he took it."

"I asked *why?*"

"I needed a stall for Caramel."

His answer momentarily stymied her. "Bill kick you out?"

Jon grinned. "No. But I'm moving in here and I needed a place for my horse." His tone was neutral, as if it was perfectly obvious and rational.

"Who says? We already settled this."

"No, *we* didn't. You stated your opinion. Mine's different."

"Who do you think you are, Jon Mercer? You can't just throw out a paying boarder and move in!" She was spitting mad.

"I'll pay for the stall, so you won't be losing money."

She took a swing at him, but he caught her wrists. "Now you listen to me, Ciana Beauchamp, I won't stand by while the people I love are threatened. It was your property this time, but next time, it could be *you* or your mother these freaks go after. I saw what they did to your fields. These are *not* nice people you're playing with."

"Let go of me." She twisted in his grip, but he held firm.

"Then settle down. I wrestled you to the ground once before, Ciana, and I'll do it again. Don't test me."

The look in his eyes stopped her. She remembered the day she'd physically attacked him, blind with grief about Arie's impending death and all her long-held pain and fury over what had happened in Italy. "Low blow," she whispered, allowing heat and fury to evaporate.

"All's fair in love and war." His grip loosened, and his voice softened. "Let me help you protect this place. I have a rifle and a pistol, and I will shoot anything that comes along to do you harm. Between the three of us, we can keep steady watch."

"Mom wants us out of here."

"Your mother will do anything to keep you safe. And so will I," he added.

Ciana shook herself out of his grip. "I just don't like to be told what to do, Jon. It's not my way."

"Okay. Fair enough. I'm not telling you right now. I'm asking you. Let me stay."

His face blurred through a sudden smear of tears. Of course, he was right. She needed his help, and having him close by was another layer of protection for her land. The logistics of his staying were another matter. Grudgingly, she said, "Well, you can't sleep in the barn like before. You'll freeze to death."

He gave her a half smile. "Full disclosure: Alice Faye already offered me a room in the house. Up on the third floor. Said it once belonged to your great-grandfather Jacob and his wife."

Ciana felt another flash of anger that quickly congealed into cold sarcasm. "Already discussed and decided, I guess. Nice of you two to consult me."

Jon dipped his head to snag her gaze, his expression turning boyish. "Discussed, but you decide. Tell me right now and if your answer is no, I'll move back to Bill's. But I'd like to keep my horse here. It'll give me an excuse to come over every day."

Her choice. Of course she needed help. She'd be stupid to

61

allow her pride to interfere and turn him away. "I can't pay you." In truth, she was just scraping by. Her credit cards were maxed with fencing supplies and she still faced upcoming charges for spring planting.

"I have some money. I rode the circuit last summer, remember?"

A great weariness stole over Ciana. Jon's constant presence would be an emotional and physical challenge for her mind and body. Yet it was necessary. Any emotional entanglement with him aside, his presence at Bellmeade was a practical one. Going it alone was an ideal, a luxury she couldn't afford. And the recent intimidation was unnerving. She had proven she was spunky. So what? She wasn't Olivia, with a backbone of steel. At the moment she felt like a little girl, in over her head, trying to hold on to and manage her land with little to no support.

"One more thing," Jon said. "I'm coming to help you and Alice Faye. I don't expect anything more than what's already been promised—a bed, food, and a warm place for my horse. You don't have to worry about me going after anything else."

She understood what he was telling her. His offer was *hands off*. She'd have his presence, his muscle, his firepower. She knew the rules were fair. She sucked in a long breath, too tired to resist anymore. "I don't want you to leave, Jon. Move on over." She offered a conciliatory smile, knowing full well that her battles with history, with herself, with her neighbors, and with her long-held desire for Jon Mercer were only beginning.

"You still speaking to me?" Alice Faye asked when Ciana came into the kitchen from the barn before supper. Jon had gone back to Bill's to get his gear, his horse, and belongings.

"Does it matter?"

"Rather not have you treat me like Olivia would whenever I crossed her will."

"I'm not Grandmother," Ciana snapped. "Look, I know having Jon here is better for us. I get it. I just wish—" She stopped, not wanting her anger to regain control. "You should have told me before you asked him to move into the house."

"I should have, but I didn't." Alice Faye rattled pots and pans, putting them atop the stove, preparing to start supper. "It'll be all right, Ciana. Having a man like Jon around might make people think twice before any more damage is done."

"You still on board for selling Bellmeade?" Ciana slouched at the table, toyed with a spoon forgotten after lunch had been cleared.

"Not as enthusiastic as I once was. It's one thing to give in when it's something that's offered. Another thing entirely when some outsider comes in to drive you away."

"Why, Mama, you sound like a Beauchamp," Ciana said with a smudge of a smile.

Alice Faye snorted. "No need to insult me."

Ciana's smile broadened. "Wonder what Eden will say when she comes home to Jon living here?"

"Used to be, generations all lived together. Don't know when we got the idea that families had to break apart and live separately. I've missed having a full house."

There was a tinge of sadness in Alice Faye's voice, reminding Ciana that ever since her father's death, Alice Faye had been alone. Certainly she and her grandmother had lived in the house with her mother, but Ciana had been a child and oblivious to her mother's inner pain. For years Alice Faye and Olivia had revolved around each other. Ciana had been their touch point; she now understood that she had also been the fissure that divided them. She had run to her grandmother, not her mother, for most everything, further isolating Alice Faye. A mistake, Ciana realized. But how could she undo the damage now that so many years and memories stood between them?

"Did I ever thank you for handling the hay harvest while I was in Italy?" Ciana asked, suddenly remorseful over the divide. "Maybe I shouldn't have run off and left you."

Alice Faye looked up, startled. "Goodness, I've done it before, Ciana. It's what we farmers do . . . plant fields, gather in crops, muck stalls." She scraped corn bread batter into a baking pan. "And at the time, I had enough money to hire help. I was glad you and your friends were on vacation. Besides, you're here now. In time for spring." She put the empty bowl in the sink under running water. "Turned out for the best. What with Arie getting sick and all."

And dying, Ciana thought, filling in the unspoken. "Sure can't hire anyone this year. Jon will be a big help come April."

Alice Faye caught Ciana's eye. "He's a good man."

"I know."

"Man should have a reason to stay around after planting season."

Ciana bristled at the implication. She wasn't about to discuss her and Jon's complicated relationship with her mother. "Man loves the rodeo circuit," she said curtly, leaving the conversation and the kitchen.

11

"We're going to have a good time today!" was pretty much how Garret greeted Eden every morning when she came bleary-eyed into the kitchen for coffee, and after her first cup of caffeine, she was ready for any itinerary. He took her all around Sydney, showing off his city like an art dealer with a prized collection. They rode public transportation when possible, partly because it was simple and plentiful, and partly because gasoline was expensive and made driving costly. They rode buses, city trolleys, trains, and they walked—for miles. As a benefit of the exercise, his body began to fill out. The gauntness left his face, and he began to look more like the Garret she'd met in Italy. Maggie beamed continuously, and Trevor, a quiet man, often peeked from behind his newspapers and legal briefs to flash approving smiles at Eden and his son.

"You're good for him," Maggie often said to Eden.

Eden basked in the approval.

Lorna and Tom invited Eden and Garret over for a

Saturday afternoon at their apartment, so they went into the city early and walked across the famous Sydney Harbour Bridge. There was a sidewalk protecting walkers from traffic, and at the midway mark an opportunity to don an elaborate harness and scale the metal heights to the bridge's top. Eden rejected Garret's suggestion that they try it. Instead she ogled the famed Opera House in the harbor below, its white roof gleaming in the sun.

On the far side, they paused at the Circular Quay, where ferries shuttled people across the sparkling blue water. The area teemed with pedestrians. "We'll catch the Manly ferry one day soon," Garret said. "Now it's on to the buses and out to Tom's place."

The ride took them to an area of apartment buildings, none of them as tall as many Eden had seen in Nashville. Tom and Lorna's rental was on an upper floor that looked out over treetops and houses.

"I like your place," Eden told Lorna. "It's cozy." They were in the kitchen preparing a salad and sipping wine while the guys were on the balcony minding the grill. Tom had dragged a TV plugged into a long extension cord outside so they could watch a cricket match while they cooked and drank beer.

"Cozy is a polite word. We're crammed in here. Been looking for a place of our own to buy for months. Everything's so expensive, and right now we'd have trouble covering a mortgage even with our two salaries together. But we persevere."

Eden thought of the house she and her mother had once lived in. She had no warm, cozy memories of it, or of living with bipolar Gwen. They hadn't communicated in months. "I'm sure you'll find a place."

"Tom's up for a salary increase. Hope he gets it."

Eden sliced a radish paper thin on a cutting board of eucalyptus wood. "Can I ask you something?"

"Ask away."

"What can you tell me about Alyssa? She keeps popping up like a garden weed."

Lorna laughed. "You've pegged her perfect. I don't care for her . . . never have, and I'm not just saying that. She thinks she's so much better than us common folk. She and Garret got together in school. Hate to say it, but he fell hard for her."

Eden didn't like hearing that. "Well, she is pretty. And a model."

Lorna stabbed the air with her paring knife. "And she never lets you forget it either. Some talent agent 'discovered' her when she was thirteen, signed her to a contract. They used to tart her up for a photo shoot so she'd look older. Now that she's in her twenties, they tone her down to look like a twelve-year-old. And airbrush her face too! Never believe there's truth in a magazine picture of a model."

"Garret says she's successful."

"Depends on how you qualify success. She makes money and her face gets plastered over ads, but I think she's about as interesting as chewing gum. After a few chews you just want to spit it out."

Eden smiled but said, "Regardless, Garret likes her."

"For a while. There was a time she led Garret by his nose. Until you came along," she added with a broad smile. "Could see that he went bonkers over you plain as day back in Italy."

Lorna's endorsement made Eden feel better. "We had a good time. I didn't know what to make of Garret back then. He comes on strong, you know." Eden picked up her wineglass, took a sip.

"He can't help it; his nature is enthusiasm. We all could see he was fallin', but you kept backing away."

"I was a little overwhelmed."

"And Ciana watched over you pretty fierce." Eden didn't want to go into why Ciana had been protective of her. "But Arie—she seemed to understand Garret right off. We used to talk, me and her. Sad about her dying."

The mention of Arie made Eden nostalgic. "Arie never met a stranger. That was *her* nature." She went back to work cutting up salad vegetables.

From the balcony, they heard a shout and cheers. Lorna glanced toward the noise. "Guess their team scored. Not like rugby, where the guys pounce on each other. Mean sport."

So is finding your way through a relationship, Eden thought. "I get the feeling that Alyssa isn't on best of terms with Garret's family, though—especially his mother."

"That's true. Alyssa is so hoity-toity. Not to Maggie's liking at all." If Lorna knew any other details, she didn't offer them. "Ignore Alyssa if she comes around."

Eden washed a couple of tomatoes, turned off the tap with her elbow. "That beach party's coming up. Not sure how I feel about going, knowing she'll be there. Plus there's the bathing suit thing."

"Rubbish! You're being silly. She's tall and thin like a bird. Has to be because of modeling. She used to starve herself, maybe eat a lettuce leaf for lunch. But you . . ." Lorna smiled at Eden. "You have a great body. Just look at yourself."

"Oh, Lorna—"

"You've got curves and boobs. Alyssa's flat as my hand. I've seen her in the locker room. That girl has no titties. Tom says guys like their girls with some meat." Her eyes twinkled. "Something to hold on to in the dark."

Eden laughed. "Back home, we say, 'a man don't want to have to shake the sheets to find you.'" She picked up her glass, swirled the ruby liquid.

Lorna whooped. "That's why Tom and I get on so well." She patted her backside. "He can't miss me in the dark or in a crowd."

Eden laughed so hard wine splashed over the top of her glass.

"What's so funny?" Tom asked, coming in the kitchen.

Behind him Garret stood holding a platter of grilled meat and shrimp. "Must be quite a funny salad. Didn't know carrots and lettuce could say funny things."

But the girls couldn't stop laughing.

"I think it's going to be a while before we eat," Tom said over his shoulder.

Garret set the platter on the counter, took Eden by the waist, and pulled her close. "I think the cooks have spent too much time tasting the grapes and not enough time working." He grinned, took the wineglass from her hand, and drained it. "Problem solved."

He started humming and dancing Eden around the kitchen, twirled her into the adjoining living room while she giggled. He lost his balance when he dipped her, and they fell in a heap onto the sofa, laughing uncontrollably.

"I think my best mate's gone bonkers," Tom called out, wrapping his arms around Lorna.

"No," Lorna said, pressing against him. "Fool's just in love."

Eden especially loved the day they spent at the zoo. Garret walked her through a gate into a large, grassy enclosure of free-roaming kangaroos and wallabies. "They're so cute!" she cried. Garret winked and cautioned, "Watch out for roo doo." She gave him a smirk, then bent and petted a roo that had hopped over to investigate them. A little joey poked his head from his mother's pouch, and Eden was totally charmed. "Ciana should see these. Much cuter than horses!"

That day she saw all kinds of animals native to Australia and the island of Tasmania, but she loved the koalas best of all. The fuzzy gray animals clung to eucalyptus trees, fast asleep. "How do they hang on?"

"Desperation," Garret joked. "Wouldn't want a dingo dog to grab 'em." He took Eden's hand, kissed her palm, and wrapped her fingers around the spot. "They sleep up to twenty hours a day. Not a bad life. Sleep. Eat. Have sex." He pointed to a baby koala.

"Is that your idea of a full life?"

"Well . . . how about sex, eat, and sleep?"

She punched his arm, but it wasn't a secret that when he left her at her bedroom door every night, he wanted to come in with her. She wasn't ready to go there yet, and especially not in his parents' house.

She kept notes on her electronic tablet about her adventures and every so often emailed stories to Ciana, who in turn filled her in on day-to-day life at Bellmeade. One evening, sitting on the steps in the shallow end of the pool with Garret, Eden said, "Jon, the man Ciana likes but won't let herself love, is moving back onto her property."

"It bother you?"

"No. It's a good thing. Someday that girl's going to realize she's in love with him. Don't know why she fights it."

Garret swirled the water with his broad hands, making

circles flow around Eden. "Girls can be blind that way. Can't see what's right under their noses sometimes."

Her heart did a stutter step. "Meaning?"

He caught her gaze, winked, then pushed off and started swimming laps.

12

February 10

Hey, girlfriend. Sounds like you're having a blast down under. I hate you for lying in the sun by a pool while we shiver. If you were here, I swear we'd go down to New Orleans for Mardi Gras for a couple of days and just leave the job of guarding Bellmeade to Jon. Him and Mom act like BFFs and I feel like an outsider in my own house. I tell you, it's hard with him living here and sleeping two flights up from me. We make small talk, but he keeps his distance like he promised he would. When he moved in, he said it was to help and protect us, so I guess he meant it.

Just as well, I guess. Makes it easier to stay peeved at him for bulldozing his way in and taking up residence and treating me like I'm some helpless child. Won't tell him this, but me and Mom do sleep better nights having him here. I don't jump every time something goes bump in the night, and every morning he saddles up Caramel and rides out to inspect our property. He always rides armed, and mostly he comes back and sets to cleaning the stalls. The only way I know if there's been property damage is when he comes back and loads up tools and fencing wire. He doesn't say anything about it, just goes to work fixing it. That irks me too.

I don't go into town much because people are staring at me and giving me hateful looks. Like I alone am destroying Windemere and everybody's futures. Listen to me whine! Sorry, Eden. Didn't mean to get carried away. On the bright side, Mom's covered the formal dining table, the coffee table, and every other flat surface in the house with seedlings for the garden. The little sprouts are starting to poke through the dirt in their cups. We'll plant in April, and from the looks of it we'll have a bumper crop. You will be home by then, won't you?

Miss you! Write often. Love to Garret.

Ciana

PS: Don't let that Alyssa girl get to you. I know you're better than her! And Garret likes YOU.

PPS: In reading through Olivia's diaries, I hit one juicy tidbit she wrote when she was fifteen. Seems like Roy cornered her and kissed her "ON THE MOUTH!" (Her words). It was her first ever kiss, and from the one guy she keeps writing about not liking . . . love/hate. Go figure.

"You're looking solemn this morning." Garret came into the kitchen and walked to the refrigerator.

Eden sat hunched over her electronic tablet. "Reading email from home. Ciana's having trouble at Bellmeade."

He fished a glass from a shelf and pulled out a chair across from her. "What kind of trouble?"

Eden filled him in on Ciana's dilemma with her farm, along with stories of the escalating vandalism. She gazed thoughtfully out the side window. "I feel like I should be there for her."

"Is she alone?"

"Her mother's there. And Jon Mercer—a force to be reckoned with."

"Well, if she's got help, it doesn't sound like there's anything you can do."

"Ciana plays at being strong and self-reliant, but I know she's scared. I'm her best friend. She may need me. To talk to and all."

"So what are you thinking?"

"Maybe I should, you know, head back."

She and Garret had tiptoed around the length of Eden's visit for days. She'd already been his guest for six weeks. He had told her he didn't want her to leave, and she didn't want to go.

"Don't like the idea of you going back to trouble." He poured himself a glass of juice, drank it down in big gulps. "And your visa is good for more than another month." He leaned over, took the tablet, and put it on the table. "Look, I feel the pressure too. I need to make some plans for myself. I'm hale and hearty now, and my parents don't need me hanging about. But it's summer and our beach party is coming up; picnic, surfin', and lots of sun time. All my old mates are asking to meet you. Not that I want to share, but we'll have fun, Eden. After that we'll both get serious about our futures. Stay until your visa expires. Will you do that for me?"

Looking into his eyes, knowing in her heart she wanted to be with him, she said, "If you insist."

"I insist," he said with a grin.

Eden welcomed a few more weeks with him with nothing to do but hang out. What could be so hard about that? "About that surfing thing—"

"We'll grab that ferry to Manly today," Garret interrupted. "We'll take the boogie boards and start your surfin' lessons, teach you how to skim along the surf on the shoreline. Not scary at all. Come on, now. You'll be a surf goddess in no time."

She doubted that, but went with him to a small shed at the back of the yard. Inside, through the dim light, she saw garden equipment and two large surfboards leaning against a back wall. She went to the boards while he rummaged through a stack of beach gear and mumbled, "I know the boogie boards are here somewhere."

"You stand up on one of these things? In rushing water?" she teased, making it sound like an absurd choice.

Garret straightened, came alongside of her. "On my best days, yes."

One surfboard was painted black with red stripes, the other, much more elaborate in design, sported a hand-painted stylized fish that covered its surface. "This one's pretty." She brushed her hand down the smooth fiberglass.

He nodded toward the plainer one. "This one's mine."

"And this one?"

His mood changed and his expression went flat. "Never used anymore."

Eden waited for an explanation that didn't come. Not like Garret to hold back a story, she thought, but it warned her away from more questions.

He turned to resume his search and seconds later came up with the boogie boards. "Got them! Let's go." His familiar smile and cheerful demeanor had returned.

She left with him, but she couldn't shake the feeling that the beautiful board against the wall had a story he wasn't sharing. She thought again of Tony. Everyone had secrets. And she would respect Garret's.

Late one Saturday night they met Tom and Lorna downtown and hopped the club circuit. Eden was in her element. The techno beats were different from the sounds of Nashville and Italy, but she quickly adapted and embraced the music, the crowd, and the noise. The four of them drank down pitchers of beer, shouted conversations over the beat of the music, and danced until most of the night was gone. Eden was humming and standing in line in the restroom when she caught sight of Alyssa, staring at her in the bathroom mirror. In spite of all the beer she'd drunk, Eden suddenly felt sober. She straightened, kept her back against the wall.

"Thought that was you," Alyssa said, coming over. She wore a short gold lamé dress that barely covered her crotch. "Enjoying our Aussie night life?" Alyssa's eyes were half closed and Eden quickly saw that the girl was very drunk and very high.

"What's not to love?"

"You here with Garret, I suppose?"

"And Tom and Lorna."

"Ah yes. The lovers without a cause. Two losers."

"Bitchy thing to say." The words were out before Eden could stop them, but she didn't like Alyssa's put-down of two people she liked.

"Being nice isn't my forte. Never been necessary to 'be

nice.'" She said it as if hatefulness were a virtue. "And I'm sure Lorna's told you how *wrong* I am for Garret."

"We have better things to talk about," Eden said, not wanting Alyssa to know she'd even been a blip on Eden's radar. "Work out your own problems with Garret. He and I don't have any."

Alyssa's eyes slitted. She reminded Eden of a cobra about to strike. Alyssa wedged her body between Eden and the door, leaned into Eden's face until the smell of cigarettes and liquor made her eyes water. "You do *not* matter to me," Alyssa spat. "You are nothing."

Eden flinched. Feeling like a nothing, a nobody, lonely and worthless, had once led her to cutting, self-mutilation, to manage her emotional pain. Wasn't that all behind her now? She couldn't let this hateful girl tear her down. Not in some club thousands of miles from home. Eden reached deep into herself, then said, "Why don't you ask Garret if I'm a nothing. Because that's not how he says he feels about me when we're alone. That's not what he tells me at all."

Just then another girl brushed by Eden and Alyssa, giving them sour looks. "Could you two move? You're jamming the doorway."

Alyssa suggested something for the girl to go do with herself, and the girl scampered out the door. Alyssa turned back to Eden, but her spell was broken. Alyssa knew it and tried to regroup. "But you will leave. You are going back to America."

"Not soon. Wouldn't want to miss the beach party." Eden delivered the line with forcefulness, letting Alyssa know she wasn't surrendering any time she had with Garret.

"Just listen, bitch," Alyssa said through half-clenched teeth. "I was Garret's girl long before you came on the scene, and I will be his girl long after you're gone. Trust me."

With equal venom, Eden fired back. *"Trust me.* He left you in the dust a long time ago. So get out of my way, or I'll take you down right here on the bathroom floor."

Looking shocked, Alyssa threw her head back, but she stepped aside. Breathing hard, she gave Eden the finger, jerked open the door, and left.

Eden was still shaking when she exited the bathroom. She looked around but saw no sign of Alyssa, so she steadied herself on the wall and struggled to get her adrenaline under control and lose the feeling that she might heave. She regrouped, replaying the encounter, and realized that her reaction had been telling. She cared more for Garret than she'd allowed herself to admit. *Good to know.* Anything worth having was worth fighting for—the Beauchamp philosophy was rubbing off on her. Eden gave herself a self-satisfied pat, then sobered. She and Alyssa would face off again at the beach party.

Bring it on.

13

Eden wore her best bikini to Bondi Beach, and when she removed her cover-up, the look on Garret's face told her she'd chosen well. "Outstanding," he told her, twirling her by her fingertips.

Many of his friends had already arrived and staked out their territory. Garret introduced her to a sea of faces with a litany of names she knew she'd never remember, but seeing Lorna and Tom made her more comfortable. Thankfully, Alyssa hadn't yet arrived, and Eden found herself hoping she didn't come at all. The encounter at the club still felt like a bad hangover.

Eden, Lorna, and several girls spread towels on the fine yellow sand and watched the guys hit the waves with their boards. All surfing was done in water at one far end of the beach, well away from the rocks that clustered below large bluffs soaring above the ocean. Bathers were left to swim in the blue water between two flags positioned in the sand, without fear of being run over by surfboarders. One of Garret's friends had brought along a big board for Garret, because he and Eden had ridden the bus and only brought along the smaller wave-skimming boards. Eden had gotten good on hers at Manly Beach, but the waves there had been smaller. Here at Bondi, the surf intimidated her. And while the steady roll of breakers made for good surfing, Eden decided that sitting on the sand and watching suited her just fine, and said so to Lorna.

"No worries," Lorna said. "I never liked surfing much myself. Hate the tumble when I fall. Tom and Garret are pretty good. We'll just cheer for them."

Garret had style on the board. He paddled out and waited for an ocean swell to his liking, and just as the wave began to crest, he stood on the board and rode it as long as possible, sometimes all the way into the shore. Occasionally he even tucked himself into the curl—no easy feat, Eden was told.

At one point, he jammed his board upright in the sand and jogged over to the spread of towels, leaned down, and gave Eden a salty kiss. "Care to try?"

"Maybe later."

"Come on. I'll be on the board with you."

"Try it." The voice from behind them was Alyssa's. She sauntered to the front of the towel, looked down on Eden and Garret. Her height was impressive, her bikini couture, and her hair like spun gold. *Looks like a freakin' sea nymph*, Eden thought sourly. "You might like it."

Eden forced a chipper smile. "Guess it won't hurt to try."

Garret pulled her up, gave Alyssa a polite but disinterested nod, and led Eden to retrieve the board. He put it in the water and walked it out with her in tow until the water was deep enough for the board to float freely. "Straddle it," he said, and helped her get astride it, then put himself on the board behind her. "Now paddle."

She cupped her hands into the water and together they

went farther out. She was half terrified, half exhilarated. "Water's cold."

"Pacific Ocean. Doesn't get very warm." He kept glancing over his shoulder, looking for the right wave. "Let the wave do the work," he said into her ear.

"Do I have to stand up?"

"No, we'll just ride a few in, but put your feet up on the board. Here comes a nice one. Hang on."

She felt the board lift as the water rose beneath them, and for a moment she felt as if she were on a roller coaster. She gripped the sides of the board and they coasted, then slid down and toward the shoreline. The sensation was amazing. Lorna and the other girls were there to meet them when they nosed ashore. The girls clapped, and once Eden stood, she bowed theatrically. Garret hugged her, lifting her off the ground. "That's my girl!"

She kissed him, but noticed that Alyssa hadn't stayed around for the show.

The food appeared, and everyone ate on the grass of Bondi away from the sand and surf. Eden fielded questions about her life in Tennessee, and told every story she could think of about Bellmeade, horses and bronc riding, and Ciana, her friend who drove a tractor. When the questions wound down, the men started a soccer match and the girls shopped the stores that fronted a wide thoroughfare.

"Looks like Alyssa abandoned us," Lorna said, smiling smugly.

Eden realized it was true. "Maybe it was something I said."

"Hope so. I guess she hated all the attention you were getting." Lorna linked her arm with Eden's. "Good job."

Eden bought souvenirs for Ciana and Alice Faye. She remembered that Abbie was going to have a baby and bought a stuffed koala covered with sheep's wool. Lorna said that she and Tom had to leave early, so Eden wandered back to the beach alone. The men's game was still in progress, so she slathered herself with sunscreen and stretched out on a towel.

She grew hot, looked out, and saw that the ocean was now a glassy blue and calm as bathwater. Garret's loaner surfboard was upright in the sand, and Eden thought back to Italy and the way she would lazily drift half asleep on a float in the pool. She got up, wrestled the board into the water, and walked it out until she was able to hoist herself onto the slick surface. She lay on her stomach and closed her eyes. And she thought about her life and where it was headed. The Aussie girls all seemed to have plans for their lives. They had jobs, or were returning to university. A few were married. But Eden felt just as unclear about her future as she had in Windemere. She had never loved studying and didn't want to go to college. Nor did she want to return to her former dead-end job at the downtown boutique. The money she did have wouldn't last her forever. She'd come all this way to reconnect with Garret, but although they cared for each other, she had no idea as to what he wanted for his life. And the distance between Tennessee and Sydney was mind-boggling. Loneliness crept over her. She should face it. She had no future plans. Not a single one.

The change in the sound of the surf roused her. She glanced up and saw that she'd drifted far from shore, closer to the jutting rocks. Waves hammered the cluster of stones. Alarmed, Eden sat upright. She straddled the board and paddled toward the open water, making some headway, but the tide caught her and she watched the shore recede even farther. She struggled to turn the board, aim it back at the beach, but the tide was strong and she couldn't do it. She waved her hands above her head, shouted, hoped someone would spot her.

Eden knew she was in trouble but fought down panic. Losing her head wouldn't help her. Then, without warning, she shifted and went over sideways. Treading water, she watched the board bob away in growing swells. She took in a mouthful of water, coughed and gagged, fought to stay afloat. Then the tide caught her from underneath, tumbled her over and under, sucked her down. She opened her eyes. Seawater stung and burned. She kicked hard for the surface, spun helplessly, and realized that she didn't know which way was up. Desperate for air, she scrambled, turned, and kicked, swallowed more water, breathed in ocean, not air.

Her lungs burned, begged for oxygen, and just as darkness closed over her, she felt hands grab her and haul her upward. A hallucination? Unable to stop herself, Eden breathed and filled her nose and throat with seawater. And the world went black.

Eden woke gasping, coughing, gagging up salt water, her lungs on fire. She blinked, saw men's faces hovering over her. One shouted, "She's back!" An oxygen mask quickly covered her face, and then Garret was there, hovering over her, touching her, holding her hand, tears in his blue eyes. Later she learned she'd been saved by lifeguards and that she'd gotten caught in a riptide. She was lucky to be alive.

Garret's parents came for them, their faces grooved with concern. Back at the house, Maggie helped Eden shower and dress, clucking around her until she had parked Eden on a sofa, and fortified her with tea and soup. Then Garret took over.

"I'm all right," Eden told him, making an effort to settle both of them. Her voice was hoarse from swallowing seawater.

Garret couldn't take his eyes off her. "I—I could have lost you."

"But I'm okay. Really." Her throat felt raw, and she had scrapes on one arm from tumbling against the ocean's gritty bottom. Her muscles were sore from fighting the relentless tide, but mostly she was grateful that she'd survived. She was also embarrassed, knowing she'd ruined what was to have been a kickoff party for the autumn season. What she'd done, used a surfboard as a float, had been foolish.

His face looked ashen and his eyes were shot through with remorse. He climbed on the sofa to sit behind her, wrapped his arms around her, and nestled her against his chest. His big hands tenderly stroked her arms. "I should never have left you alone for so long. I'm sorry, love."

"Don't blame yourself. It was my fault for thinking the Pacific Ocean was akin to a pool. Tennessee's landlocked, you know. No ocean for hundreds of miles. Dumb me." He placed his cheek on hers. She felt the rough scrape of stubble. "Ciana would kill me if I came over here and drowned." She heard the low sound of his chuckle in her ear.

"I won't let you out of my sight from now on."

In his embrace, she felt safe. She turned her head to catch his eye. "I know your mother means well with the tea and all, but do you think I could trade it for a glass of wine?"

A smile lit his face. "I'll get us both some." He kissed the nape of her neck, untangled himself from the lightweight blanket his mother had insisted Eden use.

Eden watched him head toward the kitchen and the wine refrigerator there. She closed her eyes, took shuddering breaths, clenched her hands into trembling fists in an effort to ease the terrifying memory of being swallowed by the sea.

14

Ciana spent many evenings in Olivia's former study, at her grandmother's ancient scarred oak desk, going through old ledgers from the days when Bellmeade accounting had been kept by hand. Nowadays she entered the numbers into a computer accounting program, where straight rows painted a picture of a farm's financial health but never the hardships of the farm's life. Over the years, many a hand had made neat entries on the paper. Ciana liked skimming the books, keeping an eye out for notations in the book's margins, some of them especially poignant.

Old Jake dropped dead plowing today. A good horse, but plum wore out.

Drought took fifty acres. Poor harvest. Will owe bank.

Hail ruined most of hay crop.

In the 1940s, her great-grandfather noted he'd bought a tractor from a bankrupt neighboring farm. But it was Olivia's notation in 1961 that one evening stopped Ciana cold.

Bought the Soder farm for back taxes today. Sheriff tossed Roy off the property. He never saw it coming. Am glad both his parents are gone and didn't have to face the humiliation, but I hate Roy with all my being. God forgive me for gloating.

Ciana pushed back in the squeaky desk chair, her palms against the well-worn arms, and mulled over the entry. What had happened that made Olivia turn against Roy? Last she'd read, Olivia had been in school and all of sixteen, getting a French kiss from the guy. In that entry Olivia had noted, *The kiss made my knees go weak and my heart 'bout jump out of my chest. My first kiss like that . . . with his tongue in my mouth. I'm supposed to not like Roy. Never supposed to be seen with him. So why do I think about him all the time and wish he'd kiss me that way again?*

Ever since reading that entry, Ciana had had to put the diaries aside. Many of the books were near ruin; apparently, the old roof had leaked at some point in the past, and water had badly damaged the delicate paper. Maybe that was when the old books had been shoved into the trunk, locked away, and forgotten. Ciana sighed. Regardless of the mildew and stuck-together pages, she'd have to go back to delving into them. She just had to know what had turned her grandmother's schoolgirl attraction to Roy into hatred so many years later.

"Knock, knock," a voice said.

Ciana's gaze shot to the doorway, where Jon stood leaning against the jamb. "How long have you been there?"

"Long enough. You looked miles away."

She closed the open book containing Olivia's note and shoved it aside. "Come in."

He did, and laid twelve long-stemmed red roses across the desk. The petals glowed under a Tiffany lamp. "Flowers? For me?"

His brow knitted; then he smiled. "Of course for you."

"But why?" His green eyes held hers, igniting the familiar warmth just his nearness could create. If there was a potion to make her immune to him, she swore she'd take it.

He looked bemused. "Did you forget? Happy Valentine's Day."

Her gaze flew to the desk calendar. *February 14.* It had totally slipped her mind. Plus, she'd worked all day and was tired. She shrugged sheepishly, picked up one of the perfect roses, and brought it to her nose. "I did forget. Thank you."

He chuckled. "You may be the only woman in the country who forgot."

She smiled. "You shouldn't have spent your money. I know roses cost a lot."

"My money. And I didn't buy them. I picked them."

She quickly eyed the perfect stems, obviously groomed to be gifted.

"I picked them from Flo's Florist on Main Street," he said.

That made Ciana laugh. "Touché, cowboy." She wanted to stand up and wrap herself in his arms. She wanted to feel his mouth on hers, his hands on her skin. All she needed to do was open her arms, invite him to herself. Instead she cleared her throat. "Thank you again."

He searched her face, and she saw his desire and his hesitation. Why did she hold back? She wanted him. He wanted her. Simple chemistry. Except it wasn't really so simple for her. She shifted uncomfortably and watched the light of yearning fade from his eyes. "I also have a request," he said after a moment of awkward silence.

Not trusting her voice, she nodded as a sign for him to continue.

"I want to get a dog to monitor the immediate grounds, the house and barn, and the nearby pastures."

"A dog?" The request caught her off guard.

"I've been asking around, and there's a rescue shelter in Nashville that takes in old police and military dogs when they're no longer able to stay in the field. Otherwise most of them would have to be put down. A well-trained dog will go a long way to keep intruders off your land."

The idea had never occurred to her. "I don't know, Jon. What if it goes after the chickens?" She'd heard stories about farm dogs with a taste for both eggs and the birds that laid them.

"It won't."

She chewed her bottom lip. Another animal to feed.

He must have sensed her thought, because he quickly added, "I'll take care of him."

Still she hesitated.

"A perimeter dog will keep trespassers away. We'll all sleep better."

She had never figured that Jon might have been lying awake nights, listening for trespassers invading the barn—or worse, the house. He was worried, so she couldn't dismiss his request. "All right. Go get us a badass dog who'll bark his fool head off."

He touched his forehead in a casual salute and left. She turned off the lamp and sat in the dark, longing to consummate what lay between them while chiding herself for letting it walk away one more time.

The dog was a German shepherd with hip dysplasia, still young and healthy enough to be useful for guarding property if not rigorous police work. His name was Soldier, and when Jon returned with the animal a few days later, Ciana saw that the shepherd was already bonding him. She wasn't surprised. Jon had a way with animals—he was a horse whisperer, after all.

Jon introduced Ciana and Alice Faye to Soldier, who thoroughly sniffed them and seemed to understand that they were to be accepted, then walked him the perimeter of Bellmeade proper.

Later, clearing the supper dishes, Ciana asked her mother, "Why didn't we ever have a dog when I was growing up? Lots of farms do."

"We did once. When you were a baby, an old hound wandered onto the property and stayed. I liked him a lot."

"So what happened?" Ciana leaned against the counter. Her interest in the family's past had grown since she'd discovered the diaries.

"When you were about three, you tried to ride him like a pony and he nipped at you. So Olivia got rid of him."

The expression on Alice Faye's face told Ciana there had been a rift between her mother and grandmother over the dog's disappearance. "Wouldn't it have been better to tell me to leave the dog alone?"

"I thought so, but Granddaddy Charles ended up agreeing with Olivia. And in the long run, so did I. One day when you have a child, you'll understand about protecting her above everything else."

Feeling sorry for the long-gone dog, Ciana crossed her arms. "Well, I sure won't let some kid get away with stupid stuff. Dog was just saying no to me. He shouldn't have been turned out."

Alice Faye flashed an indulgent smile, communicating that the incident was best forgotten, but Ciana could tell that even after all these years, the loss still hurt her mother.

Ciana added, "Well, we have another dog now. And I'm old enough to bite him back if he nips me."

Her mother laughed, making Ciana curiously happy.

Within days Soldier took up his duty, keeping watch by night and sleeping in the barn by day.

And with Soldier doing due diligence, they all slept better.

On one of Ciana's rare runs into Windemere, she bumped into Abbie in the grocery store. "Wow! Look at you," Ciana said, eyes on the girl's swollen belly. The memory of Abbie and Eric's lovely wedding and how happy Arie had been with Jon by her side flashed through Ciana's mind.

Abbie laughed. "I know. I look like I've swallowed a bowling ball."

"You look . . ." Ciana searched for the perfect word. She chose ". . . happy."

"I'm very happy." Abbie patted her abdomen. "Not much longer."

Ciana felt ashamed for not keeping in closer touch with Abbie and Eric, knowing that if Arie were still alive, she'd have kept Ciana up on every detail. "I should have checked on you."

"I'm working, you're busy—don't think about it." Her expression grew serious. "We heard you were having trouble with vandals. Really sorry, Ciana." Then her look hardened. "Don't you let anybody run you off, you hear? That's your land!"

Her fierceness touched Ciana. "No one's going to run us off. I know my decision affects a lot of people." She gave Abbie a serious look. "I know a new subdivision would mean lots of work for Eric and Swede Winslow."

"Don't know that. Hastings can hire from anywhere he wants." She took Ciana's hand. "My husband and father-in-law have plenty of work."

Ciana watched the news; she knew the national economy wasn't robust. It was sweet of Abbie to try to ease any guilt Ciana felt. She cleared her throat. "I better get along."

Abbie smiled. "Me too, but it was sure good to see you. Arie loved you like a sister."

"Same here." The girls hugged and Abbie turned to go. "Wait," Ciana said. "You'll tell me when the baby comes?"

"Course I will. You'll be getting a shower invitation soon, and you better be there!"

Ciana watched until Abbie turned at the end of the grocery aisle and disappeared. She swallowed the lump in her throat over the memory of her friend, and willed Eden to pick up on her subconscious message to come home.

When Ciana turned into Bellmeade's tree-lined driveway, she saw a car parked beside her front steps and heard Soldier barking furiously outside the driver's door. Ciana screeched to a halt, jumped from her truck, and ran to the car. She grabbed Soldier's collar, yelled, "Stay!" The dog sat and Ciana squinted into the window, but the tinted glass obscured the driver's face. "Hello?" she said.

Slowly, the window inched down and a man's voice, accented and hesitant, asked, "Am I safe?"

"Oh my gosh!" Ciana cried, her heart leaping along with a smile. "Is it really *you?*"

Just then Jon's truck came barreling down the driveway and slid to a stop behind the car. Jon ran over and took the dog's collar from Ciana's hand, saying, "Heard him barking half a mile away. What's up?"

Ciana yanked open the car door and a tall, elegantly dressed dark-haired man emerged cautiously. She stood on tiptoes, threw her arms around him, kissed him, and cried, "Enzo! Jon, it's Enzo Bertinalli, my friend from Italy!"

15

Jon nodded to Enzo, relaxed his grip on Soldier's collar. The dog stood, ears forward, on guard, muzzle up.

"He—he won't bite me, will he?" Enzo asked, leaning back against the car.

"Only if I tell him to," Jon answered, wearing a smile that didn't reach his eyes.

Ciana shot Jon what she hoped was a withering look. She hooked her arm through Enzo's. "Come into the house. Tell me all about life in Italy. And your horses."

"I have wine for you," he said, still not taking his eyes off the dog.

"I'll just mosey to the barn," Jon said in an exaggerated Texas drawl.

If looks could kill, Ciana would have laid Jon out on the ground. She and Enzo watched Jon and Soldier walk away, and once the two were a safe distance away, Enzo swung her to face him. "I did not have a way to reach you, or I would have called. So I drove over from Nashville where I am staying, and all in your town knew where to find you."

I'll bet, she thought. "Let's go inside."

Enzo opened the back door of the rental car and pulled out a Styrofoam box. "My best reserve vintage from last year."

His vineyards were famous and his wines some of the finest in Tuscany. "Thanks. Can't wait to open one." She led him up the steps, through the foyer, and down a hallway and into the kitchen. "There's usually someone here. My mom must have run out."

He set the box on the counter, took Ciana's hands in his, appraised her head to toe. "You are as lovely as I remember, *bella* Ciana."

She blushed, knowing her hair was windblown and her face makeup-free, and she figured she smelled like hay and horse feed. "Nice of you to say. I was in town running errands, buying seed. I start planting middle of next month." Reminding herself of another bill that would come due all too soon. His brown eyes caught hers, taking her back to evenings in Italy with him, when he'd held her, kissed her. She felt her face grow warm with the memories. "Let me take your coat. We'll sit in the front room."

He slid his coat off, handed it to her. The fine cashmere felt soft as silk. She led him into the refurbished parlor with its midcentury furnishings, grateful that she'd gotten it freshly painted and put back together over the winter. She draped his coat over a chair, sat on the sofa, and patted the cushion beside her. "So what brings you to Nashville?"

He eased beside her. "Often I go to New York City to a few select restaurants to sell my wines to key clients. This year I brought some to Nashville. I have heard it might be a good market."

She was surprised he'd come so far west. "Long way from New York."

"And I come also to meet with a man who wishes to buy the stud services of one of my prize stallions." His eyes crinkled at the corners as he smiled.

Enzo's horses were world-class thoroughbreds, greatly valued in the equestrian world. She was certain breeding fees would be substantial. "I'm impressed."

Enzo's hand slid over hers, making her remember that he liked to touch her. She had liked it too. "The patron has four daughters, all riders, and one wishes to ride in the Olympics one day. For that she needs a very good horse."

"Won't it take years to raise a colt?"

"She is young, and her father gives her what her heart desires." He used his other hand to gesture. "She is a—how do you say—a child with his younger wife. His other daughters are grown."

Ciana caught on instantly. Older man. Second wife. Child of their own. Indulged. "Well, you do have great horses, so she'll be lucky to have one from their bloodlines. I know I enjoyed our rides together."

He smiled. "And the picnics?"

"And the picnics." There was no forgetting the bountiful picnics on his property by the lake. Or the way he'd lavished attention on her. She fidgeted.

Just then, her mother's voice called from the kitchen, "Ciana? You here? There's a strange car in the front—" Coming into the parlor, she stopped abruptly. "Oh, hello."

Enzo stood and so did Ciana, who quickly made introductions. He took Alice Faye's hand, showered her with greetings in beautifully accented English and courtly manners.

Ciana watched her mother's face color as she smiled shyly

95

and slipped her hand from Enzo's. Ciana recognized what was happening immediately. Alice Faye's hands were a farm woman's hands, rough and callused from years of hard work, hands she thought unfit to be caressed by one such as Enzo. Somehow understanding her mother's embarrassment touched Ciana. She stepped up quickly. "Mom, I first met Enzo in one of his vineyards. He was working with his vines, and he caught me inspecting a handful of dirt and almost called the police."

Enzo laughed and together, they told Alice Faye the whole story. She laughed with them, her eyes frequently lingering on Enzo. The man oozed sexual warmth. He didn't flaunt it; he simply owned it. No wonder her mother was charmed. Ciana had been too. "Where are my manners? I haven't offered you anything to drink," Alice Faye said suddenly, looking mortified.

Enzo held up his hand. "This is all right."

"Not in the South," Ciana joked. "It's like a crime."

"I have sweet tea," Alice Faye said.

Enzo's brow puckered. "I have brought you wine, an excellent vintage. I will open a bottle if you wish."

Ciana remembered the case of wine in the kitchen, knowing her mother would be unable to drink it. She didn't want her mother put in an awkward position, but before she could say a word, Alice Faye smiled and said, "Sweet tea is the wine of the South, sir. And I make the best for miles around."

Enzo dipped his head in consent and Alice Faye exited to the kitchen. He turned to Ciana. *"Tua mama è graziosa, di buon cuore."*

"My mother is charming and kindhearted," Ciana translated smugly. "I haven't forgotten all my Italian."

He chuckled, his brown eyes dancing, lit by an inner glow. "You are her best reflection." Ciana felt her own face grow warm under his scrutiny. She couldn't deny that she was attracted to him. Enzo was beguiling. And damn near perfect to boot.

Alice Faye invited Enzo to stay for supper, but he graciously declined, saying he already had dinner plans in Nashville. Ciana had to concede that everything Enzo did seemed gracious. Night had fallen when Ciana walked Enzo out to his car, and the cold air sent a shiver up Ciana's arms. Enzo reached out, rubbed his gloved hands up and down her coat sleeves. She felt very inelegant in her barn jacket. Still he said, "I'd like to visit you again."

"I'd like that too. We'll go riding. My horses aren't so grand or finely bred as yours, but they give a good ride."

"No doubt. But I come for your company, Ciana, not a horse's."

She flushed. Charming as always. "How long will you be in the States?"

"Not so sure just yet. All is centered around business. I will call," he said, and drove away.

Before she could get up the front steps, Jon caught up with her. "Fancy guy."

His observation irked her. "*Elegant* guy. He was very kind to us when we were in Italy."

"No doubt."

"He'll be coming back," she snapped.

"I'll make sure to tell Soldier to put him on the approved visitors list."

She stamped her foot. "Why are you being so sarcastic? Enzo is an amazing horseman. Has some of the best horses in Europe. You might want to talk to him."

Light from the parlor played across Jon's features. She saw mischief in his eyes. "What's he going to tell me, Ciana? I want to raise and train mustangs, mongrels to a man like him. No, I'll leave that field open." He shoved his hands into the pockets of his jeans. "But that's the only field I'm leaving open."

"What's that supposed to mean?"

He bounded up the steps. "Come on, I smell fried chicken."

She was furious at him and his macho attitude. "You're really pissing me off!" she growled, as he opened the front door and stepped inside. He turned, winked. She shouted, "This isn't a contest, you know, Jon. I'm not a prize!"

He turned, winked. "Supper's getting cold."

She watched him disappear into the house, waited a full five minutes shivering in the dark and cold before she calmed down enough to follow him inside.

When she walked into the kitchen, he grinned.

16

After Eden's close call with drowning, Garret's family doted on her to the point of embarrassment. Maggie insisted they stick close to the house, so with long lazy days beside the ever calm pool water, Eden began to open up to Garret about her past, working backward, starting with Italy and the fun they'd shared. The gift Garret had always given her was space. He never pressed her or insisted she tell him about herself. To the contrary, when she'd tried to tell him about her past while in Italy, he had brushed it away with "Don't care. Right now is what matters." At the time she'd been fine with that, believing she would never see him again once her stay at the villa was over.

Except that now she was with him constantly, and more involved with him than she'd thought possible. She'd come to realize that she needed to be more forthcoming with her personal history—all of it, good and bad.

One morning while they stretched out on towels, he asked, "Do you think your mum will like me?"

"Sure, if she gets to meet you," Eden mumbled, lulled by the warmth of the sun.

"If? I was thinking 'when.' We could send her a picture of us in an email. I'd like for her to know who you're with. Does she ask?"

She realized that while she always talked about Ciana and Alice Faye, she never mentioned her mother. Of course he was curious. Eden raised up, measured her words, took a deep breath, and plunged into her story and uncharted territory. "She lives in Florida. I haven't seen her in almost a year."

Garret raised up too, lifted his sunglasses in order to see her unshielded. "You have a fallin'-out?"

Eden encircled her knees with her arms. "Have you ever heard of bipolar disorder?"

"I have, but don't know much about it."

"Doctors say it's caused by a chemical imbalance in the brain. It—um—it causes huge mood swings. When it's at its worst, a bipolar person goes from manic activity to extreme depression. My mother has it."

"Bad?"

"Bad enough."

"There must be medicine for it."

"There is. Psych counseling too. But my mother could never stick with either. Not even when she had a child to care for." She said the words softly, surprised at how much the old truth still hurt.

Garret's gaze went from curiosity into gentle understanding. "How did you deal? With growing up, I mean."

"I coped. Early on, I knew she was different from my friends' mothers, especially when she fell into depressions. She'd lie on the sofa for days, unable to do anything except cry and sleep. I was scared, and didn't know what to do. I learned to open a soup can when I was four, and how to warm the soup when I was five."

"You ate it straight from the can?" He looked sympathetic and shocked.

"The stove was gas. I was afraid of it. But I learned." Eden shifted. "I could do laundry by the age of six . . . a few mishaps, like suds all over the floor. How was I to know it didn't take a whole cup of detergent to wash a couple of tees and some socks?" She offered a smile and a shrug. "But we got through."

"Your dad?" he asked.

"Never knew him. She left him when I was a baby."

"She—she never hurt you, did she?" He tensed when he asked the question.

"Not physically. In truth, I sometimes wished she would hit me, because then at least I'd know that she noticed me. Her depressions were the worst. I actually preferred her manic phases, when she was hyper and music played all night." Eden could still hear some of the songs in her head. She stretched out her legs. "But when she came up for air, when the depression lifted, usually because she took a few of her meds, she was always sorry, and would try and make it up to me. Then things would be fine. Until the next time."

"Why didn't you tell someone? A teacher, or neighbor?"

"Social services would have taken me away. The idea terrified me. 'Better the devil you know than the one you don't.' Maybe you've heard that said before."

"Is that why you cut?" His question was perceptive. He knew that she'd been a cutter, and although a doctor in Nashville had greatly reduced her scarring, thin white lines of self-abuse still showed on her arms and inner thighs. These would be with her the rest of her life. So be it. Thankfully, Garret treated her as if the marks were invisible.

"Crazy, but the pain helped me, made me feel better. For a while." She retreated from the dark memories. "Going off to school, meeting Arie and Ciana when I was in middle school, changed everything for the better."

"Bugger. Poor kid."

"Now don't sit there feeling sorry for me. I can't stand that." Agitated, Eden stood.

Garret was beside her instantly. "I can if I want." His smile was coaxing. "Don't like seeing my girl hurt."

She peered up at him. "Am I your girl?"

He wrapped her in his arms. "I've caught you and I'm never lettin' go."

She buried her face in his chest, relaxed against his sun-warmed skin and the scent of coconut sunscreen. She was many years and almost ten thousand miles from her old demons. Of course, she'd hardly scratched the surface of her past. There was so much more she should tell him, *had* to tell him. *Not now*, her mind cautioned. *Not just yet.*

Eden had lost contact with her mother. Gwen's cell phone was no longer in service. All Eden knew was that she was in Tampa "with people who understood her." That was what Gwen had once told Eden. Translation: No one was forcing medication and therapy on her. Not knowing anything about her mother was both scary and heartbreaking. Bipolar was a cruel disorder, and one Eden dreaded she would develop too. The secret fear had driven her choices, many of which had been bad. Her one smart choice had been coming to visit Garret. She had him. She had Ciana. She had Alice Faye. All were lifesavers.

When Eden received a chatty email from Ciana about

Enzo's visit, she was a little sorry she couldn't be at Bellmeade to greet him too. *Give him a hug from me*, Eden directed in her return email. *How's Jon taking Enzo's visit?*

He's edgy, came Ciana's reply. *He keeps to himself and gives me a wide berth, when Enzo comes around. But sometimes he makes me crazy mad with some comment, so I just have a good time with Enzo and keep a civil attitude toward Jon. Men!*

March brought the approaching end of Eden's Australian visa. She had buried thoughts of leaving, knowing that saying goodbye to Garret and his parents wouldn't be easy. She had grown into the space they had carved out for her, and she was happy. They were out on the patio having dinner from the barbie one evening when the latch on the side gate clicked and Alyssa stepped through. Maggie rose quickly. "We're eating."

"I have a reason for coming."

"Not interested," Garret said.

"Go on with you," Maggie said. She made a shooing motion with her hand.

"What I've got to tell you can't wait." Alyssa stood her ground. With a malevolent look, she held up a manila folder. "I've gathered some information on your girlfriend, Garret."

Eden's heart was in her throat, and her hands had turned cold as ice. All she saw was Alyssa's wicked expression and glinting eyes.

Garret stepped over. "Go away, Alyssa. You're not welcome here."

Alyssa sidled around Garret, came to the table, and slapped the folder down onto the glass top. She looked at Trevor, then directly at Eden. "Thought you ought to know that your son's American girl, Eden McLauren, was once the whore of a drug lord." Alyssa turned to glare down at Eden still sitting at the table. "She's not so clean and proper after all. Are you, Eden?"

17

For a moment, time stood still. No one spoke. Eden heard every sound around her amplified: the lapping of the pool water against the tiles, the crackling of the wood fire in the brazier, the voices of tree frogs and night insects, the drip of candle wax from their holders onto the patio table. Garret moved first. He came to the table, picked up the file, and purposefully walked to the brazier and lifted the safety screen.

"You should read—" Alyssa started.

"Get out," he said, his back to her, his voice firm.

"I'm only trying—"

"Out."

Maggie stepped forward. "You heard my son. Leave."

"I was only trying to help," Alyssa whined. "I thought you should know. I'm doing all of you a favor."

"You heard them," Trevor said. "I will call the authorities if you don't go away right now."

Alyssa took the time to glare at each of them, but finally

she retreated to the gate and slipped out into the dark where she'd come from.

Eden felt nauseous, mentally hammered and cold, so very cold. She watched Garret's back, arrow-straight and rigid. She watched him hold the folder over the dancing flames, but before the thick paper could catch, she pushed her chair backward. The scraping sound of the chair grated harshly, but she moved swiftly and caught the folder as it began to smolder. She pulled it from his hand. "No. Don't. You can't burn history. You can't change the truth," she whispered. Her voice trembled, sounded foreign to her ears.

He turned, his face a mask of denial, his eyes sad. "Not important to me."

"You need to know," she managed to say. She blew away the few cinders that edged the folder, held it to her chest. "Give me a few minutes. Please."

Not certain she could make it back to the table, she dropped into the nearest patio chair and opened the folder. There was just enough light through the patio doors behind her to thumb the pieces of paper, obviously printouts of information downloaded from the Internet. It was all there: Tony's death in a shoot-out, the extensive tentacles of his drug network, stories of the lives he'd destroyed, and two stories about her, the girlfriend thought to be "hiding in Europe" and a "person of interest," wanted for questioning. Every word she read felt like a nail being driven into her heart.

She looked up and saw that Trevor and Maggie had left the patio and she was alone with Garret. Tears swam in her eyes; dread filled her heart. "I want to tell you. Please, sit and listen. I need to tell you, Garret. Really. Truth is long overdue."

"Won't care," he said stubbornly, but he dragged a patio

chair over and sat beside her, stared into the fire, his features set like stone.

She took a breath, shuddered, handed him the folder. "Read it."

He eyed the soot-edged folder as if it were a snake. "Why?"

"Because you need to. Because I want you to. And after you read what's inside, we'll talk about it. We must." Hurting him would be the hardest thing she would ever do, but it was necessary.

He took the folder, flipped it open, and read. She watched his eyes, how they darted over the news stories compiled from that painful time when she was in Italy and Tony had died in a bloodbath between rival drug gangs. When he was finished he closed the folder, leaned toward the brazier, and said, "Now I'm going to burn it." He set one corner on fire and held the folder until the flames had half devoured it, then tossed what remained into the fire. Eden watched bits of charred paper flutter upward and float away on a night breeze. In minutes nothing remained. If only the past could be so easily destroyed.

"Did the police talk to you?" he asked.

"By the time I came home, it didn't matter anymore. With a little help from the shoot-out, two drug kingpins had been taken down and almost a million dollars' worth of drugs had been confiscated." She shrugged. "But drug wars are like that creature in Greek mythology. You know, the one with all the heads that keep regrowing every time one's cut off?"

"The Hydra," Garret said.

She watched the fire with him in silence, wanting him to question her, wanting him to help rid her soul of its darkness.

"Is that why you were in Italy? Running away?"

"Yes. The trip was Ciana's idea. She planned it, paid for

it. We told Arie it was for her sake, but it was for both of us. And it saved me."

"She's a good friend."

"Better than blood kin," Eden said. "Not that I've ever known any of mine," she added dryly.

Garret continued to watch the flames consume the wood in the brazier.

"I've always wanted you to know, Garret," she said. "I should have told you sooner. I should have told you when we were in Italy. Big regret."

"I never cared about what happened before we met, or who you loved."

"Loved?" She recoiled at the word. "I never loved Tony. I might have thought I did at one time, when I was too young to know better, but when I saw him as he truly was, I had no love for him. But by then, I couldn't get out. Not alive."

After a great deal of time, he said, "I—I need some time to think, sort it all out."

"I understand." She was emotionally wrung out herself, the pumping adrenaline having melted from her body, leaving her limp. She stood, looked down wistfully at Garret Locklin, and wished with all her heart things could have ended differently. "I'd like to talk to your parents."

"Later. I'll talk to them first."

Her heart squeezed and a lump lodged in her throat. "All right." Eden liked his parents so much; the idea of their knowing that their son's girlfriend was "a drug lord's whore," as Alyssa had so accurately put it, stung like the tail of a scorpion. But truth was truth.

Eden crossed the cool patio cement and went into the house and up the stairs to the room that had been hers for over two months. All that was left for her to do now was reserve a seat on the next flight home, pack her belongings, and leave.

The smell of brewing coffee woke Eden. She'd slept fitfully, last looking at her bedside clock at four in the morning. She felt drugged and headachy and knew it was an emotional hangover from one of the worst nights of her life. Groggily, Eden went into her bathroom and splashed cold water on her face. *Garret would call it "bracing,"* she thought. The memory of telling him about her past flooded back, bringing on fresh waves of inner torture. She needed some coffee but was hesitant to show up in the kitchen.

Eden returned to the bedroom, dressed in jeans and a T-shirt, and dug her suitcase out of the closet, where she'd stashed it when she'd first arrived. She opened it on the bed, went to the dresser, and began the chore of packing. Never had she expected her trip to end so sadly.

She heard a gentle rap on her closed door. Her nerves tightened. She wasn't ready to face Garret quite yet. "Um— who is it?"

"Maggie," came the answer.

Eden groaned. She was even less ready to face Garret's mother.

"May I come in? I've got some coffee for you."

Perhaps, Eden thought, the woman would throw it at her. But it was her house, after all. Eden couldn't bar her. *Stiff upper,* she told herself, using the Aussie words she'd heard locals use when the going got tough. "Come in."

The door eased open and Maggie entered the room. She saw the suitcase and the clothing Eden was folding. "What's this?"

"Homeward bound," Eden said as cheerfully as she could muster.

Maggie came over, sat on the bed, handed Eden a cup of steaming coffee colored with a dollop of real cream, just the way Eden drank it. "You don't have to leave," Maggie said tenderly.

"I do," Eden said, sipping the coffee.

"Come." Maggie patted a section of the bed next to her. "Sit with me. We'll talk."

Eden wanted to sit because her knees had gone rubbery. She sank onto the bed, which was rumpled from her restless sleep. "I'm very sorry about last night. About ruining supper."

"You're sorry? I'm sorry about that awful Alyssa. Girl never did have a thimbleful of sense."

"Has Garret talked to you?"

"Of course. Lad came up last night and told us everything."

Eden reddened. "Then you know why I'm packing."

Maggie pressed the bridge of her nose between her fingers. "You can't go home until I tell you some things that I'm sure you don't know about our Garret."

Eden stopped mid-sip. "Garret's perfect," she said.

Maggie smiled broadly. "It may seem so, but I'm guessing he's never shared a word about his brother, Philip, has he?"

Eden blinked. "He has a brother?"

Maggie's eyes teared up. "*Had* a brother," she said tenderly. "Now, no more."

18

Eden waited while Maggie gathered herself. Maggie swiped beneath her eyes and cleared her throat. "Sorry. It's always difficult to speak of Philip."

"Take your time." Eden felt upended. Why hadn't Garret ever mentioned a brother?

"There was five years between them. Garret adored his big brother. Philip was a digger."

Eden raised a brow and shook her head.

"A soldier. Diggers are army boys. After America's 9/11, he joined. Wanted to make the world a safer place. Eventually he was stationed in Iraq, part of the UN Peacekeepers. He was almost at the end of his tour and planning on coming home to marry his girl."

Eden's heart thudded as she realized what was coming. And she recalled the beautifully painted surfboard in the shed that Garret hadn't wanted to talk about. Surely it had been Philip's.

"One of those horrible IED bombs took him out on a roadside where he was driving a jeep in front of a tank. Army sent him home in a closed casket because—" Maggie sniffed hard. "Well, you know."

Not enough left to recognize. Eden had read reports of U.S. soldiers returning home the same way. Their families never had a final glimpse of the people they'd loved. "War sucks," she mumbled.

"Garret took it very hard. Inconsolable, he was."

Eden's heart ached, understanding too well how impotent a person could feel when death was a victor over someone you loved. She'd felt helpless and angry and grief stricken when Arie had died. And there had been nothing, *nothing* she was able to do to strike back at Death. She wanted to take Maggie's hand, but wasn't sure she should. She didn't want to overstep her boundaries.

Maggie glanced over at Eden. "This is the part of the story where Alyssa comes in. She and Garret had been school chums for a long time, but when Philip died, he and Alyssa became a couple. The girl could offer comfort that we could not. I'm sure you get my meaning."

Eden did.

"I never liked the girl," Maggie added. "Everyone could see she wasn't right for our Garret. Trevor and I. My sister and I. Our close friends. We all knew she was NQWWW."

Eden sorted through her memory for the meaning of the letters. She knew dozens of text and email letter add-ons, but not this one. "I don't—"

"Oh, forgive me. Stands for Not Quite What We Wanted."

Eden laughed, her first genuine moment of humor since before Alyssa's bombshell had blown up her world. "Well, if she was as toady then as she is now, I get it."

Maggie patted Eden's hand in a show of camaraderie. "We

tolerated her because Garret was happier around her. Or he thought he was. But she never played fair with my lad. No need to go into that."

Eden wasn't up to hearing the nitty-gritty anyway. "If Alyssa helped him, that's what matters," she said, trying to be generous.

"Once the funeral was over and we were all working to pick up our lives, I could see that Garret wasn't doing well. He missed Philip terribly, and there was a hardness in him like never before. When he was midway through second year of university, he wanted to drop out, enlist, and go kill the 'bad guys.' Trevor and I were terrified. Couldn't face losing another son." Maggie wiped her eyes with the back of her hand. "That's when we offered to send him off on walkabout. I knew he'd been bitten by the travel bug when he was a little lad. When you live in Australia it's a common ailment," Maggie said as an aside. "Australians go to the world because the world doesn't usually come to us. We take the long hours of travel in stride."

"It is a long trip," Eden said. "But worth it."

Maggie smiled. "Garret is bright, always loved to write. Got that job with the travel magazine all on his own. Wrote his own job description. We're very proud of him."

"That's how we met. On his walkabout."

"Almost didn't happen, though. He wanted Alyssa to go with him. But the girl was bonkers for her modeling career. She absolutely refused. I thought Garret might beg off. But he held firm. Tom and Lorna stepped up, said they'd join him. And off they went."

"My good luck."

Maggie took Eden's hand. "His too."

Eden felt almost buoyant when the memory of the night

before crashed into her brief spell of happiness. Her shoulders drooped. She removed her hand, glanced beyond Garret's mother to the half-packed suitcase. "About last night . . . ," she started.

"Garret's told us about Alyssa's nasty paperwork. It doesn't matter to him, so it doesn't matter to us. We've all done something in our lives that we regret. But after losing Philip, I know life can be short and should be fully lived, not regretted. Whatever happened to you back in the States can't be changed. Forward's the only direction you can go." Maggie stood, urged Eden up in front of her. "Now go on down to the pool. My lad's out there swimming laps and waiting for you." She shook her head, smiled. "So many laps, I'm telling you. All morning long."

Eden searched Maggie's eyes, saw only kindness, encouragement. Eden hugged Garret's mother and hurried to the patio.

The second Eden set foot poolside, Garret burst from the water, hauled himself up, and, dripping wet, went to her. He crushed her against his body, soaking her through. She didn't care. His embrace was all she needed to find atonement. He kissed her, said, "'Bout time. Me mum must have been long-winded."

"It's in a female's genes."

He grinned but quickly sobered. "I asked her to tell you everything. Still hard for me to—to talk about—"

She shushed him. "I know what I need to know. Wasn't that what you told me?"

His expression softened. "I told her you'd be up there packin'."

113

She felt her face redden. "I was. But, Garret, I really do have to go home." For several days, she'd been experiencing an urgency about returning to Bellmeade. An uneasiness she found hard to put into words. She started in. "Ciana will be planting soon. I should be there."

"Why?"

She thought about how to best say what was in her heart. "You have an amazing family. They love and care about you so much. I've never had that. All I know about my family is in a letter Gwen left me before she ran off to Florida. Ciana and Alice Faye are more family to me than any I was born into. I love them. And I miss them." Now that the words were spoken, she felt a lightness. *Love. Yes.* She watched his eyes, saw quickly that he fully understood. "I—I need to go home."

His grin was quick. "And so you will. But not before we go on walkabout in the outback."

"All of it?"

"Course not. Just my favorite parts." He kissed the tip of her nose.

"Like we'll be camping?"

"Every night."

"And . . . and there'll be wild animals?"

"I'll be the wildest animal you'll meet."

She gave him a playful shove.

"My grandfather used to take me and my brother hiking in the Blue Mountains. I want to take you there too."

"I've never camped."

"Then it's about time you did."

She wasn't as sure about the idea as he was.

"And I'll be with you. I'll gather up our gear and we can leave today."

She offered a tentative smile.

"And when we come back, we'll talk about you going home."

She nodded, anxious about both possibilities, but for different reasons. Camping was an unknown experience that he would guide her through; home was a place she suddenly couldn't imagine without him.

19

At Bellmeade the colors of spring crept across the land—new growth to cover winter's pale. For Ciana, it meant planting time was close. She had enough seed and fertilizer for extra fields, and while it was less land than she'd hoped to plant this season, it was a step up from the previous year.

The vandals had stepped up their malice also. Jon mended fences almost daily, and once had discovered corrosive lye scattered across a field, a guarantee to destroy any new planting. The continued destruction had brought the sheriff into the mix, but although he had patrol cars regularly drive the road that fronted her property, no one was ever caught. Bellmeade property stretched too far from the road, and had too few people to constantly watch over it.

Enzo drove from Nashville to visit her, and when he showed up, Jon quietly slipped away. So Enzo's visits meant a break from the pressures of everyday life for Ciana. They rode together and shared good memories, and on sunny days sat on her veranda and sipped fine wine. He was older, urbane, and sophisticated, but the age difference between them had never mattered. She thought him handsome and charismatic, and for reasons she didn't understand, he liked her enough to want to be with her, both in Italy and now in Tennessee. She decided to ignore Jon's attitude toward Enzo altogether.

On their first ride together, she brought out Sonata for him. *"Bellissima,"* he said, giving the horse's forehead a rub. "She has intelligent eyes. A good sign."

"She's the grand dame of the stable, part Arabian and part Tennessee walking horse. Her gait is smooth as butter."

Enzo swung onto Sonata and Ciana mounted Firecracker, who snorted, eager to be given her head. "Show me your world, *bella* Ciana," Enzo said, looking as if he'd been born on the back of a horse.

Just then Jon came out of the barn. The two men sized each other up, Enzo from the back of Sonata, Jon from the doorway of the barn. To Ciana both men were physically perfect—the one lean, elegant, dark-eyed and aristocratic, the other man cowboy-rugged, green-eyed, and broad-shouldered. And she felt indebted to each of them.

Jon crossed his arms, leaned in the doorframe. "Have a good ride," he called, his gaze never leaving Enzo's. Enzo tilted his head ever so slightly at Jon, turned Sonata, and nosed in beside Ciana.

"This way," she said, feeling nervous but exhilarated. She was eager to show her property to Enzo, just as he'd once shown his to her. Their lands were different and worlds apart, yet she knew how devoted he was to his property and to its heritage, which dated to Old World Roman times. Bellmeade grew no vineyards and olive trees, but it was fertile and rich and full of promise.

They cantered toward the back of the land that

encompassed the house, through a line of trees and into a back field, where she pointed to a corral and an oval track. "We can run a bit there. No potholes."

Together, over the winter, she and Jon had put in the ten-foot-wide half-mile track, a corral, and a covered lean-to. Jon had also dug a well for watering and bathing horses. The entire place had been Jon's idea. "This will make your stables more valuable to boarders. Safer riding too." Naturally, he was right, and she'd wondered why she'd never thought of it herself. They'd done the hard work together, with Ciana creating the track aboard her tractor, first towing a plow to break up the partially frozen ground and bring up rocks that she and Jon removed by hand. Then she'd pulled a disc harrow to further loosen and soften the sod; and lastly, once they had filled in low spots with wheelbarrows of fresh dirt, a tractor rake. She raked the dirt often to keep it smooth for riding. The large corral contained small hurdles where horses could be trained to jump, along with a stack of orange cones to practice for barrel-racing events. She was pleased with the site, happy to show it off.

Enzo complimented the work and then turned Sonata toward the track's entry. "This horse rides *bene*. May I stretch her?"

"Givè her a shake. She knows what to do."

Enzo clicked his tongue, pushed the heels of his boots into the horse's sides. Sonata took off into the smooth rolling gait of a seasoned walking horse. She had been Olivia's prized mount, a blue-ribbon winner in almost every contest entered.

Firecracker moved restlessly. "We'll go," Ciana said, patting the horse's neck. "Let's give them a chance to enjoy it alone." The horse snorted and sidestepped, showing her displeasure at having to wait.

After Enzo completed the track twice, Ciana gave Firecracker her head and the horse took off in a full gallop. Ciana leaned low over the horse's neck, felt the cold wind in her face, the sting of the flying mane against her skin, heard the sound of the hooves pounding the ground. The bay was quick, and Ciana let her horse run, reveling in an adrenaline high. When she pulled up, Firecracker was breathing hard and her neck was sweat-lathered. Ciana took a lap at a canter, then joined Enzo outside the track. He had dismounted and was watching her breakneck run, a beguiling smile on his face. Laughing, Ciana swung her right leg over the saddle horn and slid to the ground. "I love a good run!"

He came close and touched her cheek. His thumb slid down and across her bottom lip. "You are beautiful. Like the wind."

Her pulse quickened, remembering the familiarity of his hands on her body and of his mouth on hers. For a moment, their eyes held. She thought he might kiss her, but instead he took a deep breath and stepped aside. "I should like to take you someplace *speciale*," he said. "A ball in Nashville for horse people. Do you know of it? Will you come with me, Ciana?"

The Horseman's Ball, the annual premier social event for Tennessee's storied and elite horse owners. Of course Ciana knew of it. Olivia and Charles had attended every year until Charles's death, but Ciana had never gone. Never been invited. His request caught her off balance. "Pretty fancy dance."

He shrugged. "The man who wants to buy the seed of my stallions has insisted that I join in this event. I cannot ignore or refuse his offer. You understand, yes? Such things are not so much to my pleasure, but I should like it better if you were by my side."

Naturally, a man like Enzo was used to such social events in Europe, so she realized he wouldn't be impressed by the all-but-impossible-to-come-by invitation. Eden had once shown her Web photos of Enzo decked out in formal wear and with different glamorous women on his arm. She was nothing like those women.

"Do not say to me, 'Enzo, I have nothing to wear.' Such an excuse comes from all women, and yet I have never seen one arrive anywhere without clothes."

His voice was light and teasing. And irresistible. She burst out laughing. "It's the heels," she said. "I hate wearing heels." In truth her mind was spinning a mile a minute, attempting to think of what she had that was suitable to wear at such an event.

He bowed slightly. "You may go barefoot. This does not matter to me."

Suddenly she remembered the dress she'd worn to Abbie's wedding. It was pretty, body hugging, the pale color of champagne, and hanging in the back of her closet. It would do nicely. "Why would I say no? Mama says I clean up good. For a farm girl."

He laughed heartily. "It will be my pleasure to take you, plain or fancy. No matter, you will shine."

She squirmed under his appreciative look. "Want to see the rest of Bellmeade?" she asked, swiftly retreating from talk of clothing and moneyed balls.

"Sì," he answered, remounting Sonata. "Show me your estate."

She mounted Firecracker with a dismissive chuckle, knowing she was holding on to her "estate" by her fingernails.

"You look lovely."

Alice Faye's voice startled Ciana, who was staring into her dresser mirror, searching her reflection and seeing what she considered to be all her flaws: too-full lips, a slightly crooked nose, freckles no amount of makeup seemed to cover. "I feel like a kid playing dress-up," she said, turning away from her image.

Smiling, her mother shook her head. "When you were little you used to dress up in princess clothes all the time and tell me you needed a horse to take you to the prince's castle. I don't think you trusted any fairy godmother to get you there."

Ciana returned her smile. "A girl's got to fend for herself."

"Is that wrap going to be enough? Still cold outside these nights."

"I wore it for the wedding and it was at New Year's." Putting on the dress had brought back all her memories of that night that made her heart ache. She remembered Arie sitting at the wedding party's special table while the party flowed around her. At that point Arie had been going downhill rapidly, so signing on as Abbie's maid of honor had been a brave and heroic feat for her.

And Ciana also remembered Jon that night—dancing with him, his eyes pouring into hers, her heart all but breaking for want of him. An "Auld Lang Syne" she'd never forget. She felt ambivalence now. Jon and Enzo. Two amazing and different men. Enzo was easy to be with, comfortable in any environment. Jon made her blood run hot.

"—your hands?"

Ciana snapped into the present, threaded her way to what she must have been asked. She held out her hands, glowing with nail polish and scented with cream. "I gave myself a manicure, but these hands will never be soft."

Just then the doorbell rang. "Sounds like your coach is here," Alice Faye said.

Ciana quickly slipped on low heels, chafing with the unfamiliar feel of any shoe except boots. "Wish me well with all the socialites."

Alice Faye said, "Forget about them. Have fun. Just remember, you are, after all, a Beauchamp."

Ciana flashed her mother a wry grin and hurried to open the front door.

20

The Horseman's Ball was held at the Hermitage Hotel in downtown Nashville, in the grand ballroom, the same place it had been held for decades. The five-star hotel was over a hundred years old, gilded and ornate, aglow with polished marble and crystal chandeliers, but also swimming in twenty-first-century luxuries and amenities. As a child, Ciana had come to the hotel for occasional luncheons with her mother and Olivia when such things had mattered to her grandmother. As a girl, Ciana had been awed, but now, after the hotels of Rome, she could see how the Hermitage architects had taken their cues from old Europe, so its grandeur did not impress as it once had.

The ballroom was filled with women in silk, satin, and glittering jewels. Tables were covered with long white cloths and set with ornate silver, fine china, and crystal. Every chair back was tied up with an elaborate lime-green bow clipped in the center with a spray of white roses. A small orchestra played music beside a dance floor roped off with velvet cording.

Enzo introduced Ciana to the man who had brought him to Tennessee, Roland Shepherd III, who gave her a questioning look. She realized she wasn't the person the man had expected to see with Enzo, but he covered his surprise quickly with a smile. "Beauchamp. You own Bellmeade. I heard that you might sell it."

Her back went up. "Rumors only. I'm not selling. I'm farming it."

Roland arched an eyebrow. "Big job." He didn't say, "For such a young girl," but Ciana saw the words in his expression.

Enzo intervened. "Are your lovely daughters here?"

"Only Mallory." Roland gestured to the masses of people. "Somewhere out there. I know she was looking forward to seeing you tonight."

"And I her," Enzo said graciously, then took Ciana's elbow. "Shall we dance?" He led her to the dance floor and took her in his arms.

"I don't think Roland is happy with your exit. Or with your choice of date to the ball, *signore.*"

He smiled. "*Sì*, but I am."

"So tell me about Mallory."

"A pretty woman, but how would you say . . . ? A woman who looks only inside herself, not at others."

"Spoiled? Self-centered?"

"*Corretto*. Not becoming in a woman." Enzo nuzzled Ciana's neck. "Yet this man wishes me to want this daughter of his. I do not."

Ciana understood. A man like Enzo was prime meat on the market of the rich and famous. "Forgive him. Southern daddies are very protective of their daughters. And when said daughter desires something, or someone, a daddy just tries to help fulfill his little girl's wish."

Enzo's arm tightened around her waist. "You do not think poorly of me for not wanting to be with her?"

"Look around. I'm enjoying the scenery. Plus, I'm hungry. When do we eat?"

He stopped dancing. "I do not wish to eat at a table full of people I do not know. I have made a reservation for us in a private dining room here. I wish to spend my time with you, Ciana, not these people."

The private room had walls of aged fine-grained polished walnut, and a single frosted-glass door through which a wait-person discreetly entered with drinks and food. A fire glowed warmly in a fireplace, while candles and wall sconces softened shadows. "Are we alone?" Ciana asked, startled to see that she and Enzo were the only diners in the room though there were eight tables.

"Do you mind?"

"You'll turn me into one of those spoiled rich girls."

His laugh was easy. "Not possible." He leaned back in the massive dining chair, rested his palms on the carved arms, studied her until she felt her face grow warm. "You are very special, Ciana."

"Bet Mallory wouldn't think so."

This made him chuckle. "Do you know my ancestry goes back hundreds of years? That I have titles?"

"Of course." His steady gaze flustered her, so she spoke quickly and confidently. "You have a ton of titles after your name. A bunch."

"Tell me one of my titles." His voice challenged, but his eyes held amusement.

Busted. She sat stock-still. "Right off the top of my head,

I—I don't recall . . . well, I'm not sure how to say them in Italian." She squirmed as heat crawled down her neck. Had she insulted him?

He laughed, reached up, undid his bow tie, unsnapped his dress shirt at his throat. "Most women know my titles. That's *all* most women know about me. What do you know, Ciana?"

She slid her hands under the table, sat on them to keep from fidgeting. "I know you're a man who loves horses, and loves his vineyards. A man who loves his land."

His brown eyes grew serious. "Exactly. And that is all you have ever seen when you look at me and when you talk to me. You are a woman who holds dirt in her fist and who can tell me of its composition. How many women do you think I meet who can do that?"

Her "talent" seemed dubious to her. She shrugged, feeling every bit the unsophisticated child. No wonder he chose to dine alone with her and away from the elite of Nashville. "Bet other women can tell the difference between Cartier and Chanel, though."

"Why should I value that? What is remarkable about a woman who can covet baubles and expensive trinkets, and not see the raw beauty in soil?"

He scowled, and his disdain for things she didn't value either made her feel better about his dining choice.

He picked up a wine bottle already uncorked on the table and poured some of the ruby liquid into her glass. "I taste the land in every swallow of wine. I savor it. Cherish it. Do you know that in parts of Europe the only thing that separates great wine from very good wine can be a few feet between the rows of grapevines?" He set down the bottle, held his hands apart to make his point. "This is the magic of the soil."

126

"And rain and sunshine," she added, then wished she hadn't. Like he didn't *know* this?

But he bent his head in tribute. "And that is why I like you, Ciana Beauchamp. Because you know these things and care about them."

A waiter came through the door with two plates of food and set them on the table. "I ordered for us already," Enzo explained. Ciana barely saw the food, knowing that with Enzo, the food was only to accompany a great wine. She didn't really care what they were eating anyway. His passion for his land was what drew her to him.

She took a few bites of some delectable morsel splashed with wine sauce. A fresh bottle of wine had been opened, and Enzo poured some into a clean glass, swirled it, swallowed it, his gaze intense and ever on her. After a minute, she realized he wasn't eating. Self-consciously, she edged her fork down to rest on her plate. "Food's delicious," she murmured.

"I will be returning to my vineyards in a few days," he said.

Of course. He'd been Stateside for weeks, and he had a life back in Italy. "I'll miss you."

"And I will miss you." He drank from his glass.

She felt the air snap between them, electric and taut.

His dark eyes brimmed with desire. She felt her heart race. He said, "I would like, *molto* . . . to take you upstairs to my room for tonight."

Molto . . . very much. In the time he'd been with her at Bellmeade, he'd not done more than hold her hand and kiss her cheek. In Italy she'd come within a hairsbreadth of going away with him to his villa in Portofino. He wanted her still, and as before, the offer was tempting. *"No puedo ir con tu para Portofino, signore,"* she had told him then. "I cannot go to Portofino, *signore,"* she told him now softly.

He searched her face, and as his expression turned to regret, he offered an understanding nod. "Again you refuse me, *bella* Ciana. You sadden my heart. After dinner and dessert, I will drive you home," he added graciously.

She smiled tenderly at him, reached across the table, stroked his hand. *Dearest Enzo . . . She would never forget him.* Together they lifted their wineglasses to one another in a toast.

The drive home was cozy inside the plush Mercedes. Ciana leaned her head against Enzo's shoulder, relaxed, but saddened knowing she would not see him again. They spoke little, listened to soft music, and before she knew it, the car was going up the tree-lined driveway of Bellmeade. The dashboard clock glowed the late hour as Enzo stopped the car. "The dog?" he asked before opening the door.

"Mom's put him inside. I'll release him after you go."

Enzo came around and opened her door. She took his hand, stepped into the night air, which made her shiver after the luxurious warmth of the car. From where she stood, she saw a light glowing in the barn's window.

Enzo pulled her thin wrap tightly around her shoulders. "I would have liked to keep you warm in other ways," he said tenderly. He glanced over his shoulder at the barn. "Someone is waiting for you."

Her pulse quickened. "Probably just left the light on by mistake."

Enzo tugged her closer, kissed her forehead. "Go to him."

"I—I don't—"

Enzo shook his head. "It is all right, *bella* Ciana. I see the way he looks at you."

"I—I—"

"And I have seen the way you try not to look at him."

Ciana felt heat suffuse her face. She had tried *not* to notice Jon when Enzo was with her, but Jon's sheer physical presence fought for her attention, and no matter what else she was doing, she couldn't escape it. "I didn't mean to . . ." She had never meant to insult Enzo.

He whispered, "It is all right. I can see what's in your heart. This man, he is the one you want. Yes?"

No use to deny it. "Yes."

"Then go. *Amore* . . . love. Both beautiful and strange. We Italians know love's ways."

She searched Enzo's face, her heart swelling with appreciation toward this man who understood her so well. She took a step backward. "You stay clear of those Mallory types."

In the weak, ambient light, she saw his smile and the shrug of his shoulders. "It is my life's mission." He returned to the car and she watched until the taillights turned toward Nashville. Then she walked to the barn.

Jon was straddling a bench, untangling a pile of ropes and untwisting old bridles. He glanced up when she entered. "You'd think people would be more careful with their tack."

Ciana kept her distance, her mouth dry, her heart hammering. "You're working late."

He shrugged. "Has to be done." He fought with a tangle of knots. "How was the ball?"

"Crowded. Full of people it mattered to."

"You didn't have a good time?"

"No. Yes. I mean, it was fine."

"And Enzo? How did he like it?"

His tone baited her, so she said, "He's an amazing man. Gorgeous too."

"And rich."

"And *eligible*."

"And gone," Jon said with finality. He stood, crossed the floor to stop within inches of her body, offering a satisfied smile, as if he surmised Enzo would not return.

She peered up at him with a smidgen of irritation. "You're pretty cocky. Pretty sure of yourself aren't you, cowboy?"

His expression went serious. He lifted her chin with his forefinger, searched her face as if absorbing her into himself. He said, "No. I'm sure of you."

She felt her chin quiver and tears fill her eyes. Jon knew her, too, and in that moment every wall she'd ever built to keep him out fell. She loved this man—loved him without boundaries, without conditions.

He put his arm around her shoulders, tucked her against his side. "Come on, Miz Beauchamp. It's late. I'll walk you home."

They left the barn with Ciana leaning into Jon, and walked across the yard together.

21

Eden spent six days and five nights in the Blue Mountains with Garret. He made the experience as easy as possible for her because after her experience at Bondi Beach, she wasn't very adventuresome. They drove a jeep Tom owned, parked, and walked easy trails, spent three nights in a tourist-friendly campsite, which had a mess hall for supper and breakfast and showers with warm water. He pointed out fauna found only in Australia, and surrounded her with a wild and awesome beauty that took her breath.

Once the sun set the nights were cool, and inside the small tent he put up for sleeping, he snuggled them into an extra-large sleeping bag, curled up behind her, and held her in his arms. "Don't want you to freeze," he whispered that first night.

She'd been apprehensive, not knowing what he expected from her. She loved him and wanted to make love to him, but she was scared. Sex had almost destroyed her once. Tony had used it as a weapon, at first being seductive and gentle with her, and then at some point she had become his possession. She never wanted to travel that road again.

But her and Garret's nights were used for sleeping, her mind settling, her body relaxing once she heard his soft snore and felt his warm breath on the nape of her neck. And after a few nights, she curled into him and fell asleep quickly, safe and protected in his arms. He always awoke cheerful, a little annoying to her because she wasn't a morning person, but he quickly made coffee in an old pot on a small, butane-burning stove. "My grandfather's gear," he said. "He used to take Philip and me for overnighters all the time."

The last night in the outback, he took her up on a bluff, where he pitched the tent but laid the sleeping bag outside on the ground. They ate ready-to-eat meals that tasted like cardboard. "People eat these things?"

"Digger food. And brave campers. But it's dinner tonight because this is where we'll be sleeping."

"Seriously?"

"You don't think what we've been doing so far is serious camping, do you?"

"I was serious." She nibbled at the food.

"You haven't really camped unless you've slept under the stars," he said with a boyish grin. "So far all you've seen at night is the underside of this old tent."

They watched the sun set, and later lay side by side in the sleeping bag, staring up at the sky. "Look. A half-and-half moon. Between waxing and waning." Garret pointed at the moon, one side bright and cream-colored, the other dark and hidden.

Looks like my life, she thought philosophically. She had struggled with darkness most of her life . . . loneliness, abandonment, fear. She knew those components well and no longer wanted to live with them. She wanted to bathe in the light, have it wash over her heart and make it whole. Like a butterfly emerging from a cocoon, she wanted to burst out fresh and new. "Beautiful," she said.

His hand swept in an arc, at a canopy of stars so vast that they seemed to run together like a smear of glowing paint. "Can you count the stars, love?"

"I've never seen so many," she said in absolute awe. "But I guess they're always there, aren't they? Can't see stars without night, though, can we?"

"Too much artificial light from cities blocks them out. But out here you can see them all. Makes a person feel small and wanting."

As he talked she was absorbing the profound truth of this night: She no longer had to remain in the dark. She could be free of it. He raised up on his elbows, pointed, and named a few of the constellations.

"I'm impressed," she said, regaining her composure. "But I don't know how those early stargazers saw those images. I can't."

"Because the stars *talked* to them, told them about other lands and adventures to be had. And the stargazers believed the stars, so when they roamed far away, they looked up and saw the same star images in the night skies looking down on them as they saw at home. It probably brought them comfort. So they named the stars into constellations. Makes sense, don't you think?"

His words raised a lump in her throat. The same night sky had hovered above the earth for eons. Stargazers sought and found order in chaos, a place and a purpose under heaven. It made her think of Tennessee and the ones she loved. "Thank you for bringing me here, Garret. Lets me see how beautiful the world is . . . here and at home."

He chuckled. "*Life* is beautiful."

It is with you, she said inside her heart.

He looked down on her. "You're beautiful."

"You're daft," she said, using the Aussie word for crazy.

"You once told me you'd come with me on walkabout. Do you still want to do that?"

"That was a while ago. I—I mean, yes, I'd like to see the world with you, but just now, I have to go home." The feeling was suddenly intense.

He took a deep breath. "I want to come with you. I can't just let you go away from me, Eden. Do you think Ciana would let me camp on her property? Maybe in the barn you told me about? I can work."

Eden's heart thumped with the sudden uptick of the unexpected, like a box found under the Christmas tree after all the other presents were opened. "You'd come to America? With me?"

"I'll need a visa. Can apply for it soon as we get back to Sydney." He pushed her bangs off her forehead.

"But a walkabout takes time. You can't see the States in only a few months."

"We'll worry about that part when I get there. We can be together, that's what's important. We'll figure out the future."

Brimming tears smudged the stars above him until they melted into glitter. "Ciana will welcome you. I know she will. And you can meet Jon and Alice Faye, all the horses—"

He pressed his fingertips to her lips. "I take that as a yes."

She wiggled her arms up from the warmth of the bag and hugged his neck, laughing. "Yes. Yes. A hundred times yes!"

Her mind started racing. "Soon as we get to your house, I'll email Ciana." A week in the outback had completely cut Eden off from communications. "It's still yesterday in Tennessee. I can't get used to this time difference."

"And you don't mind sleeping out here tonight, roughing it?"

"Not with all those stars watching over us."

He kissed her, drew back, cupped her face in his palm. "I love you, Eden. And tonight I want to make love to you, here under the stars of my country. And when we get to America, I want to make love to you under those stars too."

She gave her answer wordlessly by partially unzipping the sleeping bag to make room for their bodies to move more freely together. "Don't forget about the moon," she whispered, parting her lips to receive his kiss. "Shouldn't the moon have equal time?"

Ten thousand miles away from New South Wales, Australia, Ciana drove home on a narrow, dark county road toward Bellmeade, a line of trees on her left, open fields on her right. She could tell that her left headlight was burned out, but because it was so late, she pretty much had the road to herself and wasn't concerned about oncoming traffic. The moon flirted with moving night clouds. She'd been at Abbie's baby shower, and was still basking in the party's glow, where it had seemed as if every woman from the expansive family of relatives had been stuffed into the church's basement.

The room had been decorated with balloons and banners, and tables had overflowed with gifts. All kinds of appetizers—savory, hot, chewy, spicy-sweet—had been spread across banquet tables, along with cake and cream puffs and fruit for dipping in a small fountain dripping warm chocolate. On a beverage table sat containers of coffee, sweet tea, and punch.

For a minute, after walking in, Ciana had keenly felt Arie's absence, but Patricia quickly pulled her into the circle of friendship and spoke freely about her daughter. "She would have loved this. It is a night for happiness."

Abbie wore a coral-colored linen dress, her big belly protruding. She grumbled about being the size of a heifer, but she looked radiant. She also announced a long-held secret—she and Eric were having a boy. He would be named Aaron, the closest they could come to Arie's name, which they would have chosen if the baby had been a girl.

"So much for offering Abbie my old dollhouse," Ciana said as she drove the dark road. Maybe she could donate it to the Pediatric Oncology floor where Arie had volunteered and taught art classes. It had been good to be around Arie's extended family, good to laugh and share stories, and keep her mind off her problems. The sudden glare of headlights almost blinded her in the rearview mirror.

Behind her she saw another truck coming at her fast. It was dark colored, a bar of hunting lights mounted across the top of the cab, and riding on oversized tires. Irritated at the driver's lack of consideration, she stepped on her accelerator, but her old truck couldn't deliver the speed she needed to outdistance the one behind her. The truck drew closer. Her pulse shot up, and irritation gave way to concern. She tapped her brakes, hoping to signal the driver to go around her. But he didn't slow. If anything, he came faster. She moved onto the shoulder of the road, half on, half off the asphalt. The shoulder jarred and shook her truck, rattled her teeth, forced her to fight to keep her steering wheel straight.

She honked her horn. The truck didn't pass, didn't back

off. Fear wedged in her throat, gave way to panic as she realized that the driver wanted to force her off the road. Desperately, she glanced right, saw empty fields flying past with ravines trenched into rain runoff gullies, and telephone poles evenly spaced. If she hit a pole, the front end of her truck would cave. If she went into a gully, she could flip.

Ciana felt the truck behind tap her bumper, making her jerk forward, almost causing her to lose her grip on her steering wheel. Her bumper was hit a second time. She couldn't hold on much longer, dodging poles and gullies at this breakneck speed. She gritted her teeth.

Another quick glance ahead and to her right. She saw an upcoming turnoff and a closed gate, an entrance to a field for farm equipment. Driving through the gate would destroy her truck, but she would also avoid a ravine, spread the impact across the grille, and instantly slow her speed. With sudden determination, Ciana turned the wheel and drove onto the turnoff, letting the other truck shoot past her. With her hand on the handle of the door, she lay as far down across the seat as her seat belt allowed and struck the gate. With an earsplitting sound of metal on metal, her truck hurtled through the steel barrier, and with a momentum that shoved most of her engine into the cab. The truck stopped with a lurch. The heat of the engine scorched her legs. She gasped for breath, tasted metal-tinged smoke. Her mind screamed, *Get out!*

She somehow struggled out of her seat belt, tumbled through the door she'd thrown open and torn off its hinges by the impact, rolled across the ground. She panted, her lungs on fire, lay back against the hard cold dirt. Ciana knew she was hurt, and she was alone. She closed her eyes and lost consciousness.

22

Ciana was sitting up in the ER, on an exam table, her midsection tightly wrapped, and wearing a gown that gaped in the back, when her mother and Jon barreled behind the curtain. "Hey, you can't barge in here," a doctor barked. But there was no stopping her visitors.

"I'm okay," Ciana said, bursting into tears. She put her arms around Jon's neck.

"What happened?" She heard raw fear in Jon's voice.

"I'm doing an exam here," the doctor interrupted crossly.

"When you didn't come home . . . ," Jon said. She winced with the pressure of his arms on her sides and he quickly drew back.

Alice Faye stepped forward, her face pasty white, and peered into Ciana's eyes. "Oh my God, honey . . ."

"I'm all right, Mom." She was woozy from the pain medication the doctor had given her, and she was shaking from cold and from shock.

"How'd she get here?" Jon asked the doctor.

"Ambulance brought her in. Some farmer found her in his field about four a.m. He called 911, stayed with her until the paramedics arrived."

She was in an emergency clinic attached to a small hospital on the outskirts of Windemere, near the interstate. The ER was tiny and, except for Ciana, without patients.

"I think my truck's totaled," Ciana mumbled, still dazed, and unable to let go of Jon.

"How bad is my daughter hurt?" Alice Faye turned to the doctor.

The doctor's demeanor became patient and compassionate. "Just got her X-rays and scans. There's a broken rib that I've wrapped, and some burns on her arms, but she was wearing boots, and they protected her legs. Some cuts, already stitched, and she's going to bruise and be pretty sore from head to toe. But all in all, I'd say she's pretty lucky. No organs damaged. I've given her a shot of antibiotics and pain meds. I'd like to check her in overnight for observation."

Together Alice Faye and Jon said "Okay" at the same time that Ciana said "No way." She looked at their anxious faces. "I want to go home."

"It's just observation," the doctor said. "You blacked out. Have a good night and I'll sign you out in the morning."

Ciana struggled to scoot off the table.

Jon stopped her. "Whoa. Don't be stubborn. Do what the doc says."

"Mom, my clothes are over there." She pointed to the things she'd been wearing.

"Ciana—" Alice Faye started.

"I will walk out naked if I have to."

The doc exchanged glances with Jon and her mother. "I can't hold her against her will. And she seems capable of making her own choices."

Jon flashed her an angry look, but he nodded.

"I'll write her a pain prescription, and you can take her home. She should see her regular doctor in a couple of days, or"—he turned to Ciana—"or sooner if you have abdominal swelling or serious pain."

"I'll make sure she does," Alice Faye said, wiping her eyes on a tissue handed over by a nurse.

Ciana started off the table, but the doctor stopped her. "Not so fast."

"You said I could go." Waves of nausea washed over her.

"Nurse, bring a wheelchair."

"I can walk," Ciana started, holding the gown closed behind her, but another look from Jon silenced her.

The nurse rolled a wheelchair over and Ciana was helped into it. She knew she couldn't manage by herself at the moment. She felt battered and no longer up to arguing.

The woman settled Ciana in the chair, handed Alice Faye a paper sack with Ciana's torn and filthy clothes, too damaged to be re-worn, so she had to wear the hospital-issue gown home. The nurse pushed the chair to the door.

Jon jogged ahead and brought Alice Faye's Lincoln to the entrance and to a stop in front of the chair. With help, Ciana eased into the backseat. Jon leaned over her, snapped her seat belt, stole a kiss, brought her back to herself. She was safe now. The pain meds were working their magic. She felt numb and floaty. She leaned into the seat. "Happy to ride in this old tank," she said, drifting on the current of the drugs.

"That old truck of yours needed to be gotten rid of years ago." Alice Faye's voice quavered.

Ciana was glad her mother was blaming the truck. Jon caught her eyes in the rearview mirror. His look was dark as thunder, and questioning. She shook her head slightly to say *Not now*. And so silently she shared with him that what had happened had not been an accident.

Later that day, the sheriff showed up with a deputy and took Ciana's statement about her wreck. She was groggy on pain pills but was determined to answer his questions. Trouble was, she couldn't help much with the investigation. She could only describe the truck as "big and black," but was unable to give either a make or model. "I never saw the driver either. I was too busy trying to get out of his way."

The sheriff filled out a report as she spoke, prodded her for details, but she wasn't able to tell him more. Finally, he closed his notebook and said, "If anything else comes to you, call me. You handled things real smart, Ciana. This could have ended a whole lot different."

Once he left, she drifted off to sleep and dreamed of a large, dark beast chasing her, trying to devour her. When she woke, Alice Faye brought her lunch on a tray, offered to feed her. Ciana declined. "Mom, I'll be okay. How's Jon doing?"

He had visited her first thing after breakfast, still livid. He'd eased onto her bed, gathered her into his arms, held her, rocked her gently, then left the room without a word.

"Upset. We're both crazy upset," Alice Faye said, answering Ciana's question.

In spite of the mellowing effect of the pain pills, Ciana felt anxious. "Where is he?"

"Working the horses now, but he went out to the field earlier, to the scene." Her mother's eyes went shiny with

141

unshed tears. "This has gone too far. I'm not dumb, Ciana. I see what's happened around here. The fences. Now your accident. Someone's trying to run us off Bellmeade. It isn't right. I know I wanted to sell, but I never expected things to go this way. I never thought it would come to—to hurting *you*."

"Mom . . . we don't know for sure. I don't know why—"

"What other reason could there be for you to crash? Someone's trying to scare you . . . us . . . away. Most everyone's on board for Hastings's project. You're the holdout, Ciana. And so they came after you."

Ciana dropped her gaze because the naked pain on her mother's face had put her on the verge of tears. "We can't let this get to us. This is our land, and no one's going to chase us off it."

"Right," Alice Faye said, her chin high. "They won't."

And just like that, Ciana realized that their wills had merged. They were of one mind about keeping their land, no longer a house divided.

When it was time for supper, Ciana wanted to come to the kitchen, but neither Alice Faye nor Jon would allow it. So Jon carried both his and Ciana's plates into her room while she remained in bed. "I feel silly," she grumbled, but not without some gratitude. She hurt all over.

He ignored her complaint, looked around, and in his best drawl, said, "Never thought I'd be invited into your bedroom. I know I just barged in this morning, but I had to see you, make sure you were really here."

She gave a little laugh, groaned because it pressed against her ribs. "Would have given you a tour if you'd asked."

"I wouldn't have trusted myself to tour and leave."

She found having Jon in her bedroom incredibly sexy. Not that she could offer to do anything about it just now.

He dragged a chair to her bedside, set the tray across her lap. "You look wonderful."

"I've seen a mirror, cowboy. I know what I look like, and 'wonderful' is a huge exaggeration."

"You're alive. That's what's wonderful." He set his own tray on his lap. "I saw your truck. Sheriff had what's left of it towed to impound. Maybe a paint sample from the other truck is on the bumper. That could help pin down a brand."

"Is my poor blue beast toast?"

He nodded. "I can't believe you walked away from it."

"Rolled away like a ball," she said for clarification, and pushed her fork through the gravy on her mashed potatoes. She had no appetite. "I was afraid it might blow up."

Jon's face darkened. "When I catch up to the guy, *he'll* be toast."

"Not sure he'll ever be caught. Probably part of the same gang that's breaking our fences."

Jon blew out a lungful of air. "Let's drop it for now."

He ate, and while he did, she nibbled a few bites. "And I've lost my truck too. That really burns me. I've had that truck—"

"Way too long." Jon completed her sentence with a wry smile. "Sort of a piece of junk, you know."

"It was running," she said defensively. "Now I have nothing to drive except Mom's Lincoln and my tractor."

He grinned. "You can drive my truck."

"I accept your offer." She knew he'd worked all day without much sleep, so she let him eat in peace. When he was finished, he set his tray on the floor. She poked her tray. "I'm through. Tell Mom it was delicious, but it hurts to chew."

143

He set her tray beside his, scooted onto her mattress, and facing her, took her hand. "I don't know what I would have done if—"

The anguish in his voice and on his face stabbed at her heart. "But I'm all right. Really. I'll be out there plowing up the fields real soon and planting a new crop." Spring alfalfa was generally planted anywhere between early March and May. "I'm going to put in a field of corn too. And then there's the garden out back."

"I get it. You can't keep a good girl down." He started to stand, but she caught his hand.

"And you're going to train horses here."

"What?"

The words had slipped out, and until that moment she hadn't realized she'd even been harboring such an idea. But now that she'd said them, resolve set in, and she knew it was what she wanted. She didn't want Jon to leave, try to buy other land for a business, or decide to return to the rodeo circuit. "You heard me. This place is going to pay off, and you're going to be a part of it."

He shook his head. "This is your land. Not mine."

"But I can do whatever I want with it. And I want you to get some of those mustangs and train them, and sell them, just like you did for Bill Pickins."

"How's that help you?" He looked somewhat amused.

"I'll take a cut of your profits," she said, realizing she was acting on pure emotion with no clue about his business. "I—I mean, if you want to work out the details, we can."

He studied her. "We'll talk when the drugs wear off."

Fighting sudden exhaustion, she closed her eyes and rested against her pillow. When she opened her eyes, he was still staring at her, his look so tender that an intense physical desire stirred inside her. "I have a lot of boo-boos, cowboy."

"Maybe I should kiss them." He leaned forward, brushed his lips against her forehead, just above the stitches over her eyebrow.

She held up her arm where there was an abrasion. "Hurts here too."

He kissed the spot.

"And here." She pointed to her mouth.

He kissed her with a pressure as light as the brush of a butterfly's wing.

She thought of a hundred places on her body she wanted him to kiss. "I hurt all over."

He stroked the swell of her breast above her bedclothes, making her ache to have him kiss her there. But he pulled away and said, "Rain check."

Reluctantly, she watched him rise. "I'll probably need more therapy tomorrow."

Love for her spilled out of his intense green eyes. He said, "Count on it."

23

Visitors, flowers, and a dozen cards came during the week Ciana was recovering, taking her by surprise. Maybe everybody in the town didn't hate her after all. Patricia and Abbie came to visit, as well as some friends who had once ridden with her in the flag corps. The ones away at college texted her get-well wishes. One good thing that happened after her wreck was that the vandalism to her property ceased. "Maybe almost killing me scared them off," she told her mother.

During her recovery, she received a long email from Eden that read like a continuous run-on sentence, saying she was coming home and that Garret was coming with her and could he have a place to stay and, oh, she was crazy in love with the guy and they were going to eventually work their way across the country so they could see America together but really wanted to hang in Windemere for a while if that was okay.

Ciana told her, "Of course," and didn't mention the accident. She also wrote about Enzo's coming and going and about her finally-out-in-the-open-for-all-the-world-to-see feelings for Jon. She ended by writing, *Hurry home. The garden needs planting.*

Ciana also had two other visitors. One she knew; the other she'd heard about but had never met. She was snapping green beans on the veranda a few days after her wreck—the farthest Alice Faye would allow her to migrate from her bed—when a red sports car turned into Bellmeade. She watched it come slowly up the tree-lined drive toward her, and with the afternoon sun in her eyes was unable to make out the driver. She set down the bowl of fresh beans as the car stopped a few feet in front of the steps. When the door opened and the driver emerged, her back stiffened. "Hello, Mr. Hastings."

Gerald Hastings came closer but stayed off the steps. "Miss Beauchamp."

Ciana wondered where her dog was, and while she didn't want Soldier to bite the man, it would have been nice to have the animal terrify him. "To what do I owe your visit?"

Hastings looked distressed. "I'm just in from Chicago and heard of your accident. I'm sorry."

"I'll be just fine."

"I'm hearing that it may have been more deliberate than accidental."

"The sheriff has my statement."

"Miss Beauchamp. Ciana—"

The front door opened and Alice Faye walked quickly onto the porch. "We have nothing to say to you, so turn around and go away."

"Alice Faye . . ." He stopped, regrouped. "Are you against me too?"

With effort, Ciana stood, teetered slightly, hating to have him watch her struggle. "You heard my mother. Leave."

Hastings stepped backward, his gaze darting between the

two women. "Are you implying that *I* had something to do with the accident? I told you, I've been in Chicago."

"I don't have to imply it, but it can't help me from thinking it," Alice Faye said, her brow knitted.

"Now listen here, I'm a businessman with projects all over the country. I'm sorry about what happened, but I had nothing to do with it."

"Your offer to buy out my farmland most likely had everything to do with it," Ciana countered, holding her anger like a tight wad in her chest.

The sound of Jon's pickup turning into the drive and hurtling toward them stopped any argument Hastings was about to give. The truck screeched to a halt, but when the door opened Soldier beat Jon out of the vehicle. "Stay!" Jon commanded. The dog stood at attention, a low growl in his throat, eyes trained on Gerald Hastings, now pale as a ghost, and standing stock-still.

Jon sauntered forward, a rifle against his thigh.

Hastings's gaze moved from the dog to the rifle. "Now hold on. I just came to say how sorry I am Ciana was hurt."

Soldier's growl deepened. Jon touched the dog's head and he sat obediently. "And don't think we're not grateful for your visit, but it's over now. Best if you left."

"The accident was *not* my doing," Hastings said in a raised voice that caused Soldier to stand again. Hastings went rigid.

"No one said it was. But what has been said is that Bellmeade is not for sale," Ciana told him.

"I'm offering you a lot of money."

"And I have turned it down."

"I have investors—"

"Then you might want to tell them to invest in another one of your projects," Alice Faye said.

"You were never against this," Hastings told her, looking betrayed.

"Things change."

Jon raised the tip of the rifle. "And when you get back to town, you might want to spread the news that anyone caught trespassing on this property will be . . ." He stopped short, grinned, but his green eyes were hard as marbles. "Well, they'll be dealt with."

Without another word, Hastings climbed into his sports car and drove away.

Ciana was walking her horse on a lead line in the area around the barn, Jon by her side. Firecracker plodded behind her, and Soldier walked alongside Jon. "She was mad at me when I first came into the barn," Ciana said.

"Horses can act like two-year-old kids when they've a mind to. Where do you think we get the phrase 'acting like a horse's ass' from?"

He made Ciana laugh, which also made her wince. She was getting better, but her broken rib still hurt. "She was probably wondering why I haven't ridden her, or haven't come out to see her until today." She turned to the horse. "You forgive me?"

"Good bet she will."

Ciana let Firecracker catch up to them, then stroked the animal's soft nose. "She seems to understand I'm hurt."

"Horses are intelligent and sensitive," Jon confirmed, taking Ciana's hand in his.

The sound of a truck turning into the drive made them all look. "Now what?" Ciana grumbled. "Is the whole town coming in to see my stitches and bruises?"

The truck was painted in camouflage and had a cracked

windshield. Jon watched the approach, said, "Never thought I'd see a truck uglier than your old junker."

"Hey, watch it, cowboy. That old hunk of junk saved my life."

The truck stopped at the barn and an old man got out, seemingly unfazed by Soldier's bristling back hairs. Jon told the dog to stand down. To the man, he asked, "Help you, mister?"

The man was short and well-muscled. His potbelly hung over his belted jeans, and long white hair stuck out from under his Tennessee Titans ball cap. "Miss Ciana?" the man asked.

"I am."

His face looked weathered and grizzled. He held out his hand, "Name's Cecil Donaldson."

The name was familiar, but she couldn't recall why.

"I was Miss Arie's uncle."

The man's voice reminded Ciana of tires on gravel, but the mention of Arie brought back the time when Tony Cicero had been harassing their families. When told that her relatives had put a round-the-clock guard on her house and that someone had shot out a tire of Tony's SUV in the dark, Arie had said, *"That would be my uncle Cecil. He was a sniper in Vietnam, and he can shoot the eye out of a wild turkey at two hundred yards."*

"She spoke highly of you," Ciana said to the man in front of her. "This is Jon Mercer."

Cecil gave him a nod. "I know who you are." Jon returned the man's nod, and Cecil said, "I heard you been having some trouble out here."

"Some."

"I come to help out."

"How?" Jon asked.

Ciana put her hand on Jon's arm to hold him off. There

were ways to talk to folks from these parts and issuing a challenge in a Texan accent wasn't one of them.

"That's a kind offer, Mr. Donaldson."

"Cecil," the man said, giving her permission to use his first name. "I come because I know it's what Arie would want. Saw her in a dream the other night. She was real as you are. She was standing in the sunlight, her arms crossed, and she told me, 'You help my friend, Uncle Cecil.' She's always been our little angel, so when she speaks to me, I got to listen."

A lump formed in Ciana's throat. She saw Arie's face too, real and soft and smiling. "I miss her too, Cecil."

The old man cleared gruffness from his throat. "All those years back when she was in the hospital and them docs were pumping poison in her blood that didn't help no way, our family give her all we could. What we couldn't give her was the one thing she wanted most: a true friend. Folks were afraid they'd catch cancer if they come around her." He spat into the dirt to show his disgust.

"They were ignorant," Ciana said. "People know better now."

"Every kid shunned her 'cept you. You had that big fundraiser and you became her friend."

Fifth grade. A lifetime ago. Ciana smoothed the toe of her boot in the dirt. "I loved her."

"And then you took her to Italy. Whooie, that gal talked nonstop when she got home." A smile cracked Cecil's face, smoothed out the Etch A Sketch lines of his skin. "She'd wanted to go to that place all her life, and you took her. Fact is, you give her most everything she ever really wanted." He cut his eyes to Jon, who shifted his stance, then back to Ciana. "None of us ever going to forget that."

"So how do you want to help out, Mr. Donaldson?" Jon

asked, quietly, as if well aware that he had not been granted permission to call the old man by his first name.

"I will watch your fields at night while you're sleeping."

"You don't sleep?"

Cecil eyed Jon full in the face. "Ain't slept through the night since I come home from 'Nam. May as well make it useful to someone."

Ciana stepped forward, cutting off any further discussion. "I'd be pleased to have you help out, Cecil."

He offered a curt nod. "Start tonight."

She held out her hand. "Man's shake is his bond."

Cecil grinned again, shook her hand. "Arie always said you were good people. Even when some in the family said you being her friend wouldn't last, what with you being a Beauchamp and all."

Ciana felt her face redden. "Person can choose her friends. She's stuck with family."

Cecil grinned big, exposing crooked teeth. "Ain't that the truth."

He turned, but before he could walk to his truck, Jon said, "We don't need anybody killed for trespassing."

Cecil turned back around, measured Jon head to toe. "You can call me Cecil, too, Jon Mercer. Since we'll be working together, and because Arie liked you so much."

Jon looked uncomfortable, so Ciana intervened. "I don't want anybody shot." Ciana enforced Jon's words, before Cecil could turn away again.

Cecil said, "I won't have to shoot nobody. Hell, when the town hears I'm doing guard duty, there won't be no more trouble." He tipped the brim of his cap, and left Bellmeade, his old truck belching fumes from its rusty tailpipe.

24

Ciana sat on an old worn quilt in the barn's loft. She watched windblown sheets of falling spring rain through the large cutout window used to pass bales of hay and straw for storage. From her vantage point, she saw the barely discernable line of trees that separated the main property from the new track and corral. The track would be a sea of mud after two days of constant rain, and require resurfacing. More work she was still unable to do.

"Ciana? You up there?" Jon's voice called from below.

"Come on up." She waited for him to climb the ladder. When he did, she patted the quilt for him to join her.

"Should you be up here?"

"It's been two weeks. I'm better. And I'm bored."

"Takes six weeks for a broken bone to heal."

"I didn't know you were a trainer *and* a doctor."

He leaned over and kissed her forehead. "I'm hanging out my shingle next week. What are you doing?"

"You mean besides wishing I'd already planted spring

alfalfa?" She glanced toward the opening. "Hate to miss a good rain."

"It'll rain again." He looked to the basket of books and papers she'd managed to bring up with her.

"Some of Olivia's diaries," Ciana said. "Only good thing about my confinement. I'd given up on them, but now it seems I have time on my hands." She opened the book on her lap. "Interesting reading. Like peeking through a window into the past; life in the forties and fifties. No TV until the late seventies here at Bellmeade."

"No television?" Jon lifted Ciana's hair, kissed the nape of her neck, sending shivers up her spine. "What did people do for entertainment back then?"

"They made their own fun." She offered a wry smile. "These old books are fragile. And during the war years she often turned them upside down and wrote on the backside of any blank pages, making the ink bleed through. Some pages are unreadable."

"But still you try."

Ciana shrugged. "She wrote about everything, so this is a way for me to get to know her better. I've tried putting the books in some kind of order, but that's been really hard. I jump from reading about high school to grade school, or from after Granddad Charles died to when they were dating. She stopped most of her journaling when I was a child." Ciana riffled through pages of the book in her lap. "Some of it kind of freaks me out, though."

"How so?" He made lazy circles on her back with his broad hand. His touch was gentle and soothing.

The rain hammered the barn's roof. She felt a sudden twinge of family loyalty, reminded herself that this was Jon she was talking to. He already knew some of the Beauchamp history—the story of Charles bringing Olivia a bag of apples the day he decided he wanted to marry her. He knew

154

about Charles Jr. dying in the tractor accident when the boy was twelve too. Maybe he needed to hear more about her family, warts and all. She stared out at the driving rain. A boom of distant thunder sounded. "Mom's always had a thing about Grandmother not liking her."

"Her own daughter?" He sounded skeptical. "Alice Faye's the best!"

"That's not how Olivia made her feel. They—um—they used to fight over me. For my attention. Sometimes I felt like a rag doll pulled between them." As the child of an alcoholic, Ciana had resented her mother and had turned to Olivia many times instead of Alice Faye. She dropped her gaze. "And I regret to say that I often took advantage, played them against each other."

He stroked her shoulder. "What kid wouldn't?"

"Don't make excuses for me. I was a brat. Mom used to tell me about feeling rejected by Grandmother when growing up, but I blew it off, told her it was her imagination. Today I read this entry." Ciana stared down at the book in her lap, the veil of her hair covering the side of her face. "It's dated January, 1960. Mom was just three months old. Listen."

> Charles woke me in the middle of the night holding the baby. "Honey, can't you hear her crying? She was in her crib screaming." He was trying to comfort the baby and she was whimpering and mewing like a newborn cat. Then he sat on the bed and tried to hand her off to me, but I wouldn't take her.
> "Put her back," I told him. "Let her cry it out."
> He looked like I'd slapped him. "She's just a baby, Livy. She wants her mama."
> I couldn't take her. I'm hardly able to look at her,

and there's no way I can tell Charles that. "You take
care of her. Fix her a bottle," I told him.
"You nursed Charlie. Why not her?"
I crawled under the covers. Losing Charlie is still
as raw a wound as the day he died. But it's more than
that. How can I tell my husband that I do not love this
child? That I cannot love this child? And it has nothing
to do with our Charlie dying.
My husband thinks that the baby was a godsend.
A gift from heaven to ease our pain. How can I tell
him this baby may be a curse?

Ciana looked up at Jon. "Makes a strong case for Mother's point of view. Don't you think? Why couldn't she love my mother?"

He shook his head. "Maybe she had that kind of depression women get after giving birth."

"Postpartum depression. I thought about that, but there are other entries where she dismisses Mom. It became a sore spot between Olivia and Granddad. He adored his little girl, my mother. He couldn't be around much, though. He and Grandpa Jacob were always working the farm, or traveling to sell their crops." Ciana shivered.

He put his arm around her. "You cold?"

"No . . . just a creepy feeling. Grandmother used to say the feeling is due to someone walking over a grave."

"No more sad talk. I want to ask you something before Eden and this Garret fellow arrive day after tomorrow and life gets crazy around here."

She pulled away, arched a shapely eyebrow. "So ATV attacks on my fields, broken fences, an accident that hammered me, and night patrols by man and beast don't qualify as crazy life to you?"

He grinned sheepishly. "Point taken." He reached into his shirt pocket, extracted a small red velvet pouch, and held it out. "Then before there are any other complications or distractions, please take a look at this."

Intrigued, she took hold of the soft material, undid cording holding the bag closed, pulled it open, and dumped the contents into her other hand. Her breath caught. In her palm lay a band of gold, that even in the weak gray light, glimmered enough for her to see intricately carved images of birds and fruit.

Her heart skipped a beat and her gaze flew to Jon's. Words jammed in her throat. Rain pounded on the roof. A gust of wind swept moisture through the opening and Ciana felt the wetness on her skin, her hair, in her eyes.

"Marry me," he said.

Ciana burst into tears.

Jon recoiled, looked shocked. "I—I didn't mean to—I mean—"

She shushed him with a kiss, pulled away, said, "I love you, Jon Mercer. Dammit."

He laughed loudly. "*Dammit?* You do have a way with words, Ciana."

She wiped her eyes with the back of her hand, opened her tightly closed palm holding the ring. "I am battered and stitched and I have big ugly bruises all over my body and you think it's the perfect time to get engaged?"

He ignored her complaint, peered into her cinnamon-colored eyes. "Thought I'd pick a time when you were vulnerable. Did it work?"

157

She held up the ring, slid it on her finger, but it wouldn't slide over her knuckle. "Previous owner had small hands."

Jon watched her turn her hand to catch the feeble light on the exquisite ring. "It once belonged to my great-great-great-grandmother on my mother's side. Isabella Elena Cordoba-Cortez. According to Mom, she was from an old Castilian family, a descendant of German, Visigoth, and Roman conquerors. Her husband had this ring fashioned for her as a wedding gift."

"Tell me more." Ciana spun the ring, admired the carvings clearly created by a master artisan.

"Well, his name was Bolívar and he brought her from Spain to Mexico, and together they built a cattle empire that was said to span a third of the country. She was blond and blue-eyed and so beautiful that peasants fainted when they saw her." He grinned. "Great story. Course, the cattle empire is long gone and my mama's people are poor and living in Texas. Mom wore this ring when she married Wade, took it off when they divorced. When I went home over the holidays, I told her I'd found the one girl in the world I wanted to give Isabella's ring to, and she let me bring it back. I want you to wear it, Ciana."

She watched his eyes as he spoke, her heart so filled with love for him that it ached. "Well, since this is a wedding ring, on the day we marry, I'll put it on forever."

"Is that a promise?"

"My oath."

"Then all we're discussing here is *when*, right?"

"Can I heal first?"

His grin made his green eyes glow. He gathered her in his arms, lay across the old quilt with Ciana pressed against him. She felt the rhythm of his heart under her hand resting on his chest. Above, she heard the music of hard rain and distant thunder. Below, she heard the horses moving in their stalls. She was surrounded with the scent of spring rain, fresh hay, old lumber, and the spice of Jon's skin. She floated between her past and her future on the dreamlike cusp of all her tomorrows. In Jon Mercer she had found her soul mate. It had been written in the stars that night they'd first met, but impossible for her to see at the time. And later, when they'd again come together, her friendship with Arie had held her feelings for Jon hostage, so that even after Arie's death, Ciana had been unable to allow herself to love him the way she wanted to. No longer. From this moment on, she would face her life with this one perfect person by her side.

25

Two days later, Eden and Garret bounced into the flow of Bellmeade life inside a white camper loaded to the brim with camping gear and luggage. Even before the vehicle stopped rolling, Eden bounded out like an exuberant puppy, ran up the porch steps, and threw herself into Ciana's waiting arms. Ciana held her breath, willing her ribs to not hurt through the squeeze of Eden's embrace. Alice Faye hugged Eden next and finally Jon.

"G'day, mate." Garret's words from the porch step cracked into their reunion.

Eden whirled, grabbed Garret's hand, and pulled him up next to her for a round of introductions. "Where are my manners? This is my mate . . . my friend, Garret Locklin."

Ciana kissed both his cheeks in the manner she'd learned in Europe. "Good to see you again."

"You too." He looked around with keen blue eyes. "Nice digs."

Eden had called from the airport the day before to announce their arrival, so Ciana had watched from the porch the whole day. She'd said they'd drive over and get them, but Eden had insisted they'd arrive under their own power. "A camper?" Ciana now asked, looking out at the truck with metal housing that could sleep two.

"Bought and paid for in Nashville. Figured we'd need it to get around the country," Eden explained. "Plus we can stay in it while we visit."

Ciana understood the unspoken message. Eden and Garret were lovers and the camper would be their nighttime home. "You'd better stay a while!"

"We're here as long as you want us."

Garret said, "Won't wear out our welcome, though."

Alice Faye intervened. "I have fresh sweet tea and a homemade cake waiting to be cut in the kitchen. Come inside. And later you two bring in your luggage. No guest of ours is going to sleep in my driveway in a truck. It's uncivilized. Eden, your old room is waiting, clean sheets on the bed. And Garret, you're on the third floor in the room with Jon Mercer."

Ciana saw Garret and Eden exchange glances, a look of panic passing between them. With unmistakable charm, her mother had just laid down the house rules—no cohabitation allowed. Ciana suppressed a smile as Alice Faye hooked her arm through Garret's and walked him to the door. "Welcome to America, and to Bellmeade, Garret. So *happy* you're here."

Eden lingered in bed, stretched, reached for Garret, then remembered he was upstairs in another room. She sighed. It was the first morning she'd awoken without him beside her in many weeks. They'd slept together at his house throughout the long process of telling friends and family goodbye while waiting for tickets and Garret's visa. Even on the long flight from Australia, they'd slept holding on to each other. Eden formed dark thoughts toward Alice Faye, felt contrite and quickly erased them, realizing the woman still embraced the Southern morality code: propriety above all else. Even Gwen, not always the best reflection of motherhood, had complained about appearances when Eden had moved in with Tony. Eden knew there had been other reasons for her objections, but with Garret, it was different. They were madly in love, and being in each other's arms every night had only strengthened their bond.

"It is what it is," she told herself, and tossed off the covers. Olivia's former room was just as she remembered it— quaint and cozy, decked out with lace pillows and old quilts and highly polished mahogany furniture over a hundred years old. And despite not being able to have Garret in the room with her, it felt wonderful to be back. To be home. She saw the alarm clock, realized she'd overslept, dressed quickly, and hustled downstairs to the kitchen where all except Jon sat around the table talking and drinking coffee.

Garret got to his feet, kissed her soundly. "Ciana's mother thinks I talk funny," he said, seating Eden and going for coffee.

"No way," Eden teased. "He speaks four languages, including Aussie."

Alice Faye had turned bright red. "I didn't say funny. Just different."

"You only need to know a few phrases, Mom," Ciana said. " 'G'day' is good morning or good afternoon or good evening—"

" 'Short black' and 'long black' refer to the size coffee you want to buy," Eden interjected.

"A 'bloke' is a man," Ciana added.

"A 'sheila' is a girl—"

"'Billy boil' is a teapot of hot water."

"'Ear bashing' is something a nonstop talker does—"

"And in the south we say 'kiss my grits' when people are heckling you," Alice Faye announced with a flourish.

Everyone laughed. Alice Faye went to fixing breakfast, and soon the smell of bacon mixed with the aromas of coffee and baking biscuits. Garret turned to Ciana. "My bunk mate was gone when I woke up. Maybe I was snoring."

"Jon went to tend to the horses. He'll have breakfast with us," Ciana said.

Jon did, but as soon as he was finished, he headed back to the barn. Eden poked Garret. "Go see if he needs any help. Ciana and I are going to settle in for a nice long chat. Lots of catching up to do."

Ciana had barely closed her bedroom door when Eden pounced. "What happened to you? Did you think I might not notice your bruises? Or the way you favor your right side?"

Ciana stretched out on her bed gingerly, leaned against the headboard. "Gee, and I thought you'd tell me about your near drowning experience and Garret's hateful old girlfriend first thing."

Eden had emailed Ciana about the beach party and Alyssa's outing her dark secret but had insisted that she was doing fine and that she'd fill in details when she got home. The two friends stared at each other, then simultaneously threw their arms around one another and sniffled, telling of how each had missed the other and how glad they were to again be together. When they finally settled down, Eden grabbed tissues, blew her nose, and said, "You first, Ciana."

Ciana started with the vandalism, which Eden knew about, and ended with the accident, which she hadn't known about. "You should have told me."

"Nothing you could have done from so far away except fret. You're here now and can see for yourself I'm banged up, but fine."

After grumbling at Ciana anyway, Eden recounted her story, finishing with the camping trip.

"So I guess Mama's edict about separate rooms for you two seems prehistoric."

"We won't go against your mother's wishes." Eden conceded defeat. "But we'll find private time together because we need to be with each other. Maybe drive the camper someplace where we can be alone. You and Jon can borrow it if you wish," Eden added, cutting her eyes to Ciana.

"Not going there with Jon until I can move freely. I want our first time together to be perfect."

"When two people are in love, it is perfect," Eden said.

Ciana tipped her chin. "And no need to use your camper for alone time. There's a loft in the barn, and an old trunk with a quilt and throw pillows in it. Barn's mostly empty all day, and after Jon shuts it down, place is empty most nights, too . . . except for the horses, and they won't talk. Take a bottle of wine with you," she added with a wink.

Eden grinned. "I'd have never thought of that. Any reason you have a quilt and pillows in the loft?"

"I go there when I have downtime and read Olivia's diaries."

"The diaries!" Eden smacked her forehead. "How's that going? You discovering all about her past?"

Ciana grew somber. "Maybe more than I need to know."

"Tell me."

164

Ciana sighed, shook her head. "I think . . . I believe she had an affair with Roy."

Eden's eyes widened. "Really?" She saw the tortured impact of the revelation on Ciana's face, decided to tread softly. "What makes you think that?"

Ciana shifted to try to get comfortable. "For some reason, she was all alone for almost a week during a January ice storm. Roads were impassable. She had no electricity, not much food. She had to melt ice for drinking water in the fireplace, and actually burned some furniture to stay warm. It wasn't long after Charles Junior had been killed. She wrote that she thought she was going insane with loneliness." Ciana looked up, shook her head sadly. "She was trapped, couldn't leave Bellmeade, but in spite of the weather she had a visitor."

"Roy?"

Ciana nodded. "He got out here somehow. Somehow knew she'd be alone. He stayed for three days. And he 'comforted' her. That's how she wrote it in the diary—comforted. There were no other details. I think I know what she meant. What about you?"

Sunlight spilled across Ciana's bed in buttery yellow pools as Eden took a minute to formulate what she wanted to say. What had happened during those days between Olivia and Roy was speculation, and yet knowing how Olivia had been drawn to Roy, Eden could not come to any other conclusions. She took Ciana's hand, which felt cold in spite of the warm sun. "From all we've read, the two of them were on a collision course. We know she was fascinated with him. They were hung up on each other—love-hate, fatal attraction—call it what you will, but maybe this encounter, and how it turned out, was inevitable."

"Why didn't she make him go away when he showed up?

She was married! And from other things she wrote, Roy was married too. Had a child too."

"I know how you worshipped her, but I also know what it's like to be in someone's snare . . . in their *thrall*. I felt that way about Tony in the beginning. He was . . . addictive. I wanted him so bad, I was physically ill over it. And I sure lived to regret it." Eden's admission came with physical pain, yet she couldn't stand seeing Ciana's disillusionment with the grandmother she had idolized.

"You were a *kid*. My grandmother was a grown woman." Tears of anger and frustration brimmed in Ciana's eyes. "She loved my grandfather. She told me so many times."

"I'm sure that's true. But Roy wanted her. And she was vulnerable. Alone, grieving, scared. He took advantage." Yet Eden knew there was more to the story by the look on Ciana's face. She waited.

"She—she wrote about it again, but not until months later." Ciana reached into her bedside table's drawer, pulled out an old water-damaged book, opened to a bookmarked page, and read, " 'This is my punishment. This is divine retribution. Oh God, what have I done?' " Ciana closed the book.

"Okay. See? Whatever happened with Roy, she regretted it."

Ciana offered a tired, indulgent smile. She had to help Eden understand the awful importance of what Olivia had written fifty-four years before. "She wrote these words in April, three months after the ice storm. And right after she'd found out she was three months pregnant with my mother."

26

Ciana's words hit Eden like a splash of stone-cold water. "Don't you get it?" Ciana asked.

Eden racked her brain for a kinder spin on Olivia's assessment of her pregnancy. Eden leaned forward, took Ciana by the shoulders, forced Ciana to look into her eyes. "Olivia was married. And as you said, she loved her husband. There's no reason for you to think Alice Faye isn't Charles's child."

"Olivia thought so."

"No. Guilt and shame drove her, not certainty."

"So? It built a wall around her heart, and Mom paid the price." Ciana hugged her knees, chewed her bottom lip. "Should I tell Mom? It might help her understand Olivia's rejection, which as it turns out was absolutely real." She buried her face against her knees. "I—I don't know what to do."

Eden wanted to ease Ciana's hurt, but she didn't want Alice Faye, who'd been so kind to her, to suffer either. "What's that oath that doctors say? 'First, do no harm.' I mean, what purpose would it serve to tell her? She's a recovering alcoholic.

She's happy. Why drag this up? How can knowing this help? It isn't like she can go to Olivia and hash things out, you know."

Eden's logic made sense, but still Ciana felt guilty withholding information that might bring her mother insight into Olivia's motives and feelings.

Seeing Ciana's hesitation, Eden pressed her advantage. "And now that you know, my advice to you, my dear friend, is to forget it. Don't let it color your feelings toward your grandmother. I never had a grandmother I knew. I've always envied that you loved yours so very much."

Ciana saw the wisdom of Eden's words, but still her anger simmered. She'd slavishly clung to her image of Olivia, unwavering, defended her religiously to her mother. And now, seeing her in a different light, Ciana felt sorry for being so blind to the woman's flaws. Sure, the knowledge might vindicate Alice Faye's feelings, but what good would it do? Wasn't it bad enough that her image of Olivia was tarnished? She remembered the old woman's last days, her dementia and confusion. In spite of everything, Ciana still missed her. "I guess you're right."

"Exactly," Eden said with a smile. She stretched her legs, felt the needles-and-pins sensation of blood flowing into cramped muscles. She leaned back on her hands. "So now tell me something happy."

Ciana brushed aside her troubled feelings, offered a sly smile. "Well, you and Garret can't go rushing off on your tour of America anytime soon."

"We can't?"

"I'm planting extra fields this year. Corn. I've already had the soil samples tested and analyzed for pH levels. That way I know how to best amend the soil—"

"Yikes! My eyes are glassing over," Eden yelped.

Ciana grinned impishly. "Okay, if you don't care about hanging around watching corn grow, how about hanging around for my wedding?"

Eden startled, then launched forward, grabbing Ciana. "How could you have not told me this the second I came in the door?"

"I'm a drama queen."

"Have you picked a date?"

"This summer, before the corn harvest." Eden rolled her eyes. Ciana continued, "Of course, I also need to line up a maid of honor."

"Me?" Eden pointed to herself. "I'd be honored," she added smugly. "Found a dress yet?"

"Haven't had time to look for one."

All at once, Eden's eyes went wide. "Then you haven't looked for my dress either." Her expression turned panicky. "Oh, Ciana, please, *please* put me in a dress, not coveralls!"

Ciana burst out laughing.

Around lunchtime, Ciana and Eden took a picnic basket to Jon and Garret at the new corral and track. The men had ridden Caramel and Sonata, and Soldier rested beside the water trough. Both men were seated on the ground, and Garret was drawing on a pad of paper in his lap as Jon looked over his shoulder. Ciana asked, "What's up?"

"We're designing stables," Jon said. "If I'm bringing in horses to train, they'll need a place to stay. Turns out Garret has a background in construction."

Garret looked up, grinned. "Growing up I spent every

169

summer with my uncle, who owns his own building business. I learned how to handle every job. Just need to research your building codes. Jon and I will get a stable up in no time."

Eden settled on the ground beside him. "Guess that means we'll be staying awhile."

"Looks like it."

"Soon as the plans are finished, we'll go into town and order the lumber," Jon added.

"Maybe I should buy me a cowboy hat," Garret mused, attempting a western twang. "And a pair of boots. I like the boots."

More laughter. Garret's enthusiasm was infectious, and Ciana's heart swelled. She shoved memories of Olivia's diary to the back of her mind and decided that happiness was right in front of her in the form of friends, family, spring sunshine, fresh earth, and horses. What had happened years before she was even born was history. And no one could change history.

Once the threat of frost was over, Eden helped Alice Faye plant the backyard garden. The dirt had been tilled and turned, the tiny seedlings spaced and planted on raised mounds, away from drowning rain. She had seen the results of these early days of hard labor the summer before, the lush and abundant growth, the almost daily harvest of food that, when blanched and put into glass jars and stored properly, guaranteed that no one on a farm would go hungry. And with Garret living at Bellmeade too, she felt totally content. In the cool of the morning, she heard the echo of his hammer and the buzz of his handsaw. At the end of the day, she made the long trek from the back of the garden through the stand of trees to the newly rising stables, where Garret would shout, "Come to give me a kiss and a cold beer for a hard day's work?"

On occasion they would steal away and find a private place to be alone, to make love, to plan for the trip they'd take once Ciana and Jon were married. If it rained and no one could work, they'd meet in the barn up in the loft and while away the afternoon.

Eden gave Ciana money even though Ciana at first refused it. "Take it! Until the garden comes in," Eden insisted. "I know this place doesn't run on fresh air." Late at night, after being with Garret in the camper, Eden saw the lamp glowing from the room she knew was Ciana's office, and knew Ciana was poring over ledgers and working with cost containment. Bellmeade was a fearsome burden, and Eden swore to do whatever she could to help her friend carry it.

One evening while the night air was still cool, Eden and Ciana sat on the veranda, sharing a bottle of Enzo's wine. Jon had built them a small fire in a brazier for warmth, and Alice Faye had sliced fresh bread and cheese for a snack.

Eden propped her feet on the porch railing, held up the glass, watched the fire gleam through the ruby-colored liquid. "The man sure knows how to make good wine."

"Let's toast us," Ciana said.

Eden's glass clinked against hers. "To all of us," she said.

"And to our futures," Ciana added.

"And to finding a great wedding dress for you. A pretty maid of honor dress for me."

"And to—"

"Oh for goodness' sake," Eden said. "Let's just drink our wine before the fire goes out!"

They both laughed. Ciana again clinked her glass with

Eden's. The new fields were planted. The fence cutting and vandalism had evaporated, thanks to Cecil's diligence, and now, with the new stables nearing completion, Jon was eager to get married, go west, and buy mustangs. Combining Jon's horse business with her agribusiness would give Bellmeade a real future. All it would take was hard work, patience, money, good weather, and a whole lot of luck. But Olivia had always said, "Just because something's hard, doesn't mean you shouldn't do it." On that point, Ciana agreed with her grandmother wholeheartedly. She could do this! With a little help from her friends.

27

Another long workday was over, the old house lay quiet, and darkness had chased away daylight. Ciana wandered into the kitchen, lit by the open refrigerator door, where Jon was searching the shelves. She stood in the doorway, enjoying the view of his bare torso. The man had a great butt. "Help you?" she asked after watching him hunt for a bit.

He bumped his head retreating from the fridge's interior. "Oh, hey. Looking for the leftover casserole."

The light from the refrigerator silhouetted him. She thought he looked good enough to eat, or at least to lick all over. "Look in the lower right drawer."

"Where is everybody, anyway?"

"Mom's at an AA meeting. Garret and Eden went into town to catch a movie."

Jon kept stock-still, measuring Ciana across the length of the kitchen. The fridge's motor kicked on. "So we're alone in the house?"

"That a problem?"

He flashed a wicked smile, stepped away from the fridge, shoved the door closed with the heel of his bare foot. "Not for me."

Ciana's mouth went dry and her heartbeat doubled. He sauntered toward her, his hair still damp from a shower. Her gaze skimmed down his chest to his flat, hard abs and then to the denim waistband slung low on his hips. She felt her skin heat up. When he was standing in front of her, she said, "I thought you said you were hungry."

"Different appetite reared up."

Her breath went shallow. "Really?"

He edged closer, flipped her hair off her shoulder. "So you're saying I'm all alone with the girl I'm engaged to. What should we do about that?"

"Make the most of it?" she ventured, positive she wanted no other choice. The fire between them had burned for a long time.

"You're healed?"

"Perfectly."

"You love me?"

"With all my heart."

"I love you, too, Ciana Beauchamp. And right now, I want to do something about it."

"Like what?"

"Let me show you." He lifted her, surprising her as to how easily he did it, and how seduced she was by the low rumble of his words in her ear.

She clung to him as he walked down the hall to her bedroom, laid her on her bed, and stretched out beside her. The room's only light came from a horse head night-light she'd owned since she'd been a kid. In the soft glow, his eyes stared

174

into her. She felt his fingers push her tangled hair away from her face, then trail down her cheek and along her neck.

"You're beautiful," Jon said.

"So are you." It was the only thing she could think to say at the moment. He *was* beautiful. She touched his bare chest. He kissed her deeply, slowly.

He broke the kiss. "You know you ran away from me once before, and fell asleep on me after that when we got this far."

"It won't happen this time."

He gave a throaty laugh; then his voice turned serious. "I missed you this summer. Out on the circuit you were in every thought under the stars."

"I missed you too." She had long forgiven him for not calling. All that was behind them now. He was here with her. They were engaged. They were alone. "You just going to spend this time talking?"

He flashed another smile, lifted her T-shirt. "Reckon not."

He ran his palm, rough from handling ropes and leather, from her throat to her waist, resting the tips of his fingers along the band of her jeans. She held her breath, her skin burning with an exquisite fire, and torn between wanting him to hurry and wanting him to move slowly. "Don't leave me again." Her words came from down deep, throaty but soft.

"Never going to happen."

From far away, she heard a car door slam.

Beside her, Jon tensed.

No-o-o! "Not now!" Ciana said with a breathy moan.

They heard Alice Faye come into the kitchen, and call out, "I'm home!"

"Other people do live here," Jon said, nibbling on Ciana's shoulder.

"But—but—I don't want to stop."

He rolled onto his back, his face in a grimace. "You think I do? You're going to have to go out there and distract her until I can sneak out."

"Ciana? Eden? Guys? You here?" Alice Faye's voice drifted down the hall past Ciana's bedroom.

"Meet you in the kitchen!" Ciana shouted, hoping to stop her mother's advance. She gave Jon a hurried kiss and swung her legs over him. He groaned.

Leaving him wanting her hadn't been her intention. She made it to the door, and over her shoulder teased him as he'd once teased her with the words, "Rain check?"

He heaved her pillow at the door as it closed behind her.

"How was your meeting?" Ciana asked, coming into the kitchen, raking her hand through her tangled hair and sitting at the table across from her mother hoping she looked more pulled together than she felt.

"Good. No one's fallen off the wagon. Tea?" she asked as the kettle whistled on the stove.

"Sure." Ciana couldn't care less about drinking a cup of tea, but it would give Jon plenty of time to make his escape and herself time to cool down. She kept her smile to herself because it was all so high school. Why couldn't she simply say, "Mom, Jon and I want to be alone tonight—you go on to bed"? But of course, she couldn't and wouldn't.

"Where is everybody?"

"The 'children' are at the movies and Jon's hanging around somewhere."

Alice Faye set two mugs of steeping tea on the table along

with sugar and milk and a container of honey. "What have you been up to?"

"Nothing. Slow night." Their teatime was cut short by Eden and Garret coming through the front door and noisily tromping through the house into the kitchen. Garret was saying, "No one's cooler than James Bond, my love."

"Puh-leeze! All those fights and explosions and not a scratch on him. Get real!"

"Doesn't have to be real, does it Mum Alice?" It was Garret's pet name for Ciana's mother.

"What's reality got to do with a Bond movie?" Alice Faye asked. "Tea?"

"Exactly!" Garret said.

Eden patted her tummy. "No thanks. Had a sundae after the movie."

Just then Jon walked into the kitchen, looking disheveled and sleepy-eyed and absolutely gorgeous in Ciana's eyes. "What's up?"

Eden homed her radar in on him. "Your shirt's buttoned all crooked."

Jon glanced down at the misaligned shirtfront, turned red-faced. Ciana glanced in the opposite direction, knowing she'd burst out laughing if their eyes met. "Just got out of the shower upstairs. Heard ya'll come home," he mumbled.

Eden looked at Jon's bare feet, then back at Ciana, and shot her an *Oh you naughty girl* look.

"I'd like some tea," Jon said, clearing his throat while fumbling with his buttons.

Alice Faye jumped to her feet. "Water's still hot."

Ciana knew Jon had never drunk a cup of tea in his life.

Eden's cell phone rang. She slid it from her pocket, glanced at the display, looked puzzled. She stepped out of the kitchen as Garret began to discuss the latest Bond girl. "Her hair never got mussed, but who was watchin' her hair?"

The others laughed and were still laughing when Eden reentered the kitchen, her face ghostly white. Ciana leaped from her chair. "What's wrong? Who called?"

All eyes turned toward Eden. "Love!" Garret said in alarm, going to her.

"A woman in Tampa. The director of a halfway house." Eden's words were barely audible. "She said . . . the woman said my mother died."

28

"Sign says there's a rest stop in a mile. Want to stop, love?" Garret asked.

Eden lay in a semi-fetal position beside him in the camper's front passenger seat, curled as tightly as the seat belt would allow. She didn't answer. She hadn't said much of anything since they'd left Bellmeade for the ten-hour drive to Tampa. She didn't want to talk because there was nothing to be said. Gwen, her mother, had up and died over seven hundred miles away from her only child, who might have never known except for a phone call from an absolute stranger. The woman's question had been "What do you want done with her body?"

"Well, I want to stop," Garret said, putting on the blinker and turning into the rest area. Late-morning sunlight poured through the windshield. Garret pulled into a parking spot. He turned off the engine, unsnapped his belt, reached over, and released Eden's. "Come on, love. Let's stretch our legs. There's a picnic table. We'll eat something."

Eden's stomach rebelled at the mere suggestion of food. Except for coffee, she had refused breakfast too.

As the sun had risen that morning, Ciana and Jon and Alice Faye had seen her and Garret off. Alice Faye handed them an enormous basket of food for the road, and Jon had policed the camper, cleaning it out and readying it for the trip. Ciana had printed maps that would take them to the doorstep of the halfway house called Crossroads House, Gwen's last address according to the caller. She had also helped Eden pack. In actuality, Ciana had packed while Eden sat listlessly staring into space. "Not sure what you'll need, Eden, so I'm throwing in a little of everything. And take your time coming back too. I hear Florida's beautiful. The beaches in the panhandle are supposed to be some of the best in the world. You and Garret should check them out. Oh, I'm shoving your tablet into the side pocket. After you know what's happening, you call, all right?"

"The stables—" Eden mumbled.

"Don't you even think about it. Jon and I can finish up. Almost done anyway."

Now, hours later, she and Garret had left Tennessee far behind. Garret opened the passenger-side door, urged Eden out of her seat, took her hand, and retrieved the basket with his other. He walked them to a sun-dappled picnic table under a stand of trees, seated Eden, then began laying out sandwiches, carrot sticks, and apple slices. "You need to eat, love." His tone was tender.

She rested her elbows on the table, covered her face with her hands. "I'm really not hungry. You eat, though. Where are we, anyway?" Her words came with effort. She was numb, felt like a sleepwalker unable to wake up from a bad dream. She'd hardly slept the night before, her head filled with a kaleidoscope of memories of Gwen, of a childhood lived mostly on her own. She might have felt numb at this moment, but she had yet to shed a tear. Eden didn't know how to mourn for her mother, wasn't sure how to both hold on to her and let her go. She hadn't seen the woman in over a year. Nor had she talked to Gwen in about the same amount of time. What constituted "goodbye"?

"We're in Georgia, heading south on I-75," Garret was saying. "A sign said Georgia's the Peach State. I like peaches. Guess it's too early just yet."

Eden knew she wasn't being fair to Garret. Her withdrawal was rude, and he didn't deserve it. He was an innocent by-stander, someone who loved her. Because she felt guilty, she tried to make an effort. She took a bite of her sandwich, a ham and cheese on Alice Faye's home-baked bread. Immediately emotion clogged her throat. Ciana's mother had treated Eden more like her child than Gwen had. Her months of living at Bellmeade had been her happiest. Bellmeade was where she'd learned to grow things, especially herself. "I'll be all right. I'm not going to break like glass, Garret. Me losing my mother isn't like it would be if you lost yours."

"Your mum's your mum. Can't be replaced, you know. I'll cry like a baby when mine goes."

While in Australia, she'd given him a glimpse of her life with Gwen, but no amount of telling about it could fully de-scribe how it had felt to be the child of a mother who couldn't connect with either her daughter or the real world. "And so will I. You have a great mother," Eden said.

He gave her an odd look, making her ashamed. She was coming across as callous, and that wasn't who she was. "Can we go now? I was hoping to make Tampa before dark." Before he could answer, Eden headed back to the camper while he cleaned up and repacked the basket. *Keep your mouth shut*, she warned herself. There was no explaining a relationship she'd never understood herself. Gwen had disappeared forever. She was gone, and this time, she wasn't coming back.

They crossed into Florida in late afternoon, blew past exits for Gainesville and Ocala, ignored the cutoff that would have taken them to Orlando and Disney World. Garret looked wistful and Eden realized that he would have liked to have visited the Magic Kingdom, a place where adventurers lived and childhood dreams came true. He was such a kid at heart, while she had never been a kid. Just north of Tampa they became ensnared in a giant traffic jam that destroyed any hope of reaching their destination at a reasonable hour. The Crossroads House was at the extreme southern end of the city.

"We'll get a hotel nearby," Garret told her. "One with a pool."

By now, Eden's numbness had turned into a stupor, and lack of sleep made her feel dull and witless. "Yes . . . a pool and a glass of wine. Good idea."

"And some supper," he added.

The motel he chose had a Tahitian theme, with smooth tile floors and no carpet. Because April was so much warmer in Tampa than in middle Tennessee, the pool water revived Eden, while the wine mellowed her out. She swam, crawled into a lounge chair, and drifted in and out of sleep. At some point, Garret took her back to the room, helped her out of her damp suit, and tucked her into the king-sized bed. "I'll watch a little telly, then turn out the lights," he said. She didn't care.

Later, when he snuggled in the bed beside her, she burrowed closer to him, saying, "Hold me."

He needed no urging. He wrapped her in his arms, smoothed her hair, kissed her forehead. "It's all right now, love. You're safe."

Eden felt an involuntary shudder in her shoulders that quickly spread down and through her body. A low, pitiful wail escaped from her mouth. She fought to hold back another but lost the battle. Tears came pouring out, great racking sobs that shook her, made her gag, made her nauseous. Over and over, like a small lost child, she cried, "Mama . . . Mama!"

Garret clutched her tightly, rocked her, absorbed her choking, gushing sobs into his skin. "It's all right. I'm here. Let it out, love. Let it all out," he repeated like a mantra. She cried until she was spent and drained and limp, until her ocean of tears had escaped, then moved away like the tide from the pull of the moon. And finally she slept, but even then, Garret Locklin didn't let go.

29

The next morning Eden changed three times trying to decide what to wear to a meeting about what she wanted to do with her mother's body. Her nerves were stretched as taut as piano wire. How could she do this and not fall apart? Garret waited patiently on the bed, flipping through television channels and sipping coffee he'd brought back from a café a block from the motel. He wore jeans and a short-sleeved dress shirt. Men had it so easy.

"How's this?" she finally asked. It was already midmorning and time had her in a pressure cooker. Part of her wanted to get it over with; part wanted it to never happen.

He eyeballed her. "Nothing's more warmin' than a pretty girl in a summer dress on a sunny day," he said with a grin.

"Too casual," she muttered, pulling off the dress and changing into a knee-length black skirt and a white blouse with a Peter Pan collar. She kicked off her strappy sandals and buried her feet in closed-toe Mary Janes. Ciana had certainly given her a variety . . . bless her heart.

She grabbed her purse off the dresser. "Come on. Let's get this done."

Garret sprang off the bed, and together they left the room.

In the car, Garret drove and Eden navigated from the maps Ciana had printed. The day was bathed in sunshine that sparkled off windows of buildings as they rolled through light traffic. She pushed down her window to allow a balmy breeze into the camper's cab and calm her jittery nerves.

"Turn left at the light," Eden said.

Garret turned and soon they were on narrow, bumpy brick streets lined on either side by older houses and parked cars. Scrub palms and live oaks dotted sidewalk frontage of a neighborhood on the cusp of urban change, in different states of renovation, being redeemed from age and blight. The yuppies had arrived.

As Eden searched house numbers on mailboxes and front-porch posts, she wondered how her mother had landed here in this perfectly ordinary neighborhood, so like the one she'd abandoned in Windemere. "This is it," Eden said, spotting the number on a wooden house painted goldenrod and trimmed in dark brown. Her heartbeat drummed against her ribs.

Garret parked close to the sidewalk, then got out, came around, and opened her door. They stood on the cement walk, staring up at the house that Eden realized was actually three houses connected by newly built closed passages that served as hallways. A small sign on a porch post read CROSSROADS HOUSE. WELCOME.

"Ready?" Garret asked, intertwining his fingers with hers.

"Never," she answered, dizzy and feeling faint.

Yet they went together, past blooming hibiscus bushes and a bed of bright white daylilies. Thick vines, heavy with purple and white morning glory blossoms, wrapped around a picturesque low picket fence. The porch stretched across the front of the house and smelled of fresh paint. Chairs were set in clusters, some around card tables, some facing the street. This is where the residents gather, Eden told herself, trying but failing to imagine Gwen becoming social enough to do such a thing. Except for her job at Piggly Wiggly, Gwen never went out. Eden couldn't remember a time when a neighbor came over for coffee or a chat. Which was why she had never had Arie and Ciana over when they'd been in school. Her house was off-limits, the boundary set by an illness that for Eden had long passed pity and morphed into loathing.

Inside, a woman at a desk offered to help them, and when Eden told her her name and purpose, the woman said she'd get the director, and left the alcove. Eden looked through to a larger room and saw well-worn furniture set up as a traditional living room. The furnishings were obviously hand-me-downs, some covered with throws or quilts and softened with pillows. The space smelled like new cotton and sunshine, which settled her nerves. She hadn't known what to expect, and was surprised at the hominess of the facility.

The receptionist returned accompanied by a tall, slim woman with steel gray hair up in a bun. She wore a caftan that brushed the tops of sensible shoes. Her smile was warm as she held out her hand. "Liz Sheehan, director of Crossroads House. I was the one who called you. Thank you for getting here so quickly."

After introductions, she led them to her office, which was smaller and more cluttered than the open space out front. "Please sit." She pointed to two chairs, then settled in the one behind her desk.

Eden felt ready to jump out of her skin. She licked her lips, but her tongue held no moisture. "My mother lived here?"

186

"Sometimes." Liz steepled her fingers. "Crossroads is a halfway house to give homeless, special-needs women a place to live instead of the streets."

"It's very homey," Eden said.

"Thank you. That was always my goal. I started it years ago because so many of these women had no place to go. The house is actually three houses strung together, each with three bedrooms and a kitchen. We offer a safe place for mentally ill women who might otherwise end up in jail or the streets. We have three requirements." Liz held up three fingers. "They must take their medication if any has been prescribed, hold a job if possible, and stay off drugs in order to keep a room with us."

"And my mother stayed on her meds? She never would back home."

Garret soothed Eden with a touch.

"Off and on," Liz said. "But she was on them and living here when she passed. The coroner said she had a heart attack while she slept."

Dying in her sleep on clean sheets in a safe house. Eden was glad for that. At least Gwen hadn't been discovered in a gutter, murdered. That worry had nagged at Eden every time Gwen had left home. If Gwen never came back, how would Eden ever know what happened to her? "She—she always talked about Tampa. When I was growing up. I never knew why."

"It's warm here mostly year-round, and that attracts a lot of homeless people."

Eden's chin trembled. "She wasn't homeless."

Liz leaned forward. "Eden . . ." She paused, and Eden looked up into the woman's soulful brown eyes. "Your mother was ill. You didn't cause it. You couldn't fix it. You were a child born into her condition."

187

Tears filled Eden's eyes. "I—I know that. I used to read everything about bipolar, so I *know* it's not my fault. But . . ."

The word hung in the air until Liz broke the silence. "I, too, was a child of a mentally ill parent. My father. He was schizophrenic. And paranoid. My mother and I went through hell trying to help him. This place"—she gestured—"is the fulfillment of my dream to help others like him. I exist on donations and grants and do my best to make a difference. Some of the victims want to be well, but not all."

"She wouldn't take her meds."

"Chronic problem. Better the demons they know than dealing with a world that they don't know how to fit into."

Eden sagged, and Garret held her hand. "I'm here, love."

Liz gave him a smile, then turned her attention back to Eden. "There is a correlation between bipolar and schizophrenia. On the DNA helix, the genes are almost twins. People with extreme bipolar disorder can often slip over into schizophrenia. It's called schizoaffective disorder. Research is ongoing. New medications must be developed for it. I believe your mother fell into that category."

Little comfort. Eden took a tissue from a box on Liz's desk, wiped and dried her eyes. She'd thought she was all cried out. *Wrong again.*

Garret cleared his throat. "What do we do now?"

We. Eden heard him take on her burden.

Liz shuffled paperwork on her desk. "Her body is being held at the city morgue. You have choices. You can find a cemetery here, fly her body home for burial, or you can cremate her remains and take her ashes with you."

Choices. How could she decide? Why had it been left to her? *Because I'm the next of kin.* She answered her own question. If there were others, she didn't know them. Never had.

"You can take a little time, Eden. Maybe another day, but the morgue will only hold her body for so long," Liz said kindly. "It's the law."

Eden felt like crawly things were inside her head. She had the money to do anything, but if Gwen were sitting there with her, she would not have cared less about what happened to her earthly remains. And who would come to a funeral in Windemere for Gwen McLauren? Eden's friends? Why would Eden ask that of them? Better to take her home in a box and scatter her ashes. That was what Eden wanted to do.

"Cremation," she said, through barely parted lips.

"I'll make the arrangements. Also," Liz said softly, "I'll have her remains sent here. Much better than you having to go downtown. There's paperwork for you to sign, of course." She fanned out several sheets of paper. "I'll call your cell phone when you can come pick her up."

It sounded more as if she were to return and retrieve a sick animal. *All better now.* "I'll wait for the call." Eden quickly signed the papers and stood, and Garret got to his feet beside her. Eden's knees went wobbly. He intuitively braced her arm with his.

Liz came around the desk and held out her hand. "I'm so glad I got to meet the two of you. And Eden, when she was lucid, Gwen often spoke of you."

"You're kidding."

"She was very proud of you."

Eden wasn't sure she believed that. Maybe Liz was simply being nice.

"She said you had gone to Italy and that you gave her the most beautiful scarf when you came home."

Eden recalled buying the fashionable item in Florence, the great city of the Renaissance, from a vendor at the Ponte

Vecchio. "Near the Duomo, the church," she said, as if it mattered to anyone in the room. The same day she and her friends had stood in line to see the David, Michelangelo's masterpiece carved from fine white marble. Eden had bought the scarf quickly, almost as an afterthought.

"Well, she wore it every day she stayed here."

Eden's eyes misted, but she made it to the office door before turning around and asking, "Your father? How did things turn out for him? Has he seen this place and what you're doing?"

Liz offered a sad smile. "My father committed suicide when I was fifteen. He never saw me grow up. For a long time, I felt like I should have done more to save him. I shed a lot of tears and carried a heavy load of guilt. But now I know I could have done *nothing* to save him."

Absolution from a woman who had walked in her shoes. "I understand," Eden whispered.

Liz offered Eden a beautiful, hope-filled smile. "Now go be happy, Eden McLauren."

30

"Soon as the Aussie and his 'sheila' come back, let's set our wedding date."

Ciana was brushing Firecracker after a long ride, when Jon's words came from the barn's tack room as he stood watching her. She turned, gave him a beguiling smile. "Is that a request or an order?"

He came over, took her in his arms, and took her breath away with a kiss.

"Wow," she said, coming up for air.

"Wow, yourself. I want to get married. Sooner the better."

She poked at him with the brush. "Plans are in the works. These life events do take a little planning, you know—a dress, a location, a guest list, food, a minister."

"Look, I don't care if we hire an Elvis impersonator and get married here in the barn."

That made her laugh. "What about guests? Who's on your list?"

He shrugged. "My mother, my grandparents if Granddad's able to travel. Oh and Bill and Essie Pickins."

"That's all?"

"I don't have a lot of friends. The rodeo crowd breeds competitors, not close friends. And other than family, there's no one back in Texas I want here either."

She tossed the curry brush aside. "What about your father, Wade? Do you want him to come?"

Jon scoffed. "No love lost there."

It hit Ciana then that she had no father to walk her down the aisle. She'd grown up without one. Losing him at age six had turned him into a shadowy memory. He and Grandpa Charles were always flying away in their little airplane to sell their farm produce. Her earliest memories were of going to and from a little airfield with her mother and grandmother to wave goodbye. She had images of waking late at night to him bending over her bed and kissing her forehead and saying, "Daddy's home, sweetheart." Then one day, the plane didn't come back and everyone around her was sobbing. She'd been confused, frightened, but as time passed she understood that her daddy and Grandpa would never come home. After their deaths, Olivia became an overwhelming presence, and Alice Faye sank further into the background, retreating into her sweet tea drinks. Olivia hung tough, and Bellmeade was such a ton of work, Ciana adjusted to it being the three of them. Friends, chores, school, the flag corps, her horse had filled any daddy void she felt. In time she had to look at old photos to remember what her daddy had looked like.

Now she told Jon, "Maybe I can hire that Elvis impersonator to give me away."

Jon looked stricken. "Hey, I'm sorry. I forgot about that part. Were you thinking Wade might do it?"

"No. I guess not." The vivid scene of Wade once yelling for Jon to stay clear of Beauchamp women returned in a flash as she recalled the day she'd met him in an extended care unit and he learned she was a Beauchamp. "Did you ever learn what he has against us Beauchamp women?"

"Who cares? He's just crazy." Jon pulled her to himself again. "I, on the other hand, just want to marry this Beauchamp woman and take her to bed."

"You don't have to marry me to get me in bed," she said.

A lazy smile drifted across his face. "I want to take a whole night with you. And after we sleep a bit, I want to take the whole next day to do it all over again."

She met his eyes, spoke her heart into her answer "Sounds like a very good plan to me."

He laughed, twirled her away, then back to himself. "And then I'm going to take you to Montana."

"Rodeo?" she asked, half joking, knowing how he liked following the circuit and riding broncos.

Jon laughed. "A honeymoon."

"Sounds romantic."

He winked. "And a wild mustang auction. We'll buy a few horses, make arrangements to have them brought here. Now please set a date, woman."

Ciana loaded the dishwasher that evening while Alice Faye sipped sweet tea at the kitchen table.

Her mother asked, "Have you heard from our road warriors?"

"Eden sent me a text. They're going to take a few days in the Florida panhandle. I suggested it before they left. It'll do them both good," Ciana said.

"I miss them. It's been wonderful having this house full of people again. So much company and all your comings and goings. That Garret is a dear. He just walks in a room and fills it up, doesn't he?"

"He does," Ciana conceded. But listening to her mother voice her satisfaction about everybody living under the same roof gave Ciana new insight about all the years Alice Faye had spent alone since her husband's death. Just two women raising one child—her—and holding Bellmeade together. Suddenly, now that Ciana was in love with Jon, she grasped just how long and lonely the years must have been for her mother. She'd never dated that Ciana could recall.

She finished cleaning the kitchen, went to the table, and pulled out a chair. "Okay, Mom, here's the thing. The fields are planted, so the rest is up to Mother Nature. It's time to plan this wedding."

"I've been wondering when you were going to get around to that." Alice Faye patted Ciana's hand and smiled. "What are you wanting to do?"

"Mom, I'm not into any Cinderella syndrome. I just want to get married with as little fuss as possible." Ciana hoped she wasn't disappointing her mother. She thought back, but couldn't dredge up family stories about her mother and father's wedding day. "What was your wedding like?"

"It was Olivia's show." Alice Faye leaned back in the chair. "Jackson and I were simply decorations for a Bellmeade social event. Olivia expected a certain degree of 'festivity,' and I complied. I'm not bitter," she added quickly. "Just stating facts."

"I know you aren't," Ciana assured her. With what Ciana had discovered in her grandmother's diary, she clung to Eden's counsel. *Do no harm.* Best to forget the entry and protect Alice Faye. "What about your dress?"

"This was back in '79, and the hot new look was bustiers, with the bride showing cleavage. The gowns had lace appliqués, sequins, and lots of beads."

"That doesn't sound like you."

"It wasn't. Plus Olivia would never have let me step inside the Baptist church with even a hint of my boobs showing."

Recalling how dour Olivia could look when she disapproved of something, Ciana laughed. "What did you do?"

"We found some dated frilly concoction in Nashville with lace that went all the way up under my chin and lacy sleeves that fully covered my arms. I almost passed out from heat exhaustion."

Ciana giggled. "What happened to the dress after the wedding?"

"Eventually, I made curtains out of it. They're hanging in Olivia's bedroom. Eden looks at them every day."

Ciana laughed harder. "Priceless."

Her mother's expression turned stricken. "You weren't going to ask to wear it on your wedding day, were you? Oh my gosh! I hated the thing. Never thought about you wearing it one day before I cut it up for curtains."

"It didn't cross my mind," Ciana said. "Frankly, I'd wear jeans if I could."

"It's your wedding, but for what it's worth, a groom likes to see his bride in a pretty dress. Your father did." She stopped, and Ciana watched Alice Faye's eyes grow soft with memories. After a moment, she cleared her throat, asked, "Assuming you do decide on a dress, what would you want it to look like?"

"Simple. Clean lines. Nothing froufrou. And no lace up to my throat."

Her mother nodded sagely. "We can run into Nashville on Saturday afternoon and look around if you'd like."

"We can do that. Maybe Jon and I should elope," she mused.

"Your father and I thought about that, too, but in the end, we danced to Olivia's tune. Don't get me wrong. It was a lovely wedding," she added quickly. "Besides, maybe Jon's mother wants to see her only child get married."

Ciana straightened, thinking of the magnificent family ring Jon's mother had given him to bestow on a complete stranger. She grew anxious. "I've never even met her. What if she hates me?"

"She won't hate you. How could she? You're a Beauchamp!"

Ciana shook her head, bemused. "That bromide can't be the answer to everything."

"Okay, so tell me, what kind of wedding do you and Jon want?"

Ciana told her Jon's wishes, adding, "I don't want anything big. And the only people I care about showing up would be Arie's mom and dad, Eric, Abbie, and the new baby. I just want to get married. I want Jon, plain or fancy."

"If that's what you want, then that's what you shall have," Alice Faye said emphatically. She reached over and smoothed Ciana's hair. "One more question. Would you like me to move into town once you're married? There's a new condo complex going up—"

"*What?* You move? This is your home." She'd never thought about living arrangements until this moment, and to dispossess her mother of the only home she'd ever known would be barbaric.

"Ciana, it's all right. The two of you may not like having me hanging around all the time. House isn't big enough. Maybe a change would be good—"

Ciana held up her hand. "I can't think about this now."

"Lot of work in this old house."

"Not now, Mom."

"Fair enough. But do think about it. Talk it over with Jon. He gets a say now too."

Ciana slept fitfully, waking and dreaming, her head flooded with thoughts and worries. Her marriage would change everything. Growing up, she had been a bystander, someone looking at Bellmeade from the sidelines, certainly one who belonged, but belonging as a child had belonged, not an adult. True, Olivia's death had impacted the farm's dynamic, but marrying meant her life would make a drastic turn. Like the changing of the Swiss Guard she'd watched that afternoon in Italy at the Vatican, the old left . . . the new came. Her friends would leave. Her mother might move and would one day die. She and Jon would build the future. Doubts assailed her. Was she ready for this? Was she willing to share her heritage, her ownership?

She tossed and turned, twisted the bedding into wads, kicked off her covers, only to grab and pull the sheets over her head minutes later. She stared at the clock that glowed with accusatory, crawling hands. Dawn was coming, and with it a hard day's worth of work, and her not ready or rested for it. She was still wrestling with her thoughts when a noise made her bolt upright. In the distance, out of the darkness, she heard the unmistakable blasts of a shotgun.

31

Eden sat on the edge of the bed, staring at the blue duffel bag beside her. *All that remains . . .* This bag contained what was left of Gwen McLauren's worldly goods, the scraps and pieces of her life and existence. Pitifully little. Across from the bed in the motel room, on the dresser, stood the plain gray box that held Gwen's ashes, a human body, once flesh and blood, muscle and bone, heart and soul, now reduced by fire to a fine gray dust.

When Eden and Garret had returned to Crossroads House to claim the ashes, Liz had also given them the bag, saying, "These were her things. She kept everything she held dear stored in it. Took it with her if she left here, brought it with her whenever she returned." During the drive from Tampa to Destin in the panhandle, Eden had set it between her feet, sometimes touching the handles, sometimes recoiling from the sudden flop of the handle against her bare ankles. The once-hated duffel that had always taken her mother away was hers now.

Eden sighed. Her and Garret's motel room was spacious and nicely furnished, and on the ground floor of a beach on the Gulf of Mexico, facing due west. Through the patio doors, a path led over a sandy berm speckled with wild sea oats, and down through powdery white sand to a rolling turquoise surf, where late-afternoon sun glinted off the water.

Garret was taking a long walk on the beach, giving her time to be alone with her memories. As if she hadn't spent much of her life with them already. He had left her alone out of consideration, to let her go through the contents of the duffel. Like a moth to a flame, her gaze kept drifting to the old duffel bag, a symbol of all her childhood fears and teenage loathing. She decided to wait for Garret before opening it, and when he let himself in the room he looked surprised to see her sitting exactly as when he'd left her. He came to her swiftly, sat on the bed, and took her hand.

"You all right, love?"

She shrugged. "I didn't want to do this by myself. Sorry."

"No problem. We'll do it together." His skin and hair smelled of sea brine. His Aussie accent soothed her, helping her find the comfort zone that came with his presence.

Eden set the duffel on her lap. With trembling fingers, she unzipped it, pulled it open, and peered inside. She pulled out the scarf she'd bought Gwen in Italy, saw that it was dirty and torn. She dangled the filmy scarf from her fingertips, saw clearly that street life had been hard on the delicate silk fabric.

"Must have been pretty once," Garret said.

"It's garbage now." Eden tossed it aside, reached into the bag, pulled out a broken compact, worn-down lipsticks, and a shattered eye shadow palette. She grabbed wadded paperwork held together in a stack with a rubber band, along with a bank book and photos. The paper on top was a scrawled note that left Eden all her mother's worldly goods, including the money that was in the bank. She flipped open a bank statement. Much of Gwen's portion from the sale of the house was still on deposit. Eden shook her head, felt a flare of anger, followed by sadness. "She was supposed to spend this. She didn't ever have to live on the streets."

"Liz said it was going off the meds that drove her to the streets, not lack of money," Garret reminded her.

Eden thumbed through the photos. The first was an old black-and-white snapshot of people she didn't know standing in front of a two-story clapboard house, an enormous fir tree to one side.

"Family?" Garret asked.

"If so, she never talked about them." She raised the photo, searched the blurry faces for any resemblance to Gwen, or maybe even herself. "I think she grew up in Washington State. Like I told you in Australia, she left my father when I was a baby. He was abusive and she ran away . . . brought us clear across the country on a bus. She had an aunt in Windemere who took us in, but she died when I was two, so I don't remember her." Eden looked into Garret's sympathetic gaze, then quickly looked away. "She wrote me a letter once with some information. I still have the letter, but don't care about her family. I mean, if they knew she was in a bad relationship, why didn't they take her in? Why didn't they help her?"

Eden had no answers, not even a supposition. Garret stroked Eden's cheek. "Don't feel sorry for me." She repeated the warning she had given him while in Australia.

"What's in the other photos?" he asked, distracting her.

She sorted through them, looked up in surprise. "Me. All of them are of me. School pictures." She fanned them out on the bed, watched herself morph from a first grader into a high schooler. The last picture was of Eden, Ciana, and Arie in their caps and gowns, looking happy. The series of photos made sense to Eden in a strange way. Photos could be managed, unlike a real flesh-and-blood child. Tears filled Eden's eyes. She sniffed.

"Looks like she carried them around for a long time." He picked up one of Eden at age seven. Her hair was a mass of black unkempt curls and a front tooth was missing, but she was smiling cheerfully. "You look happy here."

"Might have been a good week at our house at that time. Between bouts of mania and depression, life was a bowl of cherries," she said with a trace of irony. "Who remembers?"

He put the pictures down, took her hands in his, and pulled her up. "It's dark out. Let's take a breather and sit by the water. It's beautiful, you know."

She wanted to crawl into bed, but she was too drained to argue with him.

He grabbed a couple of large towels and took her through the patio doorway, over the berm and down to the beachfront. She figured the tide was out, because the sand felt hard and packed under her bare feet as they went toward the shore. They walked for a while, until lights from the motels were behind them. The water was too dark to see more than just the occasional white crest of a wave catching light from a partial moon. The sound of the waves was constant, enduring.

Garret spread the towels near the bottom of the berm on the soft part of the sand, still warm from the day's sun. "Come, love. Let me hold you."

She needed no urging, and snuggled into his embrace when they lay down together. Without artificial light to interfere, she could see a smattering of the overhead stars. She nestled against his chest. "It's like all the chapters in a book have ended and I can't open it again. She's gone, and so are all the stories I should know. I'm so sad," she told him.

He kissed her forehead. "I'm no stranger to grief, darlin'. I've been down that road myself."

Philip. Eden felt guilty. "I—I don't mean to make you relive your bad times."

"No worries. Who else can I share them with? We're in this together, Eden. Every step of the way."

She wept a little while he held her close. Together they listened to the roll of the surf. The sound was a salve to her spirit, and Garret a balm to her soul.

After a few minutes, he said, "I have some good news to tell you. Been saving it."

She pushed up onto her elbows, looked at him stretched out beside her. "I could use some good news."

"Before we left Bellmeade, I got an email from my former editor. Seems the chap landed on his feet after all. Has a new job in Melbourne with a webzine that's all about travel. Magazines on the Web are what's happening in that market these days. No paper, no postage, just a monthly fee and a download. He wants me to send digital photos, too, just like I did when we were in Europe.

"When I told him I was in America, he got all excited. Asked me to pitch him an idea. So I did and he liked it. It's called *An Aussie in Love*, all about traveling here with an American girl and seeing the country through our eyes."

A giggle slipped from Eden. God, it felt so good to smile, to feel a surge of happiness. "Oh, Garret, that's fabulous. But I can't write."

"You won't have to. Take notes about our travels. Pass them to me and I'll do the writin'." He shifted. "A little paycheck comes with the job. I'm starting the series with Bellmeade, with meeting Jon and building the stables."

Impulsively, she straddled his stretched-out body, resting her palms and knees on either side of him. "We should celebrate."

He grinned up at her. "I'm in favor of celebrating. We'll go get some Ambers in one of the bars. Maybe some dancin'? I can wear my boots!"

Her heart felt lighter. Garret was irrepressible. He made her feel whole even though she wasn't. He chased away the darkness in her head, refilled her heart with hope, gave her back to herself. His effervescence, his love of life, and of her, dragged her back from the edge of grief. "Later," she said. "I have something else in mind right this minute."

"I'm open to suggestions." He traced his finger along her temple and across her lips.

She looked down at him, grew serious. "A while back you made love to me under the stars of your country. And with all the stars looking down on us, talking to us, you said—led me to believe—that you would make love to me under the stars of my country too." She glanced upward. "Pitiful few stars out tonight, but are you a man of your word, or not?"

In one smooth move, he flipped her onto her back, hovered over her, dipped down, and gave her a long, passionate kiss. "I am a man of my word, my dear Eden. I love you, and there are plenty of stars to testify to us cementing my pledge. And believe me, the stars never lie."

32

Several more blasts from the gun shattered the rural night. Ciana threw on jeans and a sweatshirt, her heart racing, her hands trembling. She grabbed the shotgun that she kept in her closet and rushed to the front door. She was tugging on her boots when Jon clambered down the stairs, almost mowing her over. "You heard that?" she asked.

"I heard it. Sounded like it came from behind the tree line, by the track." He took a second to shove his revolver into the waistband of his jeans, then grabbed the doorknob.

She followed him.

"Where you going?" he barked.

"To the truck with you."

"Like hell! Stay here."

She grabbed his arm. "*Not* going to happen!"

He wrenched away. "There are live guns out there. I don't want you shot."

"My house, my rules," she said through clenched teeth. "I'm going with you."

He growled something unintelligible under his breath that she knew wasn't charitable and took off toward his truck, parked by the barn. She ran after him, made it in the cab just as he shoved the gear into drive and headed toward the new stables. The ride was rough because the road was nothing more than a pig trail, ruts worn into the ground by tractor wheels. Usually they rode the horses or walked, but taking the better frontage road would have taken longer. "We need to put in a decent road," she said over the noise of the engine.

At the stables, Jon lurched to a stop. The truck's headlights nailed Cecil standing beside the stables, his shotgun slung over his shoulder. In the glare he looked washed out and colorless. Jon killed the engine, but not the lights. He grabbed his pistol, told Ciana, "Stay put." She ignored him and bounded out of the truck. In seconds Jon was beside her. "What happened?"

Cecil spat, cradled his gun in his arms. "Had some visitors. Two men. They won't be back."

He nodded toward the stables, where Ciana saw a gas can sitting on the ground. She gripped Jon's arm. "Oh my God. Were they going to burn it down?"

"Looks like it," Cecil answered.

"You scare them off?" Jon asked.

"Better. Filled their backsides with buckshot, and their truck too. Left my mark all over its shiny black doors. Should be easy for the sheriff to track them."

"Are you hurt?" Ciana's adrenaline overload receded, and her knees turned to jelly.

He snorted. "They never saw me coming. Be picking buckshot out of their asses for days. Not like I didn't warn everybody in town I'd be out here at night."

"You think it was locals?" Ciana hated to face the idea.

"Can't say."

Jon walked to the can, squatted, but didn't touch it. He leaned over it and sniffed. "Gasoline, all right. Would have made a hell of a fire."

All their hard work up in flames. Ciana tasted bile, and fury. She wanted to shoot the men too.

To Ciana, Cecil said, "They were driving a badass big truck with off-road tires and hunting lights 'cross the roof. Bet it's the same one that forced you off the road awhile back."

Her stomach roiled. Jon returned to her side, put his arm around her waist. He shoved his pistol back into his waistband. "Come on to the house and we'll call the sheriff."

She touched her pocket, realized she hadn't brought her cell phone. She nodded, crossed her arms, hugged herself for warmth. The two of them walked to Jon's truck. She stopped, turned to Cecil. "Thank you."

He grinned. "Satisfaction guaranteed. Fools shouldn't have messed with this old army grunt."

"Come with us. Least I can do is give you some coffee."

His weathered face broke open in a grin. "That would taste mighty good right now. I'll drive up in my truck and meet you there."

She glanced nervously at the can left beside the wood structure.

"We need to leave things as they are for the sheriff. These guys won't return," Jon insisted. The first streaks of dawn had lightened the sky in the east. Stars were disappearing, and the night was giving way to grayness. "They're like roaches—they only come out in the dark. Light makes them scatter."

When they got to the house, Alice Faye was in the kitchen dressed in her bathrobe, and the smell of freshly made coffee saturated the air. "Tell me," she said, worry creasing her face when Ciana and Jon came inside. Jon headed for the wall phone.

"Before we do, Cecil Donaldson is on his way up," Ciana said. "In case you want to change."

She arched an eyebrow, stood firm. "That old man's seen plenty of us old farm women in our bathrobes in the mornings."

The words and their implication startled Ciana. Cecil? Good grief! Had Alice Faye been one of those farm women? Ciana didn't dare ask.

"Tell me what happened," her mother demanded, just as Cecil knocked on the back door.

Alice Faye let him in, got him a clean mug, and gestured to the pot while Ciana told her what she knew. Her expression turned grim as she listened. After Jon hung up and announced that the sheriff was on his way, Alice Faye ordered everyone to sit at the table, and started fixing breakfast. Ciana was certain she couldn't eat a bite, but her mother wouldn't hear of it, and sent her to the hen coop, guarded by Soldier, to gather fresh eggs. In no time the smells of country ham, fried eggs, and baking biscuits, turned the morning into another normal day.

The Southern way, Ciana thought. *In times of great stress, feed people.* In truth, once the platters of food were set on the table, and because of her restless, sleepless night and harrowing morning, her appetite returned with a vengeance. By the time the sheriff arrived, she felt fortified and ready to deal with what had happened.

"We'll catch those sons of bitches," Jon said in her ear as they went out to meet with the sheriff and his deputy.

Ciana nodded, but questions gnawed at her. Who was behind the terrorism? And what would happen when the truth came out? Was it really neighbor against neighbor, as Jon had once suggested? Or was it sinister men for hire, intent on driving her to her knees and taking by force what she would not sell?

The next day, Ciana and Jon started building a roadway to the stables. Jon laid out the route, marked it with stakes and orange twine, turning it south to skirt the stand of trees. A longer distance, but he said it would be easier than cutting through the tree line. Ciana had hooked up the chisel plow to the tractor in order to cut through the hard ground and carve out a bed for the road. The road would be crude, made of packed sand and crushed rocks, but easier to drive on than the current rutted path.

Two days later, Jon drove his truck heaped with supplies for the day's work and Ciana rode Caramel to the newly formed roadbed. The horse needed the exercise but seemed nervous, difficult to handle. "Calm down, girl." Ciana tried to soothe her. "You'll be with your friends in a little bit." The other five horses had been turned into the pastures near the barn to graze, and Ciana suspected Caramel wanted to be with them. Ciana tied the horse to the outside rail of the corral's fence.

Jon parked beside the water trough. They still needed a well to be dug and a waterline to be laid so the animals could drink after a workout. Another chore, Ciana reminded herself. It had to be done because toting water back to the trough in the truck was heavy, hard work. Ciana brushed aside what had to be done in favor of what they were here to do.

She and Jon began to unload the truck. The day was cool, and held the threat of a thunderstorm. Jon glanced at the sky.

Ciana asked, "Think we'll get rained out?"

"Probably. Weatherman said a front was coming through."

Farmers lived by the weather forecasters' predictions, but she'd been in a hurry that morning and hadn't listened to any reports. "We can still get something done before it hits," she told him, hating to let a little rain stop their workday. Still, Jon kept searching the sky, watching the fast-moving banks of low-hanging gray clouds. Finally she asked, "What's bothering you?"

"My horse. She's acting strange, and when I turned out the others, they were acting squirrely too."

Jon read horses like Ciana could read a book. She glanced at Caramel, saw the way the buckskin was sidestepping and how the whites of her eyes showed. "She looks scared," Ciana said.

Jon jogged over to calm his horse. Caramel neighed, a deeply distressed sound. Ciana felt goose bumps crawl up her back. Horses had a sixth sense. "What do you think is wrong?" she called to Jon.

He leaned into the horse, trying to calm her with his familiar voice.

Seconds later Ciana felt the air grow still, heavy, clammy, and thick, and watched the gray sky churn and morph into the color of aged copper. The wind picked up. Caramel jerked, broke Jon's hold. She reared, pawed the air, with a look of absolute terror. The leather reins went taut, then broke.

Impossible! The power of the horse's muscle to snap a

leather strap left Ciana stunned. She watched the frightened animal gallop away. The wind's fury whipped Ciana's hair into stinging strands that felt like whip marks on her cheeks.

Jon whirled, yelled something Ciana couldn't hear above the roar of the wind. From the corner of her eye, she saw a funnel-shaped cloud in the sky skimming the ground, heard what sounded like a freight train bearing down on metal tracks.

Jon leaped across the distance separating him from Ciana. He hit her sideways, tumbling her into the nearly empty water trough. She landed hard, breathless, scrunched in a ball, shouting, "Jon!" and clawing at him to pile atop her. The awful screeching wind was deafening and her voice was swallowed. Daylight vanished. The world turned dark. What felt like a hundred bee stings pelted her exposed skin. Again she screamed out for Jon.

Just as suddenly as it had come, the roar of the wind abated, and an eerie silence fell. Ciana fought for breath, struggled to process what had happened. As her head cleared, she realized that she lay in a few inches of steadily rising water. She shivered. She was alone with a cold rain falling. Jon Mercer had vanished.

33

*J**on!*** If she didn't move, Ciana knew she could drown in the rapidly rising water filling the trough. But her muscles had cramped and frozen in place. She couldn't straighten her legs. "Move," she whispered. Then louder, "Move!" Her muscles balked, but slowly, through sheer force of will, her body began to obey. First her legs, then her arms unclenched and stretched out. Her teeth chattered as her body began to shake as she sat up.

She blinked, looked around. Destruction lay in every direction. The truck was battered, filled with rubbish. Yards from the truck, the new stables still stood, but a large tree branch had partially crushed the roof. In the other direction she saw fields littered with chunks of wood, leaves, paper—stuff she couldn't even identify. But no matter which direction she looked, she couldn't see Jon.

Fear for him wiped out the remaining dullness in her brain. Panic gave her strength to boost herself up and slide over the side of the trough. Her legs were too weak to support her. She hung on the edge of the water trough, waited for waves of nausea to pass. She had to find Jon.

She tested her legs. She was wobbly, but her legs worked. She examined her hands, arms. Cuts and scrapes, but no gushing blood. Ciana pushed back her tangle of wet hair, her eyes darting in every direction. No sign of Jon. She limped forward, calling his name. The farther from the truck and stables she went, the more scared she became. He'd been right beside her when he'd pushed her into the trough.

She kept moving slowly and methodically, forcing herself to not run willy-nilly screaming and yelling for him. *Control.* She had to stay in control of her fragile will, so close to shattering. The world looked surreal, like some willful child had pitched a temper tantrum and kicked a well-ordered play space into shambles. To add to the insult of wreckage, the rain had stopped and sunlight spilled generously from blue sky through pockets of gray clouds, so that the damage stood out in sharp relief.

In the distance she heard the sound of a siren. Tornado warning. Had it been going all along, and was just now registering? She didn't know. She resumed her search. Thirst burned her throat. Her head ached and her vision blurred. Her knees gave way and she fell into a standing puddle. Mud splattered. She pushed herself onto her hands and knees, fought the urge to vomit, then to cry. Neither would help. She held up her head, took deep breaths, but seeing the area from a different vantage point allowed her to recognize a man-shaped lump about twenty yards to her left. Jon!

Relieved, she staggered upright, but when she got to him, she saw that while his right leg lay straight, his left was twisted, obviously badly broken. He was bleeding from a deep cut on his forehead. And he wasn't moving. Her relief gave way to fear, then terror. *What if . . . what if?* Her heart beat like a trip hammer.

She warned herself away from the dark precipice of such a thought, dropped to her knees beside him. She bent, said his name into his ear. No movement. She wanted to touch him, was afraid to touch him. Screwing up her courage, Ciana pressed two fingers to the side of his neck, searching for the sign that would herald life. Her breath caught. She felt a flutter and sagged. His pulse was weak, but it was there.

She crouched, kissed his cheek, his lips. No response. "Jon, I'm here, honey. I'm here." She realized he was unconscious, and if he woke, he'd be in terrible pain. He needed medical help, and he needed it quickly.

Her cell phone! For the first time since the storm struck, she remembered it. She dove into her pocket, jerked it out, punched in 911, and heard only the frantic noise of a busy signal. She punched in the emergency number three more times, finally heard a repeating automated message, "All circuits are busy. Please try your call later." The scope of what had happened slammed her. What had happened was not a storm. They'd been struck by a tornado. Surely many others needed help too. She'd have to go get help and bring it to Jon. But that meant leaving him. How *could* she leave him unconscious and broken and hurt out here in an open field? She needed to stay with him, wrap herself around him, keep calling the emergency number. She couldn't leave him! What if he woke up, tried to move? Tried to find her?

For a moment she was immobilized, torn between what she wanted to do and what she must do. Her mother had gone grocery shopping in town. She wasn't even on the property. No one knew they were out there. No one was even looking for them. Getting help was up to her. She thought of the house. It wasn't very far. She could go to the house, find blankets. She'd get water and anything else she needed to make Jon comfortable. Maybe the house phone, the old landline, was working, and she could get through.

Urgency shot through her. And hope. She took a second, smoothed Jon's forehead, and although she knew he couldn't hear her, she was compelled to say, "I have to go for help. I'll be back soon as I can. Please hold on, darling. I love you, Jon. Hold on!"

Ciana rose, turned, and started walking as swiftly as possible through the torn earth and over debris. In seconds the exertion turned each breath into panting gasps. Her lungs were on fire, and she felt a hitch in her side. She ignored her pain, kept moving, forced air inside her mouth and nose in great gulps. It seemed like an eternity, but eventually she arrived at the garden so lovingly planted weeks before by her mother and Eden. Most of the orderly rows lay shredded by the wind, and yet other areas stood unscathed. On the far side the poles for beans to climb were arrow straight, a testament to the wind's capriciousness.

She had stared at the ground until now, being careful not to trip. At the edge of the garden, she glanced up toward her home, then stopped and stood stock-still, not believing what her eyes were broadcasting to her shell-shocked brain.

There was no house.

Eden lay stretched out on the beach, soaking up the warm, soothing rays of the Florida sun on gorgeous white sand as fine as sugar. Garret had been right. Staying a few extra days in Destin was what she had needed to get back in touch with herself and her everyday life. Her mother was gone, and Eden hoped, finally at peace. She would take her ashes to Bellmeade and scatter them across the fertile earth Eden had grown to love. *At least I'll always know where you are, Mom*, she thought with a wry smile.

The sound of the rolling surf became lulling music, the salty air a heady perfume. A gull swooped low, tossing its cry into the sky. Eden closed her eyes, was half asleep when she felt a shadow fall over her face. She blinked, saw Garret leaning over her. She raised her arms in an invitation for him to hold her. He plopped down beside her onto the sand, his knees drawn up. She raised up on her elbows. "No hugs for me?"

Without the glare of the sun on his face, she saw that he looked troubled. "Been watching the telly. That's why I didn't come out to be with you on the beach right away."

"Your team losing?" She flashed a grin, but he didn't return it. She sat up, turned toward him. Her pulse began to race and ratchet up her anxiety level. "What's up? You look serious."

"It is serious. Announcer on the telly from your national news been breaking in all morning. There's bad weather slamming Tennessee. Worst of it hit less than an hour ago." Garret took her hand, held her gaze without blinking. "Tornadoes on the ground all over. But one made a direct hit on your town, Windemere. Damage is bad, love. Very, very bad."

34

Ciana stood dumbstruck, staring at the heap of rubble she had once called home. The house had a long history, once a modest cabin built by the original French Beauchamp owners, then a two-story farmhouse that was rebuilt into an antebellum mansion in the mid-1800s, and years later saved from rot and ruin and turned into a Victorian showpiece. That version was eventually reshaped and modified for life in the twentieth century. It had endured the Civil War, drought, floods, even a nineteenth-century fire, only to be reduced to ruin in seconds by an act of nature. Now all that stood amid the piles of broken wood and brick that even resembled a house was a partial fireplace chimney. She walked closer to the ruined house, saw that the chicken coop had been decimated, too, and averted her eyes from the carnage of the dead birds.

Ciana let out a tortured sob, forced herself to face reality—the house was no more. Jon still needed help. She knew better than to venture into the ruins. Too dangerous. She needed another plan. She turned to face the other direction, where the barn was supposed to be. Her heart leaped when she saw that it was still standing. In its whimsy, the wind had spared the structure, skipping over it entirely. The horses! She trotted to the old barn that opened into grazing pastures. At the far end of the open field, the animals huddled in a herd, heads hanging low. She whistled and their heads came up. Firecracker and Sonata started toward her, and the boarders' horses followed in a cluster. Briefly, she wondered about Caramel and where her terror-driven run had taken her, and if she was safe.

At the fence she stroked a few noses, gave each horse a quick look over. Some had cuts, but none acted badly hurt. Ciana heard a noise behind her, spun and saw Soldier crawl on his belly from a hole under the barn. She dropped to her knees, threw her arms around the shepherd's neck, and hugged him hard. "Are you okay?"

The dog licked her face. She checked him over and he seemed fine. She surmised that like Caramel, the dog had sensed the approaching disaster and found safety. "Good boy," she said, ruffling the thick fur. Seeing the dog had buoyed her spirits. "Jon's hurt," she told the animal. Soldier's ears pricked.

Precious seconds had passed, so she darted into the gloom of the barn and the darkened tack room. There was no electricity, but she knew the space like the back of her hand. She gathered an armful of saddle blankets, bottles of water from the small refrigerator, and a first-aid kit.

Outside she halted at the sight of the long driveway leading to the front road. Her breath caught. The path of the tornado was evident. Several of the grand old trees that had stood over Bellmeade for as long as two hundred years lay uprooted or snapped like kindling, broken, supine offerings to the wind gods. Nothing had stood in the way of the powerful wind's advance to the house. Nothing could have. The sight was staggering, nauseating.

The approach to the main road was impassable. Sweat trickled down Ciana's back and her knees felt too weak to hold her. She staggered under the weight of what she was seeing. Her body begged for rest and her thirst to be quenched. She refused to do either until she could return to Jon's side. She tried her cell phone again. No luck. Overloaded circuits still busy. She considered her few options to getting back to him. Her way off the property to the front road was blocked, and she assumed the country roads were also.

She dropped the load in her arms, ran into the barn, snatched a bridle from the orderly cascade Jon kept arranged on hooks, ran outside and pulled Firecracker from the pack grouped at the fence. She slipped the bit into the horse's mouth and spread blankets across the animal's broad, bare back. She balanced the other items on a wide nearby fence post, tangled fingers in the horse's mane, and with all her remaining strength slung her body onto her horse's back, almost overshooting and taking a tumble. The horse sidestepped, snorted, but Ciana righted herself and pulled the reins taut. "Steady, girl," she said, stroking Firecracker's neck, hoping to calm the spooked horse.

Once Firecracker quieted, Ciana nestled the water bottles and the first-aid kit against her chest with one arm, and with the reins in the other hand turned the horse in the direction of the backfield. She looked down at Soldier, said, "Come," and set off at a walk, knowing it was simply too dangerous to hurry the horse around the wreckage, through the ripped garden, and back to the field where Jon lay bleeding and unconscious.

Garret and Eden threw their belongings into the camper. The urgency to get home was tangible. "How long?" Eden asked when Garret had pulled away from the motel parking lot.

"My guess . . . about eight hours."

"So long?" she wailed.

"We'll get there, love." He clicked on the radio, found a news station broadcasting frequent reports about the devastation in the Tennessee area and then about numerous tornadoes blowing into Kentucky and lower Illinois. The wind's deadly rampage had already killed fifteen people, and the body count was expected to rise. Untold property damage was also reported. Eden's heart lurched with every new word, every horrific revelation. Apparently Windemere had taken a bull's-eye hit. And what of Bellmeade? What of Ciana? "I can't raise anyone on my cell," she told Garret after hours of trying.

"Cell towers must be down. Just keep dialin'," he said in a soothing voice.

They stopped only for gas, bathroom breaks, and road food.

"Can't we go faster?" she begged.

"We'll get there."

Afternoon shadows crept over the highway as they passed from Alabama into Tennessee, and turned northeast toward Nashville. Soon the tornado's path became obvious—a line of trees lay crushed, fences were down in pasture land, billboards were flattened, roofs were torn off and smashed. Then, just as suddenly, the land looked normal and untouched. It was as if some capricious giant had walked over the earth, destroying at his pleasure, leaving some areas devastated, other areas unscathed. No rhyme or reason. No plan, as a general might have plotted to subdue a population. The closer Garret drove to Windemere, the more the landscape resembled a war zone.

Traffic slowed to a crawl. State troopers massed at roadblocks, forcing motorists to turn around. Eden thought she'd jump out of her skin. When a cop tried to turn their camper, Eden cried, "But we live here. At Bellmeade."

"Sorry," the man said. "No one's getting through. You'll have to go back for now."

She whipped out her driver's license, jammed it under the cop's nose to persuade him that she was telling the truth. "See? I live in Windemere."

"Sorry," he said, his expression intractable. "No one's getting by except emergency vehicles. Best to go to Nashville and find a place to stay until the wounded are evacuated and roads are passable and safe. No exceptions."

Garret whipped the steering wheel, turned the camper around on the shoulder of the road, and sped toward Nashville.

"We can't leave!" Eden cried, almost in hysterics.

His face was set like stone. "We'll come back, but just now, we have to do what they tell us."

Eden shrieked in frustration.

At Jon's side, Ciana quickly began covering him with blankets. Soldier lay with his muzzle on his paws on Jon's other side, soulful brown eyes flicking from Jon to Ciana. "Good boy," Ciana said, surprised at how much the animal's presence comforted her. She opened the first-aid kit, cleaned Jon's head wound, and smoothed antibiotic salve over the gash. He never moved, and she was afraid to move him. What if his spine was broken? All she could do was talk to him, hoping that somehow he'd know she was there with him and that she loved him. She begged him to hang on, told lies about help coming soon. In truth, as the day stretched on, she was certain no help was coming.

She wept. She grew angry. The phone's busy signal became a pitiful drone that made her want to hurl it away. At some point she knew that it was up to her to once more leave him and go find help. The idea made her sick, but he'd been unconscious and unmoving for so long. He was very hurt. Her body ached all over, but she knew she must suck up her pain and go. She bent over, explained how she must again leave him, went to the fence where she'd tied Firecracker. She gave Soldier the "Stay" command, mounted the horse's bare, sleek back, and headed toward the main road some two miles away.

She rode over decimated land that in areas had been drenched in rain, but not blown to smithereens, and began to think that more than a single tornado had touched down. She saw too much damage for any other explanation. Ciana stuck to open fields, following the parallel road, where she saw downed trees, poles, and electrical wires. Going through the fields was slower, but it was safer. Her horse had to work harder to slog through the soggy earth, and soon the horse's legs and belly were caked with mud and her sides heaving. Ciana encouraged Firecracker continuously with words and strokes, but the going was slow and strenuous. The longer the journey took, Ciana grew more heart-in-her-throat anxious. She'd been away from Jon far too long. She considered turning around. Suddenly, in the distance, she saw a flash of blue lights. Police! She drove her heels into Firecracker's flanks and the horse picked up the pace. Ciana cut toward the road, hovered nearer the fence line until she saw a squad car marked as one of the local sheriff's.

A deputy leaning against the hood straightened as she approached. "Ciana? That you?"

Weak with relief, she slid off the horse. She knew this man. She and Lloyd had gone to high school together. "I—I need help at Bellmeade." Her voice cracked. "I need paramedics. I tried to call, but can't get through." She explained about Jon.

Lloyd looked grim. "Road this way is a mess, but I'll radio for a team. Maybe they can get in from the other direction."

"Lot of trees down on the property," she said.

"They'll get there," Lloyd assured her.

She nodded, and with effort remounted her horse. "I need to go."

"Keep your phone on. It's also a GPS—they can find you through the signal."

Thinking of their small town, she asked, "It's bad, isn't it?"

"We lost much of Main Street, and so far nine dead, five unaccounted for. Whole string of tornadoes came through, then headed north."

She closed her eyes against a stab of sickening pain and helplessness, remembering that her mother might have been in the grocery store when the twister hit. All she could do was blink away tears, turn her horse, and start the arduous journey back to Jon's side.

35

Ciana lay on the hard ground next to Jon. Twilight was falling, and the wool blankets were damp from the wetness leaching through from underneath their two bodies. She stroked his cheek, checked his pulse—still weak—moistened his lips with water, whispered her love for him. And waited. If no one came soon, she'd have to ride back to the barn and scrounge for dry blankets, a flashlight, maybe some dry wood she could use to build a fire to keep them warm into the night. She remembered the quilt in the loft, the old diaries. The paper would make a good fire starter—if she had the strength to climb the ladder.

Every muscle in her body throbbed, and she longed to sleep. She kept drifting off and jerking herself awake. Fear was all that stood between her and longed-for oblivion. Jon's injuries . . . her mother . . . and what of Arie's parents . . . Abbie, Eric, and the new baby? Her neighbors? What had happened to them? Had they been spared? Her one consolation was knowing that Eden and Garret were in Florida and far from the disaster area.

Ciana glanced at her horse, caked with dried mud. Firecracker's head drooped, and Ciana knew the animal was done in. Yet the animal stood quietly, her reins looped to the rail of the fence corral, seeming to understand that her keepers were hurt and unable to change the circumstances. Soldier had sensed the same, for the large dog stood watch faithfully without a whimper. Jon had always told her that animals had senses absent in humans. She saw with her own eyes now how right he was. Ciana had found a bowl in the bed of Jon's battered truck and shared some of the bottled water with the dog. He'd drunk greedily, but she had no food for any of them and knew they were in dire straits.

All at once, Soldier's ears pricked forward, the ridge of fur along his back stood up, and a low growl came from his throat. "What, boy?" Ciana asked. "What do you hear?" Seconds later, she heard the whine of engines coming from a distance. She stood on quivering legs, faced toward the approaching noise. Then she saw ATVs heading from the direction of her house, or rather, the rubble of her house.

Soldier went stiff and menacing, his growl deepening. Her heart tripped. She remembered ATVs tearing up her fields at night only months before. Was this help or trouble heading toward them?

As the vehicles closed the distance, she saw that the men riding them wore bright blue jackets, and when one turned to avoid a nasty rut, she read the word PARAMEDIC on the jacket's back in bright yellow. She sagged with relief.

"Stand down," Ciana said, touching the dog's head. Soldier instantly obeyed.

Three men and four vehicles, one a stretcher on off-road tires and being towed, ground to a stop in front of her. "You all right, lady?" a man asked, eyeing the dog.

"My fiancé's hurt bad. The dog won't hurt you."

In minutes, the men had set up a portable triage and set to work on Jon while Ciana and Soldier stood back. She watched as the team poked in IVs and hooked up small machines to gauge his vitals. She heard one whistle low when he lifted the blanket and saw Jon's leg. "Good thing he's out," the man said.

Two of the men gently straightened the leg, then put it in an air cast. Because Jon didn't even groan through the procedure, Ciana became even more concerned for him. How far under was he?

In no time, Jon was prepped, laid on a backboard, and placed on the stretcher. One of the men radioed to say, "Bringing in two."

Ciana rubbed her eyes, confused. "I—I'm all right—"

"No, miss," one of the rescuers said kindly. "You're not. You need to come with us." He motioned for her to climb behind him on his ATV.

She felt torn. She desperately wanted to go with Jon, but the animals . . . Her brain went woozy. The medic took her hand and seemed to understand her concerns. "They'll find their way back."

"The—the reins . . . trip . . ."

"I get it," one of the other men said. "You don't want the horse to step on her reins." He came forward, removed Firecracker's bridle, draped it over the fencing. "Go on," he told the horse, slapping her rump.

Numbly, Ciana watched her horse start in the direction of the barn. "Go," she told Soldier. The dog tagged behind the horse, but Ciana knew that even back at the barn, there was no one to care for the animals. No food, no access into their familiar stalls and shelter. No Jon.

"Ready?" the man driving her vehicle asked once she climbed on behind him. He revved the engine and followed the stretcher out of the field, past the broken house and the fallen trees to the frontage road, where an ambulance waited, lights flashing in the rapidly darkening night.

The ambulance ended up taking them to Nashville, to the same hospital where Arie had spent so much time having cancer treatments. During the ride to the hospital, listening to the calls coming over the paramedics' walkie-talkies and battery radios, Ciana began to grasp the scope and size of the disaster. An estimated two hundred twisters had touched down over a ten-hour period through three states. Emergency forces were reeling from the toll of death and destruction. The numbers were too large, the reports too overwhelming for her mind to wrap around, so she tuned out what she could and held Jon's hand, watched fluids flow into his arm, and answered questions for the ambulance tech, who held a sheaf of forms. At some point, the tech stretched masking tape across Jon's forehead and wrote *head trauma* in black marker. "Lot of walking wounded," the man explained while tucking the paperwork under Jon's blanket. "Guys like this can't speak up, and this will expedite his examination process. The two of you will be separated at the hospital."

"Please, no—"

"No choice. The worst cases must go first. You can walk and talk."

The hospital scene was chaotic. Jon was swiftly moved up to intensive care, while Ciana found herself in a large room that had been converted into a triage center for those victims with less serious injuries. She was placed on a cot, and in spite of the glare of overhead lights and the noise of doctors, nurses, and tearful victims, she fell into an exhausted sleep. At some point her soiled clothes were removed and bagged and she was put in a hospital gown and taken to Radiology. Afterward she was moved into a real bed in a quieter, darker space. The experience was dreamlike, as she tottered between wakefulness and oblivion.

No one knew where she and Jon were, but they were alive, which was more than could be said for so many others. For the moment, it was all she had to hold onto.

Eden and Garret landed a motel room barely the size of a closet, old and smelling musty. Garret secured it for a week. When Eden protested, saying they should be back at Bellmeade in another day, he said, "May be a while, love. Authorities have clamped down on the town and say no one comes in until they've searched the place completely for the wounded."

"But how will we know about Ciana and Alice Faye?"

"We wait for them to get hold of us."

"No one can get through!" she cried.

He put his arms around her. "That might take a few days too."

"What should I do? I can't just hang around doing nothing."

He kissed the top of her head. "I'd search to see if she's been hurt. If she has, she'll be treated and might be easier to find."

His idea made sense. Yet it was frightening too. "What if—"

Garret refused to let her finish her sentence. "Just do a search."

Names of patients were being posted online by medical officials on different hospitals' Web pages. A patient's condition

227

was not listed, only name and location. And yet the growing lists of both "John and/or Jane Doe," meaning the patient hadn't been identified, was alarming. Social media pages were filling with requests of people looking for family and friends too. Eden was diligent, surfing from site to site, and also calling medical facilities. Twenty-nine hours later, she got a hit on Ciana's name in the Nashville hospital she knew well.

"Found her!" Eden cried to Garret, coming in the door from making a food run. "And she's not far from here."

"Let's go."

Eden needed no prompting.

The rattle of food trays woke Ciana. She felt groggy, but slowly reality returned and she remembered everything. Her first thought was for Jon. How was he? Where was he? The room was full of beds and patients like herself, so she turned to the bed next to hers to see a man shoveling food into his mouth. "You have the time?"

"'Bout noon," the guy said. "That's your tray on the table. Where you from?"

She wasn't interested in food or talking to the stranger. She pushed the button for the nurse on her bedside remote.

"They're real slow at showing up," the man offered. "The place is on overload."

As her head cleared, pain returned to remind her she had been hurt. An IV line was set in her hand, and the bag hung on a metal pole jutting from her bed. The hospital gown that opened in the back and modesty kept her from bolting out of the bed. She felt like a butterfly pinned under glass. She wanted to find Jon. She turned to the man. "You have a working cell phone? Mine got lost in the shuffle of getting here."

"Mine's dead and no way to charge it here."

She tried to think of a next move. "I've got to get out of here. I'm just sore."

The man said, "Doctors are coming through and checking people out of here like you and me who aren't so hurt. Red Cross and area churches and synagogues are setting up temporary food and shelter for us until we can reconnect with our families."

The news alarmed Ciana. How would she find Jon if she was shoved out the door? "I need my clothes." She looked around as if they might suddenly materialize.

"Bags of our stuff are stored under our beds," the man said, pointing downward.

She leaned far over the side of her bed, saw a shelf mounted to the bed's bottom, and a paper sack jammed on it. She snatched it up, tore it open, and found a heap of filthy-looking rags that she vaguely recognized as her jeans and shirt. She shuddered just to think about putting them on again, but at the moment, she didn't have a choice.

"Maybe you should wait for a doc," the man said. "Risky for you to pull out your IV."

Her eyes followed the line, knew the man was right. She growled in frustration, punched the button for a nurse hard and often.

Just then she heard a ruckus from the doorway of the over-sized room. A woman's voice came loud and sharp, "You can't go in there!"

Another, and familiar female voice, shot back, "Watch me!"

Ciana looked up to see a dark-haired girl walking briskly around the sea of beds. She yelled and began waving. "I'm over here! Eden McLauren! I'm here!"

36

After a brief and teary reunion, mostly of the let's-talk-details-later variety, Eden left to buy Ciana new jeans and a couple of shirts. While she was gone, Ciana was examined for release and given prescriptions for an antibiotic and pain medication. She was signing paperwork when Eden returned. After dressing and wiping off her muddy boots, she met Eden and Garret in a waiting area.

"We have a room here in Nashville," Eden told her. "You can stay with us."

He grinned and hugged her. "Ready to go?"

"Not until I find Jon," Ciana said, hitting the bank of elevators, her nerves tight as barbed wire and just as prickly. As the three of them rode upward, she briefly told of her and Jon's harrowing experience. "The paramedic said he'd be sent to the ICU."

Just as the elevator dinged their arrival to the ICU floor, Ciana asked, "Have you heard anything about my mom?"

Garret shook his head. "Town's still under lockdown. Your National Guard's on patrol too. Not much in the way of communications coming out yet, but I'll drive over tomorrow and see what I can find out."

"The animals . . ." Ciana poured all her worries into the two words. "They need food. Care."

"Tomorrow," he promised, squeezing her shoulders. "Even if they try and shoot me."

They stepped onto the floor for the ICU. Doors into the unit were locked, so Ciana stopped at the nurses' station and asked about Jon. One of the nurses looked up his name. "Yes, he's here."

"How is he?" Ciana's heart was in her throat.

"Guarded condition."

Ciana's heart fell. "Can I see him? We were brought in together, but I've been discharged. He saved my life."

"Usually only next of kin is allowed."

"I'm his fiancé. Please." Tears swam in Ciana's eyes.

The nurse glanced at Eden and Garret. "Just you, then. And for only a few minutes."

Ciana was buzzed into the unit, a large dimly lit room off a short hallway with beds set in a semicircle. Every bed held a patient, and state-of-the-art equipment kept diligent vigil beside each one. She found Jon, moved to his bedside, stopped cold. He was on a ventilator, the tube protruding from his mouth and taped in place. His broken leg had been set in a cast and was being held aloft by a pulley system. Her insides turned to jelly.

A nurse materialized beside her, holding a clipboard.

"What's wrong? How bad is he hurt?"

"I'm writing down his doctors' names for you. The

231

neurologist is Dr. Patel, and he'll be in tomorrow morning to check on Mr. Mercer," the nurse said kindly. "He'll answer your questions."

"Please! Is he going to be all right?"

"Only his doctor can talk to you about his condition. Just know that his vitals are strong and he's resting comfortably."

Ciana nodded numbly. It wasn't nearly enough information, but at the moment, it was all she was going to get.

After extracting a promise from the nurse at the ICU to call the motel room if there was any change in Jon, Ciana returned with Eden and Garret. There she took a long, hot shower, willing the soreness out of her muscles and joints, and re-dressed. It was easy to wash away the dirt of her ordeal from her hair and body, but nothing could rinse the pain and trauma of it from her mind. When she emerged from the steamy bathroom, she saw bags of food from several fast food places. "Didn't know what you might want to eat," Garret said. "So I bought some of everything. Soda and beer too."

Eden patted a place for Ciana beside her on the bed. "Come and eat something. It'll help."

The aromas of burgers and fries, Chinese take-out, barbecue, and even fish and chips made her stomach rumble. She couldn't remember the last time she'd eaten. She was suddenly ravenous. And very grateful for Garret and Eden.

While the three of them ate, Ciana went into detail about the tornado. Even to her own ears, the story was spellbinding, and more than once caused herself and Eden to weep. "The house is gone," Ciana said finally. "And so is everything in it."

"Not the most important stuff," Eden said. "You and Jon are here."

"You two had all your belongings in the house, and nothing's left."

"Just stuff," Garret said. "We'll go through the remains. Might find a few things that escaped. Plus we have the clothes we took with us to Florida."

Eden's loss flooded back to Ciana. "I—I'm sorry. . . . I forgot . . . ."

Eden shushed her. "We'll talk about that later."

Ciana sniffed. "I'm worried about Mom."

"Your phone's recharging." Garret nodded toward the desk where the charger was positioned. "We'll keep trying her cell. News channels say communications won't stay down much longer."

"I—I just hope she's . . ."

"How about Jon's mother?" Eden asked, interrupting the direction of Ciana's thoughts.

Ciana shook her head. "It's crazy, but I know so little about Jon. Tried to think about getting hold of her last night, but couldn't. Jon's cell is missing. I've met his father, Wade, but not her. All I know is that Jon loves her and that she allowed him to give me the family heirloom ring." Fresh tears welled in her eyes. "And now that's gone too."

Garret slept out in the camper, giving Ciana and Eden the bed. Somewhere in the night, a beeping sound woke Ciana. She raised up, saw that her phone was glowing. A text had come in, meaning circuits had been restored. She grabbed her cell and shook Eden awake. "It's from Mom!"

Groggily Eden leaned over Ciana's shoulder. "Read it to me."

"R U SAFE? ME OK. CALL ME. PLZ. LUV." She texted Alice Faye her whereabouts, sent it, not knowing either when or *if* her mother would get it in the dead of night. Relief, gratitude, and fear all melted into one overwhelming emotion. She dropped the phone, put her hands over her face, and sobbed.

Ciana and Eden returned to the hospital and the ICU floor as soon as it was light the next morning. "You don't have to come," Ciana told Eden. "Nothing for you and Garret to do. I just don't want to miss talking with his doctor."

"I'm not leaving you alone," Eden insisted. "Garret and I'll be busy figuring out your next move. We'll be in the waiting area surfing the Web."

Her next move. No idea what that might be. She hugged Eden, who was sitting on a settee in a waiting area lined with chairs and sofas and a row of vending machines around the corner. The wait time between visits into the unit was excruciating. "I haven't asked you about your trip," she said at some point. "Your mother—"

Eden covered Ciana's hands knotted together in her lap. "My mother's ashes are coming with us to Bellmeade when we can get there. We're going to scatter them over the garden together."

"Garden's pretty wrecked too."

"So was my mother," Eden said with a wry smile. "No disrespect. Just the truth."

Eden recounted everything about the journey, about Tampa, Crossroads House, their side trip to Destin, the news reports on the long drive back, of the tornado damage seen on the drive, of being turned away from Windemere when they'd been mere miles away. She finished with, "I was a basket case. If it weren't for Garret, I'd still be wandering the back roads."

"Aussie Gold," Ciana said, also very grateful for Garret.

A man in a white coat came into the waiting area. He was short and swarthy, with soot-black eyes. "Miss Beauchamp?" He stopped in front of the settee. "I'm Dr. Patel. I understand you desire information about Mr. Mercer." His words held the lilt of someone from India. He sat beside her. "I was told you and Jon are engaged."

"Yes. How is he? Please tell me the truth."

His voice held compassion when he answered. "Be assured I will be absolutely truthful with you, Miss Beauchamp. I will not try to spare your feelings. That is not my way, nor what a patient's loved ones wish to hear. Is this acceptable?"

"Yes." Her voice cracked over the word. How much honesty could her heart stand?

"Jon is in a coma. His brain has been battered. He is on the vent to make it easier for him to breathe, for his lungs have been traumatized also. His leg is in a cast and his orthopedist, Dr. Cruz, believes it will heal nicely." He patted her hand. She gripped his. He offered an encouraging smile. "The first twenty-four hours after a brain injury are the most telling. Jon's Glasgow Scale—which is how we rate comas—is the best indicator we have to judge him by during this critical period. A normal person, awake and aware, is a fifteen, so the closer to that number, the better the chance of full recovery."

The words rocked her. Jon had been unresponsive well past the twenty-four hour mark. "Tell me his number." She tightened her hold on the doctor's hand. His dark-skinned fingers became a lifeline.

"Jon's score is hovering around eleven. I have every reason to believe that if I can relieve the swelling inside his head, he will awaken."

Hope flared. "How long?"

"Ah, the most difficult thing to answer. Perhaps days. Perhaps longer. Maybe a month."

Breath strangled in her throat. *A month!*

"This is not always the case," Patel amended soothingly. "But I tell you truthfully. Comas are tricky. I will continue to do brain scans and tests. I will visit him every day. If necessary, I will insert a shunt to drain accumulated fluid, but only if it is absolutely necessary."

A wave of nausea choked Ciana. "But probably not?"

"Maybe not." Dr. Patel extricated his hand from hers, flexed his fingers. "You have strong hands, Miss Beauchamp."

Self-consciously, she slid her hands into her lap.

"Jon is young and physically fit. This is in his favor." The doctor stood. "And he is loved. This I can clearly see. When you visit him, talk to him. Tell him of your love. Call him back to you."

"I can do that."

His heartwarming smile revived her optimism. "It is a fact that unconscious patients can hear, and when they awaken, they often recall what has been said to them. This may not sound scientific, but it is most assuredly true. I can only help his body. His heart, his spirit, is beyond my medical reach. Now go be with him. I will tell the nurses you may stay with him as long as you wish this day."

Ciana was on her feet and following, trying not to knock the man down or beat him to the nurses' desk, her head full of all the words she wanted to say to Jon, her heart full of so much love for him, it shoved aside all fear.

236

37

Pounding on the motel room door woke Ciana and Eden the next morning. With her heart banging in her chest, Ciana staggered to the door. "Garret? We're not up yet."

"Honey, it's me!"

Her mother's voice galvanized her. She unlocked the door, flung it open, and threw herself into Alice Faye's arms. They had talked on their cells the day before, but briefly. Ciana had given Alice Faye the motel's address. Ciana quickly dragged Alice Faye into the room. From the bed, a sleepy-eyed Eden mumbled, "Hey, Alice Faye."

Ciana switched on lamps as it wasn't yet daylight. "Sit here." She dragged the room's only chair to the side of the bed and sat cross-legged facing her mother.

"Sorry I couldn't get here any sooner. Roads along our property just cleared. Here, I brought coffee and doughnuts." Alice Faye thrust an aromatic sack into Ciana's hand. "Just sit and let me look at you. Oh, baby, I was so worried."

"We're all right."

Eden rubbed sleep from her eyes, reached for a cup of coffee.

"Tell me everything, Ciana," Alice Faye said.

Haltingly, Ciana brought her mother up to date about her ordeal and Jon's condition. She couldn't remain unemotional even now days later. "Jon's cell phone was lost in the storm, and I don't know how to reach his mother in Texas," Ciana confessed. "She's probably frantic, and she needs to know where he is."

"I can get ahold of her," Alice Faye said. "Remember, I mailed him a paycheck that time he left to go back home right before Arie passed. He put her number in my cell before he left."

Ciana remembered throwing herself into his arms before he'd driven off. He'd not returned until the following October, bringing apples and laying them at her feet. She shook off the memory now threatening to make her break down. "Okay, Mom. It's your turn. What happened to you?"

"I was in the Piggly Wiggly when the tornado siren went off. The store manager herded us into a food locker, where we all hunkered down. There were around twenty-five of us, and we were terrified. Oh, honey, we heard the most awful sounds . . . like a train passing through."

Ciana nodded. A freight train bearing full bore on her and Jon—it was a sound she would never forget.

"When we came out, half the roof over the store was gone and everything was in shambles. I couldn't believe my eyes."

"But you were safe," Eden interjected.

Alice Faye took Eden's hand. "Only that man's quick thinking saved us." She looked at Ciana. "Outside, Main Street looked like a bomb had hit it. Buildings were just crumbled, heaps of bricks and drywall everywhere. And the ones still standing had no roofs. The hardware store's gone. And the dime store, Flo's Florist, the diner, Cooley's department store, and . . . and . . ." Alice Faye's voice broke. "How will Windemere ever come back?"

Fresh tears trickled down Ciana's cheeks as she saw in her mind's eye every shop her mother described. "Could you get home?" She had avoided telling Alice Faye about the devastation at Bellmeade, wanting to hear what her mother had to say first.

"Not that first night. Those of us who weren't injured but were homeless were herded into any place that hadn't been wrecked. I slept on a pew in Cornerstone Presbyterian Church." She grunted. "I almost went on a hunt for the Communion wine."

"Mom, no—"

"Don't worry," her mother said, giving Ciana a reassuring pat. "I fought the urge. And my sponsor was in the church with me, so we talked most of the night. But the next day, I ran into Cecil in the church basement in the Red Cross food line. The tornado was fickle, wiping out some areas, skipping over others. People who weren't destroyed turned out to help us, God bless them. Arie's parents, Abbie, Eric, and the baby are fine. Their homes lost roof shingles and a few trees fell on their properties. The whole community's affected one way or another." Her eyes went misty. She cleared her throat. "Of course, there was no way to call anybody and the roads were blocked in Bellmeade's direction, so we were stuck. The cops wouldn't let us leave. Just emergency vehicles allowed."

"Met one of those cops myself," Eden grumbled. "Garret held me off from attacking the guy. Cop got lucky."

Alice Faye offered Eden a smile. "They tried to keep us out, too, but people with farms had animals to look after.

They needed to get to their homes. Report was that the dairy farm lost six cows in the field. And you know how close the dairy is to Bellmeade property. I was sick with worry about you, our property . . ." She paused, overwhelmed.

"You get out there yet?" Ciana's pulse skipped a beat.

"I have . . . late yesterday. Went with Cecil. Who's going to stop him?" Alice Faye smoothed the bed sheet and picked up doughnut crumbs. "Took us over an hour because he had to stop his truck every few miles and chainsaw some trees off the road, but we made it."

"The horses? Soldier?"

"They're all right," Alice Faye said softly. "Hungry and thirsty, and in need of a good scrubbing—especially Fire-cracker."

Ciana let go of the breath she'd been holding. "Poor things. Glad they're okay, though."

"Oh, and Caramel had found her way home too. Cinch was torn on her saddle, so it was all lopsided and her hide rubbed raw, but I got it off her and smoothed some salve on her wounds. Cecil helped and we got them all cleaned up, fed, and settled in their stalls. I know the boarders must be going crazy wondering about their horses."

Ciana would tell Jon his horse was safe soon as she was alone with him. Maybe the news would penetrate the dark-ness that held him captive. "Can a vet check them over?"

"Not right away. There's too many hurt animals for a doc to get our way for a spell. I'll watch 'em until one can come."

"Where are you staying?" Her mother hadn't mentioned their demolished house, but she couldn't have missed see-ing it.

"I'm living in the barn tack room Jon fixed up," Alice Faye said, skirting the house issue that neither of them seemed to want to bring up. "Decent cot and a bathroom. I have plenty of candles, and Jacob's old hurricane lamp until I can get gas for the generator and stock the little fridge."

"You going to be all right until we can get back there?"

"Course we are."

"We?"

"Cecil's staying up in the loft, and we're both armed."

Ciana gulped. "Is that necessary?"

"National Guard won't be hanging around forever. And for all the good people helping, there'll be some who'll take advantage of the disaster. Looters," she said, her mouth set in a grimace. "They better not put a toe on Bellmeade. Cecil's loaned me his Colt .45, and I know how to use it. Together with Cecil's rifle we'll settle any score we have to settle with thieves."

Later Alice Faye drove Ciana to the hospital. Eden said that she and Garret would come after finding a Laundromat to do the wash. Ciana went in first to see Jon. There had been no change in his condition, but she learned that Dr. Patel had lifted the visitor ban. Two at a time could come in and visit him.

When Alice Faye joined Ciana beside his bed, she wept quietly. "Poor man. A coma? He just looks to be asleep, like if I called his name, he'd wake right up." Alice Faye stroked Jon's forehead. "Let's go sit in that waiting area. Don't think my heart can stand seeing him like this."

Ciana bent, whispered into his ear, "Be right back."

They weren't the only people in the waiting area. A sleeping woman was curled on a sofa, and a couple drank coffee silently in side-by-side chairs. Ciana and Alice Faye took chairs against a far wall. *Peace and privacy*—Ciana had already learned what the people waiting in this space wanted and needed.

"Tell me everything his doctor told you," Alice Faye said.

Ciana did. "My goal is to get an update every day, and be here whenever his doctor shows up. I don't know when I'll come back to Bellmeade."

"You stay long as you want. I can handle the horses. And the house." She'd finally brought up the elephant in the room.

"What house? It's gone."

"Gone with the wind."

Ciana groaned. "Bad pun, Mom." Ciana rubbed her temples, stared down at the floor. She'd fought so hard to save Bellmeade from Hastings's buyout, positive it was the right thing to do. Now she felt utterly powerless, as tossed and rootless as the ancient oak trees on the Bellmeade driveway. "What are we going to do, Mama?"

"You just concentrate on Jon for now. Mess back home isn't going anywhere anytime soon. Eden told me she and Garret will come on back soon as they can get there. Cecil says he can get Jon's truck up and running, and we'll get it over here so you'll have transportation."

Alice Faye's words gave Ciana a much-needed boost, as she hadn't thought much further ahead than a day at a time. Of course her mother was right. Her energy should go to Jon. Everything else could be shouldered by family and friends. "Thank you." She leaned her head on Alice Faye and her mother cradled her like she might a small, frightened child.

"We'll get through this, honey. We might be bloodied, but we're unbowed and unbroken. Now go be with Jon while I get back to Bellmeade."

The next morning there was still no change in Jon. Frustrated and frightened, Ciana made her way to the one area of the hospital dedicated to the wounded spirit. The chapel and its outdoor meditation garden, a walled enclosure for quiet reflection. She used to come with Arie. "Helps me forget what's going on upstairs," Arie would tell Ciana.

The enclosure was square, generous in size. The stone walls were covered with climbing vines, now bursting with new growth. Meandering walkways led to benches or an occasional piece of metal artwork. Along the paths were small reflective pools of water, melodious fountains, Zen patches of pure white sand with candles to light. The garden's beds had been planted with spring flowers. Arie once confessed, "This is where I talk to God."

Although the morning had started cool, the sun had chased away the chill. Ciana watched the joyous, carefree dance of butterflies fluttering over flowers, listened to tingling wind chimes in a nearby stand of bamboo. She closed her eyes, let her mind drift and meld with the solitude, gradually felt her heart grow peaceful and her soul grow light, weightless. She might have remained in this place under the warming sun for hours, but for a woman's voice that asked, "Are you Ciana?"

Ciana's eyes snapped open, and she looked up to see a tall, pretty woman with brown hair and blue eyes. She appeared frazzled and stressed, very upset. "Yes?"

"I'm Angela Mercer, Jon's mother. I got here as soon as I could. How's my son?"

38

The set of her eyes and high cheekbones were Angela's true calling card. Flustered and so unexpectedly dropped into reality, Ciana leaped up from the bench. "I—I'm so glad you're here."

Angela took Ciana's hands in hers. "Left Amarillo soon as your mother called me yesterday. Flew into Dallas, then to Nashville, drove a rental car to the hospital. Trip took all night, but this was as soon as I could make it."

Ciana felt a rush of guilt over not being in the ICU. "How did you find me?"

"The information desk in the main lobby sent me up to the ICU and the nurses there told me where you'd gone. Will you take me to my son?"

Her voice held no rebuke, only concern, and Ciana clearly saw that along with being exhausted, Angela looked frightened. "This way." Ciana led the way out of the garden and to the elevators.

On the ride up, Angela said, "I heard on the news that Windemere took a direct hit. I've been calling and calling, but couldn't get through. I—I hadn't heard from Jon, knew he'd call when he could. I just figured—" Her voice broke. "I didn't know . . ." She gathered herself. "I was coming up anyway, just to check on him, then got your mother's call."

Ciana's heart went out to Jon's mother, and she explained about Jon's missing cell phone.

The ICU was as Ciana had left it, and Jon was as she had left him—unresponsive, on a vent, in a coma. Seeing him, Angela clamped her hand over her mouth. Tears filled her eyes. The sight was wrenching.

"Oh, my son," Angela whispered. "My precious son."

"Talk to him," Ciana urged. "His doctor says talking's a good thing."

Angela leaned in, smoothed Jon's hair on his brow tenderly. "Jon . . . it's Mom. I'm here, honey. Look at me, Jon. Will you look at me?"

Jon never moved. To encourage Angela, Ciana said, "I know he hears us on some level."

"You think?" Angela closed her eyes, rocked back on her heels, ran her hand along his arm, cupped his hand resting on the white sheet. "I always feared this day would come. That I'd be standing alongside his hospital bed." She turned to Ciana. "I just thought it would be because he'd been thrown by some bronc. You know? He loves the rodeo and living on the edge. I was prepared to hear that kind of news. But not of him being smacked by a tornado."

Guilt swept through Ciana. Jon had saved her, not himself.

Angela said, "Life never happens the way we think it will,

does it?" She forced a teary smile. "I'm just glad you were with him. He—he loves you very much, Ciana. You were all he talked about when he was at home."

Ciana's own eyes filled. "I love him very much too."

Not letting go of Jon's hand, Angela sat in the straight-back chair beside Jon's bed. "Do you . . . would you mind if I stayed with him by myself for a few minutes?"

"Stay as long as you want," Ciana said quickly, emotion raw in her throat. "I'll be in the waiting room. When you're ready, I'll tell you all I know about his condition." She bent, kissed Jon's mouth, and left the man she loved alone with the woman who had given him life and loved him first.

When Angela emerged, she looked pale and fragile. Ciana's heart hurt for the woman. Except for Ciana—a girl she had only heard stories of, Angela Mercer knew no one. She was far from family and friends, alone with a terribly injured son. Ciana's sense of pity for Angela morphed into feelings of responsibility. Jon would want Ciana to treat his mother as her own. "Let's go down to the cafeteria. I'll bet you haven't had a meal since you left Texas."

"Not hungry."

"Doesn't matter. Atmosphere is better down there." She put on a smile, urged one out of Angela. "And the food here is pretty good. I'm not making that up."

In the cafeteria, Angela chose soup and a small salad, and Ciana chose a table by a window that looked out on a sloping slice of lawn. The lunch hour was passed, so the room held just a smattering of employees working cell phones and laptops.

Wearily, Angela stirred her soup. "Tell me what you know."

Ciana explained what Dr. Patel had shared with her. "You'll like Jon's doctor. He's honest and truthful and very kind." What Ciana didn't say was that while Patel was forthright with the truth, he didn't divulge it all at once. He released it in bits and pieces. Maybe it was easier on the listener to get the truth in small doses, but it was also nerve-racking. She explained what she'd been told about comas, where Jon was on the Glasgow Scale, and then told the best news from her morning consult with Patel. It didn't appear as if surgery would be needed to relieve inner cranial pressure.

Afterward Angela's spirits looked buoyed, so Ciana shared the most difficult pieces of information. People in comas were often left impaired to some degree, especially if the coma lasted several weeks. "But some are perfectly fine," Ciana added hastily, recalling how deflated she'd felt when Patel had told her as much.

Angela pushed away the half-eaten salad and bowl of soup. "Thank you for telling it like it is, Ciana."

Ciana chewed her bottom lip. "I know it's hard to hear, but I hang on to knowing that Jon's in there somewhere under all that trauma. And I believe with all my heart that if there's any way out, he'll find it."

Angela bobbed her head and smiled, but Ciana noted that the smile didn't make it into her sad blue eyes.

Ciana drove Angela's rental car to the motel, where Eden and Garret met them. After a round of introductions and hugs— Garret was a natural-born hugger—Angela said, "Good to put faces with the people Jon's told me so much about."

"He's a good bloke."

Eden said to Ciana, "We've heard that the roads are clear enough for us to return to Bellmeade. We're going tomorrow."

"What's left of Bellmeade," Ciana said.

"Guess you'll be staying here," Garret said. "Motel's cleared out a bit, too, so I know you can corner an extra room."

He said this to Angela. She said, "I'm not leaving until Jon's out of the woods."

"We'll bring his truck over soon as we can," Eden promised Ciana.

A feeling of homesickness rolled over Ciana. She pushed it down, reminding herself that there was no home, just rubble and ruin. "We should go out and get some supper."

"Great idea," Garret said.

"Not me," Angela said. "I just want to get a room and get some rest."

"Come with us," Ciana begged, not wanting to leave her alone. They were all in this life drama together now.

"Next time," Angela said. "You kids go enjoy yourself. You deserve it." To Ciana she said, "Let's meet in the motel lobby early and go to the hospital together. I want to be sure and be there when his doctor comes through." She went to the lobby desk to secure a room.

Garret trailed after her, telling Eden and Ciana, "I'll get her bags up to her room for her."

Eden wrapped her arm around Ciana's waist, and they leaned against a nearby wall to wait.

By the end of Jon's first week in a coma, his vent had been pulled, he was breathing on his own, and he was out of the ICU and into a private room. His vitals had improved. His

Glasgow score had risen a point. Patel was encouraged. Everything looked positive—with one exception. He wasn't waking up. Jon moved, even thrashed, "normal and expected" Patel told Ciana and Angela. He moaned. But he never opened his eyes and seemed totally unaware of all that went on around him. Still Ciana and Angela talked to him, stroked him, willed him to come back to them.

Jon was assigned a physical therapist, who arrived daily and performed various exercises to keep Jon's joints limber and his muscles active. Soon Ciana and Angela helped with the exercises. Something, anything, to keep up their spirits because the longer Jon was under, the harder it was to believe he'd awaken fully recovered. "About eighteen percent have no lasting effects," Patel told them. The number seemed infinitesimal to Ciana. He could suffer memory loss. What if he didn't remember her? Or them? She'd cried herself to sleep the night she heard the statistic.

The days and nights blurred together. Alice Faye came to visit, bringing news of Arie's family showing up at Bellmeade, of Eric and Swede and various aunts and uncles bringing food for meals and chain saws for clearing. "Swede is saving the best of the old trees for cabinetry when we rebuild," Alice Faye said. Ciana was grateful, but the idea of rebuilding was too much to think about just now.

Eden and Garret brought Jon's truck as promised, and stayed the day. It broke the monotony, but made Ciana feel lonelier than ever once they left. Still, she and Angela kept their vigil, talking, watching, waiting for a change that didn't come.

A few days later Alice Faye marched into Jon's hospital room and took Ciana by the elbow. "What are you doing?"

"I'm taking you home for the day."

"Not happening."

"I'm your mother and I can see you're at your breaking point, Ciana Beauchamp. Don't argue with me."

Angela came quickly to Alice Faye's side. "Your mother's right. You need a break. I'm here and if anything changes, I'll call."

"It's almost two hours there and back," Ciana cried, hoping they'd see the lunacy of the plan.

"Not the way I drive," Alice Faye snapped. "Now, don't argue with me. I'll bring you straight back after your visit. Come on, honey. . . . Have a nice long ride on your horse. Animal's miserable for you."

That got inside Ciana as nothing else could. How she longed to ride! "That's a low blow."

Alice Faye gave a self-satisfied smile. "All's fair in love and arguing with a stubborn child."

Angela touched Ciana's cheek. "Go on, girl. Hug Jon's horse for him, hear?"

Weary to the bone, Ciana knew she couldn't fend off both these women. *Home.* She wanted to go home to Bellmeade, and to touch the land that rooted her. She kissed Jon's mouth, and followed her mother out the door of Jon's hospital room.

39

Once out of the unit, Ciana balked because it was late in the afternoon. She promised she'd come first thing the next morning, and her mother agreed, but threatened severe consequences if she didn't. The next day Angela put Ciana in the truck and saw her off. Ciana never let up on the gas pedal on the drive, chose to bypass her town, and take a country side road to her property.

Ciana set foot on Bellmeade thirteen days after the tornado, remembering how she'd left it, hardly believing what she saw now. The devastation and destruction had been put mostly right by days of hard work by friends and neighbors. And yet the scars remained. The grounds looked as if a giant animal had left claw marks on defenseless trees and earth. Along the driveway were empty spaces or stumps where the great oaks had once proudly stood. In place of the house she again saw the lone standing chimney, deemed still usable, according to her mother. She saw orderly stacks of bricks salvaged from the old house. Otherwise the earth where the house had stood was barren. All the king's horses and all the king's men could never put things back as they had been. She drove to the barn, sadness blanketing her homecoming.

She parked, and Eden and Alice Faye hurried out to meet her. "We're just getting ready to replant some of the garden," Eden announced, brandishing her gardening gloves. "Garret's down working on the stables."

Ciana heard the whine of a far-off saw. "The place looks good," she said, her voice quavering.

"Better," her mother corrected. "We still have a long way to go. How's Jon?"

"The same. But Angela is with him, so if he wakes up . . ." She let the sentence trail.

"Come see how we've fixed up the barn," Eden said after a brief, awkward silence.

Ciana went in with them, let out a low whistle. "Nice job. Looks comfy." The stalls were empty as the horses were out to pasture, but parts of the barn had been turned into make-do housing. A dining table had been created from several long planks of wood laid across two sawhorses, with folding chairs set on either side. A full-sized refrigerator and a mini camp stove were sitting just outside the tack room door. A battered, salvaged piece of furniture served as a surface to stack paper plates and plastic utensils, alongside a pile of candles, for although the gas generator was running, it was only used for essentials such as the fridge and fans. Ciana recognized two candelabra of ornate silver from Bellmeade's storied collection, given to various brides as wedding gifts through the years. There was even an old sofa and two cushiony easy chairs donated by someone.

"If we need extra seating we just move the sawhorses," Eden explained, looking proud of their accomplishments.

"Not ideal," Alice Faye said, "but I can shackle a meal together. We've heard that electricity's supposed to be back by tomorrow."

Ciana had heard in news reports that utility trucks had been dispatched from all over the south and east to help with the overwhelming task of resupplying electricity. The rural south would be last in line. "Where does everyone sleep?" Ciana asked.

"Garret and I are up in the loft." Eden raised her eyes upward.

Ciana surmised that the cohabitation ban had been lifted. "And Cecil?"

"At his place," Alice Faye said curtly, then added, "You going for a ride or just going to stand there and jabber?"

Ciana threw up her hands in mock surrender. "A ride, of course. Where did you park the saddles?"

Outside, she whistled to the horses. Their heads came up, but while Firecracker gazed at Ciana, she stood chewing a mouthful of grass and refusing to move. "She's mad at me for disappearing for so long," Ciana told Eden.

"You mean she's *pouting*? I didn't know horses could act like children."

"They can and do." Ciana grabbed the oats bucket and banged it on the side of the fence rail. The promise of oats brought Firecracker forward at a trot and drew a laugh from Eden. In no time, Ciana had the horse saddled and mounted. "Want to come?" she asked Eden.

"No thanks. A girl could fall off one of those things. And I think I hear tomato plants calling to me."

Ciana rode at a leisurely pace toward the sound of a power saw humming, and came up on Garret bent over raw lumber, and covered with sawdust. He was shirtless for the sun was warm, and his head of blond bushy hair was wrapped in a bandanna. The sight of him made her miss Jon all the more as she thought back to the times she'd come up on him in work mode, his muscles bunched, sweat rolling down his broad chest and flat abs, his Stetson shielding his face from the sun.

"Hey!" Garret called when she rode up. "Eden said you were coming for a day."

She reined in Firecracker, smiled at Garret, nodded toward the stack of new lumber he was cutting to replace the stable rook torn away by the storm. "You're going to be busy for a while."

He gave a grin and a wink. "Can't let a bit of wind spoil my handiwork."

"I—I can't thank you enough, Garret. I know this isn't the trip to the U.S. you planned."

"Aw, no worries. Been writin' my articles and sending them off, and my editor keeps asking for more. Lot of people in my country are keen on things American, and giving a firsthand account of the tornado and its aftermath has quite a followin'." He wiped his brow. "Miss my mate, Jon, though." He gave her a salute and went back to work.

Ciana continued on her mission. Much as she dreaded it, she had to check out the fields of hay and corn and soybeans, her crops. The storm had left damage everyplace, and it remained to be seen if she had any crop left, if she'd be able to feed her horses this summer and fall, or if she'd have to turn out her boarders and plow under the fields and replant. Alfalfa seed wasn't too expensive, but the harvest would be very late, meaning more feed would have to be bought, and that *was* expensive. Ciana heeled her horse and Firecracker went forward.

The rolling pace of the horse, the blue sky and sun, the

scent of the earth—these elements soaked into Ciana's mind and body. How did people make it day after day cooped up inside office buildings and malls without touching the outside world? Even when she'd been stuck in school for twelve years, she had sneaked outside during lunch or between classes just to grab lungfuls of bright clean air. The outdoors always beckoned and beguiled her, even from the time she'd been a small child and Olivia had walked her around and pointed to and named different plants and flowers.

She saw the planted fields from afar and her heartbeat took an uptick. She saw green cornstalks standing ankle high. Hardly able to believe her eyes, she clicked her tongue to hurry the horse, stopped at the side of the fenced field. Her corn crop was undamaged and growing! She rode to another field and saw it green with alfalfa hay. Every planted field was not only green, but unscathed. The tornadoes had passed by, dumping rain, but skipping over the fields—at least her fields and leaving them intact.

She dismounted, stood gazing out over the beautiful vision of growth. Her throat tightened as her heart swelled with gratitude. Family, friends, the blessing of escaping nature's fury, humbled her. Nothing could change what had happened, but people were strong and resilient, and hope propelled life through destruction and chaos.

After grooming Firecracker and visiting with her mother and Eden, Ciana made one more stop before turning toward Nashville. She parked at the head of Main Street in downtown Windemere and walked the length between traffic lights, staring from side to side at the damage left behind by the category four tornado. Buildings had been leveled or crushed. Many of the storefronts had been there since before the turn of the twentieth century, surviving a major flood, a few fires, and one earthquake. Now there was rubble and disaster everywhere she looked. The sight of the devastation was gut-wrenching. Still, there were people on the street cleaning up, sorting through the debris, attempting to salvage what they could. Some looked shell-shocked, others resigned.

Several called out to her. "Sorry about your property."

She went from person to person, received their sympathy, offered her condolences. A few asked, "How's Jon?" There were few secrets in a small Southern town, and people knew how gravely he'd been hurt. No one seemed to have any animosity toward her refusal to sell out any longer either. The tornado had blown that away too. They were all in this together, and grateful to have survived.

Ciana stopped in front of what had been the feed store. A bulletin board had been erected, and the townspeople had turned it into a streetside memorial. Flowers and candles, toys and stuffed animals were gathered and heaped at the base of the board. Messages holding prayers and comments had been stapled and tacked up on the wood. In the center, a list was also posted: *In Memoriam*. Ciana's heart grew heavy when she read the nine names of those who had died. The oldest had been seventy-five, the youngest eleven months. She hung her head and shed private quiet tears. *So much loss.*

At the bottom of the list were verses from the King James version of the Bible: "The Lord gave, and the Lord hath taken away. Blessed be the name of the LORD." And another: "I will lift up mine eyes unto the hills, from whence cometh my help" and another, "Bind up the brokenhearted."

Ciana was struck again by the resiliency of the people, country people. Her people.

She returned to the hospital at dusk, relieving Angela so she could go down to the cafeteria, and took up her vigil at Jon's bedside. She turned on the light above his bed to better see his face, sat, laid her head on her arm, placed her mouth inches from his ear. "Let me tell you what I saw today when I went home." She told him of her day trip, of riding the land, of feeling sunlight warm her skin, and of how people were digging out, rebuilding, starting over. She told him, not of ruin, but of hope and the future.

Finally she sighed, stroked his hair. "Come back to me, Jon Mercer. Let's go home together. I miss you so much. I love you so much. You're all I want for the rest of my life. Houses can be rebuilt, but *you* come along once in a lifetime. I want you back. Please . . . please, come back to me."

She lifted her head, leaned forward and, as she'd done so many times before, she pressed her lips to his. And his lips moved under hers. She flew backward, strangled out a cry, and stared down into his wide-open eyes.

"Jon!" Her heart thumped wildly. "Jon? Can—can you hear me?" He didn't respond and her elation turned to cold fear. She racked her memory trying to recall what Dr. Patel had told her about coma victims awakening. *Can be a slow process . . . possibly impaired . . . don't expect too much.*

Ciana leaned forward, touched his cheek, watched his pupils attempt to focus. She should ring for a nurse, but couldn't force her hand to the call button. "Jon . . . do you know me? I—I'm Ciana." She awkwardly introduced herself.

He blinked, his expression unchanged.

She took his hand, pressed her lips to his palm, dread knifing her stomach. "Do you remember me?" What if he was lost, awake, but not cognizant? Hadn't the doctor said it could be a possibility? "We . . . we were—" She paused, searching for a word that would fit.

His gaze slowly sharpened. "I . . . I . . . loved . . . you." His voice wasn't more than a hoarse whisper.

"*Loved?*" Had she heard the word correctly, in the past

tense? "Yes . . . you did." Her own voice was scarcely a whisper, too, barely audible above the thump of her heartbeat.

"Love . . . you," he said.

Tears filled her eyes. "Yes. And I love you. Forever."

Over the next few days Jon's awakening was the buzz of the floor. Angela was ecstatic. He knew her, but was confused as to why she was with him. His hospitalization was explained to him, as well as his injuries, coma, and broken leg, but the story of his being hammered in a tornado left him confused and agitated. He remembered nothing from that day. Dr. Patel told Ciana and Angela that parts of Jon's memory were damaged, most notably his short-term memory, and Patel said not to press him. He warned them that there were things Jon might never remember, even people and places. He also cautioned that Jon's confusion could likely hang on and be expressed with bursts of anger. "It's post-traumatic stress disorder," Patel said. "Like a soldier home from combat. His psyche is wounded. Be patient with him. Don't take outbursts personally. Reintroduce elements and people from his life gradually. Don't force anything."

Ciana understood Patel's message, but her only question was "When can we take him home?"

"I want him evaluated by a psychologist before I release him—just a precaution," Patel added. "And I want his physical therapist to continue to work with him too. His cast may prove problematic, and he'll need to be proficient on his crutches." Patel patted Ciana's hand. "He will come back. Give him time."

The question she was unable to ask was the one that most haunted her: *What if he doesn't come all the way back?*

Jon regained his strength more quickly than his memory. He forgot words, names of common items, had episodes of bad dreams. Sometimes when Ciana or Angela patiently explained details, his expression clouded over and he seemed to space out, which always caused Ciana's stomach to clench. She wanted him all the way back. She wanted his playfulness and the teasing glints to return in his green eyes. She wanted to lie in his arms and kiss away his confusion and doubts. While he'd been unconscious, his cuts had healed, stitches been removed, and bruises had faded. Only his mind was struggling, and no one could predict how long that journey might take.

The toughest time for all of them was when Alice Faye, Eden, and Garret came to visit. Jon recognized the two women, but although Jon tried to be friendly, it soon became obvious that he had no recollection of Garret. The big Aussie looked momentarily hurt, but his face quickly brightened. He offered his hand. "I'm Garret Locklin. We're mates, so I expect you'll recall me soon enough. We built a stable together at Bellmeade, and I've got it all repaired now, so no worries about it."

Jon nodded, and returned the smile, but his forehead remained furrowed.

Garret leaned down, said, "No worries, mate, I'll grow on you. Like a fungus." He waggled his eyebrows and everyone in the room laughed, relieving the tension.

Ciana remained cheerful and positive around Jon, but privately, with Angela and her friends, she was less upbeat. Jon couldn't recall even a minute of the day of the tornado. "So what?" Eden told Ciana when they were together in the waiting area drinking coffee during one of Jon's therapy sessions. "The day was a nightmare for you both. And I think once he gets back to Bellmeade, he'll be better. Just wait and see." Eden offered a mysterious smile. "Besides, we have a surprise for you."

She patted Garret's leg. "My man here has gotten a trailer for us, and it's parked beside the barn on Bellmeade property."

Garret gave a thumbs-up. "Your government secured trailers and doled them out to storm victims, especially you blokes who lost your homes. After a mass of paperwork, and my constant pestering, they gave us one of them. I think mostly to be rid of me . . . Woman interviewing me couldn't understand a word I was saying."

Eden nibbled on a cookie. "I went along as his translator. Tennessee Southern clashing with Aussie outback was just too funny. Anyway, we ended up with a nice trailer. It has a kitchen and a bedroom and a seat that turns into a bed."

"Nice to have a stove again," Alice Faye said. "We were thinking the sheilas"—she gave Garret a wink—"can stay in the trailer, Jon can have the tack room, and Garret can remain in the loft." Alice Faye turned to Angela. "Plan to stay with us until you return to Texas."

Angela nodded gratefully. "Just for a while after he's released, and thank you for offering."

And just that easily, the plan was set to return Jon to Bellmeade and resume the picking up of the pieces of the life they'd once known. Ciana's mood brightened, but it wasn't until the first time she crawled into Jon's hospital bed and he wrapped her in his arms that she felt her spirit totally at rest. Cradled in his embrace, she felt as if her universe had finally righted itself. No matter how long his recovery took, she would walk the road with him. Together, they could do anything.

Summer sunshine set tree leaves aglow, and a breeze cleansed by recent rain set them dancing on the day Ciana drove Jon home to Bellmeade from the hospital. Over a month had passed since the tornado. The grass had greened, and the front yard was clear of all debris, but the long driveway bore the scars. Jon said, "The trees . . . I didn't imagine so many were gone even though you told me."

"We saved the wood," she said simply. "And we'll plant more trees."

She stopped the truck beside the cream-colored trailer that they now called home. But as she helped Jon with his crutches, Soldier came bounding across the grounds, wagging his tail and wiggling for joy at Jon's feet.

"I think he missed you," Ciana said.

Jon's face broke open in a grin. "Hey, buddy." Soldier had been trained never to jump on people, but Jon tapped his chest, inviting the dog to put his paws there, and Soldier did. Jon smoothed the shepherd's fur and praised the animal, for Ciana had told Jon how the dog had lain by his side while she'd gone for help.

The trailer door opened and Angela and Alice Faye stepped out wearing beaming smiles. Angela had come back with Alice Faye the night before. Ciana's mother said, "Welcome home! Eden and Garret drove into town for groceries. The old Piggly Wiggly is mostly repaired and open for business. Folks are real happy about that."

Jon shifted the crutches, looked over to where the house had once stood. "Can I get a closer look?"

"Go on," Alice Faye said to Ciana and Jon. "We'll get your things from the truck and put everything away in the tack room."

He hobbled across the expanse of lawn with Ciana beside him, paused where the veranda had been. His gaze swept the now cleared space, stopped at the stack of the old chimney. "Hard to believe it's gone."

Ciana hooked her arm around and under the crutch. "We were able to save some things, but most of the stuff is a total loss. Swede is storing the salvage for us. Swede is—"

"I know who Swede is," he said, sounding curt. He took a deep breath. "Sorry." She waited for him to gather his temper and his thoughts. Seconds later, he asked, "You going to rebuild?"

"This is still my land. What else would I do?" Then another thought crowded out all others. She stepped in front of him, chewed on her bottom lip. "Are we . . . ? Do you still want to get married?"

He held her gaze, his green eyes serious. "That's your call, Ciana. I'm not the same man I was before the storm. I don't know that I ever will be again."

The sadness in his voice made her shiver. "None of us are the same, Jon. The storm changed everybody and everything. What it didn't change was how I feel about you."

He searched her face. "You should have a choice."

"Between what and what?"

"My head gets all crazy. I can't—" He halted, stared at the ground. "I don't know if I'll be able to work like I used to." He gave a rueful smile. "My head gets all jammed up, and things that should be simple for me to do aren't. Can't make many mistakes on a job."

She understood his fears. He was a man used to being in control. What he didn't know, what he couldn't know, was whether he could ever work with wild horses again. Dr. Patel had warned them both about the severity of his concussion, and said he should do everything possible to protect himself from another head injury. "No more bronc riding," Ciana said quietly. "Is that so terrible?" But she knew before he answered that for a man like Jon, it was. "You can still work with and train horses here on Bellmeade just like we planned."

He stared, saying nothing, and finally turned back toward the barn.

She was determined not to let him dwell on his fears. "Come with me. There's one other female in your life who wants to see you."

He scowled. "I—I don't know—"

She led him to the fence beside the pasture, where they could see the horses grazing at the far end. There were only four now. The older married couple of her boarders had lost their home to the storm and had taken their two animals and moved to Arizona to live with a son.

"Whistle for her," Ciana said, nodding toward Caramel. "She'll come. She's missed you hanging around almost as much as I have."

But he didn't have to whistle. The buckskin had caught his scent on the breeze. Her head flew up, and she came toward the fence in a fast trot. Ciana opened the gate. Jon limped in on his crutches and Ciana backed out and closed the gate. She walked away, only turning when she was at the trailer. She crossed her arms and watched.

Caramel trotted straight to Jon, making a low rumbling sound in her throat. The great animal nudged Jon, butted her forehead into the center of Jon's chest, then stood quietly, eyes half closed. He anchored his crutch in the ground, put his hand on Caramel's neck, scratched behind her ear. Ciana's heart swelled at the sight. She watched through a film of tears as Jon bent forward and began to speak in the secret language of all horse whisperers, reconnecting with the filly— old friends, separated, but never parted.

41

Over the next few days, Jon acted less angry and short-tempered. He was moody, but also able to forgive himself over memory lapses. He gave up one of his crutches, too, and although he couldn't yet ride because of the cast, he resumed many of his former chores. At first Ciana mucked the stalls, and he hobbled around and pitched in clean straw, but by week's end, he was doing both. Once he was sure of his footing and balance, the second crutch was also discarded. He and Garret worked on the roadbed to the new stables, the one he and Ciana had been shaping when the storm hit. She named the road Tornado Alley, and Garret cut a sign, burned in the name, and hammered the board to a post at the road's start.

Living in the trailer was cozy—almost too cozy. Angela was given the bedroom, Alice Faye took the cushion for a bed, and Ciana used a sleeping bag in the loft of the barn with Eden, forcing Garret into the bed of his camper truck. "Just until Jon's mother leaves," she told Eden and Garret apologetically. "I mean, I can take the camper if you two want."

"A few girlfriend sleepovers are fine," Eden told her. "Garret and I'll be squeezed into the camper together soon enough. It's okay."

"No room in Jon's bed?" Garret mused.

"It's a cot, Aussie-man. Hardly room for him." In truth, Jon was keeping his hands off her. He kissed her, continued to say he loved her, but she felt an invisible barrier between them. She knew she loved him, yet they were stalled, Jon by his doubts and memory losses, herself by the overwhelming tasks of working her fields, and shaping a plan for Bellmeade's future.

"You going to rebuild the house anytime soon?" Alice Faye asked as she and Ciana were weeding the replanted garden together. "That trailer's no home, you know, for you and Jon once you're married. And speaking of that, when are you two getting married?"

Her mother's words touched a nerve. She and Jon hadn't discussed their wedding since the day he'd returned. She was beginning to wonder if they would marry, the doubts too painful to voice, even to Eden. "Not sure how to go about it just yet. What should I build?" She concentrated on her mother's rebuilding question, purposely pushing aside the second. "What do you think? The same old Victorian? Something new and radical?"

"Radical? What's that about? What's wrong with one like we used to have?"

"Why build the same old thing?" She hedged because the details of rebuilding were overwhelming. How large a house? What should it be built of? How many rooms? And what about her mother? Would she want to remain at Bellmeade? She'd

266

talked of moving out once before. The questions churned in Ciana's head endlessly, stymieing her into a standstill. "Costs money to rebuild," she said.

Alice Faye straightened, blew out an exasperated breath. "You need a place to live, Ciana. Take the insurance money and build a house."

"Insurance money?"

"Are you serious? Your grandfather, Charles, was an insurance salesman before he married Olivia. One thing we *got* is insurance! Go see Mr. Boatwright." He was their attorney and handled the farm's legal interests. Ciana recalled writing insurance premium checks—large checks that she had resented doling out money for in lean times. Suddenly those payments didn't seem so odious. "I've never read the policies, Mom. I guess they're gone with the tornado too."

Her mother shook her head. "The company will give you a reprint of the policy. Mr. Boatwright will handle it."

Just then, a dark green truck crunched up the driveway, and without the house to impede the view, Ciana saw clearly that Cecil Donaldson was in the driver's seat. She dropped her hoe and hurried to meet him. Alice Faye waved but continued hoeing. "New truck?" Ciana asked the minute he climbed out.

"Got two. This is my Sunday truck," he said with a grin. He looked as grizzled and weathered as ever. "Heard Jon's out of the hospital."

"He is. Working back at the stables with Garret."

"Glad he's all right."

She waited for him to tell her why he'd come, because Cecil wasn't the kind of man to just drop in for chitchat. "You lose anything in the storm?" she asked.

"No, but you did, and I'm not just talking about your house."

"What else?"

267

His face broke into a grin. "Well, seems like Hastings is pulling out. Man's lost a bundle with the storm and the mood's changed in town. People who wanted to sell off their farms have changed their minds. Seems like the tornado helped Windemere to see there's more to hold on to than to let go of."

"I'd have thought they'd be all the more eager to sell."

"Don't seem like it. People's roots go deep. Can't just walk away. The legislature won't okay the highway exit either. Seems like there's too many other places for the money to go, so the exit lost its priority and its funding." He took off his ball cap, smoothed his white hair.

Ciana realized that at any other time such news would have excited her. Now it meant little. "Well, thanks for the news, Cecil. But I never will sell . . . not then, not now."

He glanced around, evaluating her progress. "Lot of work ahead for you." He resettled his ball cap. "One other thing. You don't have to worry 'bout them men coming round hassling you."

"The ones you filled with buckshot?" She smiled wickedly. "You find out who they are?"

"Always suspected who they were. Just couldn't catch 'em at it. Teddy Sawyer Junior has a big mouth."

She recalled the day she'd confronted Junior in the general store while buying fencing materials. The creep had known the perps then but hadn't said a word.

"I settled with Junior," Cecil said, as if reading her mind. He leaned against the truck's fender. "There were two of 'em, and they had a bit of bad luck with the storm. Seems as if they tried to outrun a tornado in that black truck of theirs. Can't outrun a tornado. Tree came clear across the road in front of them and they hit it. Then another tree smashed into the cab. Broke some of those boys' bones. Put them both in the hospital. Ruined that fine truck of theirs too."

"Oh no!" Ciana had wanted them caught and punished, not maimed. "Who are they? Who hired them?"

"Used to work for that Tony fella, the drug hustler."

The news hit Ciana like cold water. "But why come after me?"

"Revenge. They had it pretty sweet with that man and all his badness. You took it away from them when you hustled Miss Eden out of the country. Made that Tony punk crazy. Made him take chances on the runners from Memphis . . . the ones who took him out."

She went hot and cold all over. "I—I had no idea."

"Course not. They were fixed on ruining you, burning you out if need be." Cecil shook his head. "Them boys are dumb as a box of rocks. And once they recover, the law's got a jail cell waiting for them. I just come by to let you know you'll be safe now."

A knot of emotion filled her throat. "Couldn't have done it without you, Cecil. Thank you." She stepped closer.

He waved her away. "Aw, go on now. You be happy, Miss Ciana. For Arie." He climbed back into his truck, tipped his brim at her, and started the engine.

Ciana watched him drive away, memories of Arie, of their lifelong friendship, swirling in her head. "Miss you, girlfriend," Ciana whispered, letting the words be carried off by the warm breeze.

That night, she told Eden the whole story when they were lying in their sleeping bags. She'd only told the others the part about the two men trying to escape the tornado and getting hurt and it turning out they'd been the ones Cecil had loaded with buckshot. When her mother had asked if Hastings had put them up to it, Ciana had said definitely not, and that Cecil was positive of that much.

"Tony ruined a lot of people's lives," Eden said. "I'm really sorry you got caught up by him too."

"Even if I had a do over, I'd make the same choices." She heard Eden sniffle in the dark, added, "And how could you have met Garret if we hadn't run off to Italy?"

"I guess good stuff can come out of bad stuff after all. I can't imagine my life without Garret."

The night settled around them. Ciana listened to the horses moving in their stalls below. She thought of all the people she loved. She thought of all the people who'd struggled hard to keep this land in the family, to bring it back after every disaster. The Civil War. The Great Depression. The deaths of her father and grandfather. It was up to her now, her and Jon. "Eden, will you do an Internet search for me?"

"Sure. What do you want me to do?" Ciana told her an idea that had been brewing in the back of her head. When Ciana finished talking, unable to conceal her surprise, Eden asked, "Are you certain that's what you want to do?"

"Yes," Ciana said softly. "Let me know what you find out. I'm going into town first off next week and would like to get started if everything checks out."

"Whatever. If that's what you want, I'll get the information."

"It's what I want."

Ciana drove slowly down Main Street, glancing from side to side, seeing progress in vanishing wreckage. The cleanup was progressing, but rebuilding had a long way to go. A few streets over, she parked and went into Boatwright's office. His old Victorian house, both office and home, had been spared by the storm. He greeted her warmly, filled her in on every bit of hearsay and gossip over hot coffee. He also gave her the information she needed for her next planned stop in the town. "Miz Olivia would be real pleased," Boatwright said just before she left. "You're young and smart and everything you need to be for the future of Windemere. I'll help however I can."

Ciana drove over a few more streets. The damage was heavier because the land was lower so there had been flooding. She parked, screwed up her courage, and went into the offices of Gerald Hastings. The reception area was empty and boxes were piled on tables. Silt from flooding lay caked on warped, wooden floors. She found Hastings in the room where he'd constructed his eye-catching model for Bellmeade Acres. Now the cardboard and balsa miniature buildings lay in soggy globs across a tabletop. The man was on his knees sorting through papers, turned when he heard her enter, recoiled in surprise when he saw who it was. His face darkened as he struggled to his feet. "Come to gloat, Miss Beauchamp?"

"No, sir. The storm was a disaster and everyone was affected. I'm sorry for your losses too."

He dropped his attitude, slumped, looked weary. "Well, it's over for me. I'm salvaging what I can and returning to Chicago." He squared his shoulders. "Truth is, I like a lot of the people here. Nice town, and some real nice people."

"I know we didn't hit it off, Mr. Hastings. Under other circumstances, I'd have treated you better. But I couldn't let go of my land. It's been in my family for generations, and I'm a farmer. The land means everything to people like me."

"I get that now. No one wants to sell anymore anyway."
He paused. "You need something, Miss Beauchamp?"

She wasn't sure how to begin. She gathered her courage.

"Yes, Mr. Hastings, there is. I've come to ask you, to *pay* you, to rebuild my home."

42

Hastings simply stared at her, unable to hide his shock. She let him take his time, unsure as to whether he'd erupt in anger, laugh hysterically, or just tell her to get the hell out. She thought him entitled for any of the above. "You've come to ask me to build you a new house?" he asked. "I thought you hated me."

"Not you, just the idea of selling off Bellmeade. I couldn't do it and you didn't understand my reasons."

"But why ask *me* of all people to build your house?"

She was ready for this question, had given it some thought. "This whole town needs rebuilding. Contractors will pour in, many of them less than honest. I . . . I've been checking you out and you have an excellent reputation. Just like you told me you had that day you came to visit after my accident."

"You thought I was trying to hustle you, take advantage of you."

She nodded. "Now I realize you were only attempting to defend your reputation by insisting you had no part of the accident. You were doing an honorable thing. Not everyone acts honorably, Mr. Hastings."

He blew out a lungful of air, shook his head. "I build communities, not houses."

"And Windemere is a community in need of rebuilding. If you start with Bellmeade, it will be a stamp of approval for others to ask you." She mentally crossed her fingers, hoping she was telling him the truth, for she had no idea if others would follow in her stead. "Here's what I can promise you. I know everyone in these parts, and can get you together with excellent craftsmen—woodworkers, cabinet makers, construction workers—hard workers, all of them."

"You mean when they're not cutting hay?"

She winced with his dig, but offered a rueful smile. "Not all of us do farm labor. Some actually own stores and businesses. We're teachers and homemakers and ranchers. In summer we play softball, and hold a rodeo at the fairgrounds that tourists from all over come to see. We love our sweet tea and biscuits, our families and our country. We are not Chicago. But we have good lives here in the sticks."

Hastings looked contrite. "Miss Beauchamp, I have a deep financial hole to dig out of."

"And I have the money for a shovel. Bellmeade was once the jewel of this part of Tennessee. I want it to be so once more." He crossed his arms, studied her. She plunged ahead. "I want you to manage every phase, from drawing up the plans to painting the front porch, so you are at liberty to be creative. I want a different house from the one from the past. I'm thinking maybe something with clusters of units attached to the main house, so it can be multigenerational. So that families can grow up and grow old in the family home like they once did in America, before roads and jobs scattered them to the four corners. Show me your best ideas. I will consider all of them."

Her voice was thick with fervor, and she felt as if she was channeling her grandmother. Whatever fear she'd had about making her case to him had vanished, replaced by determination. She also knew she'd snagged his interest. "I only ask for quality. The former house stood for well over a hundred years. This one should stand for at least a hundred more."

An amused smile played across his face. "You are an enigma, Miss Beauchamp. May I ask you an impertinent question?"

She nodded.

"How old are you?"

"I'll be twenty-one this summer."

His forehead furrowed, and he gave her an *I don't believe I'm about to tell you this* look. "I'll think about your offer."

She smiled and every nerve and muscle in her body relaxed. "That would be fine. I have a crop to harvest and my wedding to plan. I can be patient." The meeting was at an end. She thought about what Olivia or her father might do in the moment, then stepped forward and held out her hand. Hastings stared down at it, slowly straightened, held out his, and they shook firmly. "Thank you," she said, and started toward the door.

"Not sure I'll ever understand you Southern women," he said.

At the doorway, she turned and, offering another smile, said, "Understanding is not nearly as important as acceptance of us."

She went to her truck, got in, grabbed the steering wheel, and rested her forehead against the backs of her hands. She took deep shuddering breaths and waited until her breathing and heartbeat were under control before driving away.

"We're having a party this Saturday night." Alice Faye's announcement at the breakfast table the next morning startled everyone.

"A party?" Ciana exclaimed. "Why?"

"Because the new road to the stable's in place, because the new chicken coop is full of new chickens, because Angela's going back to Texas on Monday"—Angela nodded to confirm—"and because we've worked like dogs for weeks and it's time to celebrate. I've invited Arie's folks, Eric and Abbie, Cecil, Mr. Boatwright and his wife, and anyone else I can think of before Saturday."

Garret's eyes lit up. "We're having a barbie?"

"And all the fixins', plus pie, cake, and watermelon, and fresh-churned ice cream."

"And beer?"

"And sweet tea too," Alice Faye said.

"All right!"

Saturday midday, Jon and Garret dug a fire pit for roasting meat, while inside the trailer the air hung heavy with the smells of tangy sauces, baked beans, buttery pie crusts, and chocolate cake. Ciana and Eden set up borrowed tables on the lawn. They draped twinkly lights on everything standing upright and set groupings of candles on every flat surface. By nightfall, the lawn looked like a fairy land, guests were spread out on chairs and blankets under the lights and stars, and ribs and burgers were sputtering on a fire.

Garret hooked up his and Eden's iPods to portable speakers. Abbie's baby, Aaron, was set into a portable baby swing beside one table, and Soldier was assigned to keep watch so that Abbie and Eric could eat and mingle. And when the fireflies began coming out, the music went slow and soft with the sound from plaintive guitars. People clustered into groups to talk about the storm, to lament those lost, celebrate new beginnings, and share their stories.

In the light of the fire Ciana watched Jon relax, was grateful to her mother for suggesting the party. She took his hand, said, "Walk with me." He had mastered walking in the cast by now, but she took her time, in no hurry to get where she wanted to go. She stopped inside the flattened ground where the house had once stood, and told him about her meeting with Hastings. "I want your input for the rebuild. What would you like in a new house?"

"You," he said, kissing her. "Naked."

Delighted, she laughed and draped her arms over his shoulders. This was the warm, sexy Jon she'd fallen in love with, before the storm had waylaid their plans. "So you still want to get married?"

"Not until this cast comes off."

"When's that?"

"I was going to surprise you. Garret and I are driving Mom to the airport, then heading to my doc's office and his cast-removal saw."

"So I should find us a preacher?"

"Hold off. Have to get the muscle strong again." He pulled her closer. "Want to be a hundred percent when I take you to bed."

She kissed him, remembering the nights they'd almost made love, when he'd made her blood run hot and set her skin on fire. She whispered, "Dance with me, cowboy. Like the first time."

He took her in his arms, nuzzled her neck. "You going to stay awake?"

"Wide awake." He chuckled, and she laid her cheek in the crook of his neck. "You smell like charcoal and wood fire."

"And you smell like heaven."

They clung to each other, swaying and talking under the stars until the silence behind them told them that their guests had gone home. The sounds of cleanup did not move them apart either, and at some point the others drifted off to bed. Garret left the music playing, and nature let the stars burn more brightly than Ciana had ever seen them shine. Jon had returned to her.

Ciana woke to the sound of Jon whistling in the barn below. She'd overslept. Even Eden was up. She raked her fingers through her hair, reveling in the afterglow from the night before, of how she and Jon had kissed and touched, and longed for a place where they might have lain down together, thigh-high cast and all. She stretched lazily, finally rose, and dressed. She came down the ladder, only to be captured by Jon's arms from behind.

"Breakfast bell rang thirty minutes ago."

"I have connections with the cook. She'll feed me," Ciana said with a laugh, and, turning, kissed Jon languidly.

"Go, before I jump your body."

She blew him a kiss and ducked away. "I must ask your mother how she raised such a sex-crazed guy before she goes!"

"Me!" he yelped. "You're the one who kept me up half the night."

"Get used to it!" She darted out the door.

In the trailer, while Angela was in the bedroom packing, Ciana wolfed down leftover biscuits and gravy. "Happy, are we?" Alice Faye asked, plopping another biscuit on Ciana's plate.

"Very happy. Get the calendar. I'm looking for a wedding date."

Just then Angela emerged from the bedroom. "Did I hear the word 'wedding'?"

"It was mentioned," Alice Faye said.

Angela was all smiles. "Come on, soon to be daughter-in-law. Take a stroll with me. I need to stretch my legs before I sit on an airplane for hours."

Outside, Angela tucked her arm through Ciana's, and Soldier fell in beside them. "I know you've been concerned about Jon's moodiness."

"I think we got over that hurdle last night. He was his old self again."

"That's because we found Isabella's ring."

"I thought it was lost."

"He *thought* he'd lost it and it was breaking his heart. At first he thought he'd left it in the bedroom at the house. Then he recalled putting it someplace else but couldn't remember where. That short-term memory business really had him torn up."

The pieces of the puzzle fell into place for Ciana. That was why he'd seemed so distant once back from the hospital. He'd been searching his damaged memory for the ring. "Good grief! I love the ring, it's beautiful, but it's Jon I want."

Angela patted Ciana's shoulder. "That's what I told him. I said, 'Son, that girl will marry you if you put a cigar band on her finger.'" Ciana laughed, and Angela leaned closer. "But good news. We found it in some old trunk up in the loft."

Ciana stopped. Olivia's trunk. The quilts, diaries, and memorabilia. She'd all but forgotten the trunk since before the storm.

Angela said, "I guess he tucked it in there for safekeeping, but the concussion erased the memory. He was so happy when we dug it out."

Mystery solved. "Me too. I'm sorry that you'll have to come all the way back for the wedding, but Jon refuses to limp down the aisle." The warm sunlight sharpened the edges of shadows cast by the barn.

"Don't care."

"Well, this way you can give me a guest list. Jon was no help. And I need your advice on inviting his father. Jon . . . He didn't sound in favor of it. But it doesn't seem right to me not to ask him."

Angela sighed. "I understand. The stroke has not dealt kindly with Wade Soder. He's a bitter man."

Time slowed then ground to a halt. And Ciana's world turned upside down.

43

"Excuse me . . . What did you say?"

Angela puckered her brow. "I—I'm not sure. Did I upset you?"

"You called him Wade *Soder*."

Ciana suddenly felt rooted to the ground, unable to move. In the distance a horse whinnied.

"Oh that!" Angela sounded relieved. "I see how you can be confused. Soder was my married name. Mercer is my family name. I took it back after the divorce, and Jon said he wanted to take it too. He and his dad never did get along. Wade was hard on the boy. When Jon was little we used to fight about how he treated our son." Angela crossed her arms. "The only thing they had in common were horses. Wade was good with animals, not so much with people. Even after we were divorced, Jon tried to connect with his dad. Spent a summer working with Wade here in Windemere when he was seventeen, but it was a bust."

The words rolled over Ciana like the freight train sound of the tornado.

Angela glanced at the silent Ciana. "Good to meet Bill Pickins last night, though. Jon liked Bill and Essie a lot, plus Bill knew Wade from when he was growing up."

"Wade once lived in Windemere?" Ciana struggled to keep her tone even, her voice steady.

"Roy Soder, Wade's daddy, was adopted and grew up here, but he hated this place. Apparently he left here under a cloud. He always said someone had stolen his family's land, but I never knew if it was true or not." Every word pierced Ciana like hammer-driven nails. She almost staggered. Olivia had bought the Soder land for back taxes. And, now she realized, as an act of revenge.

"Roy was married to Dovey, a girl he'd gotten pregnant and was forced to marry in an old-fashioned shotgun wedding. I never knew her, but I always felt sorry for her. She died from cervical cancer when Wade was just a child. By then the three of them lived in Texas and Roy worked in the oil fields. Once Dovey died Roy couldn't care for Wade, so he was shipped back to her relatives."

Angela's voice droned on, telling a story that was dismantling Ciana's world, brick by brick. At least the storm's damage had been swift.

"Then one day Roy got hurt on the job and got a settlement from the oil company. Right about that time Dovey's family—they lived back in the hills somewhere—decided to move east and Wade went back to Texas to live with Roy. He was fifteen, and Roy was a poor excuse for a father, an alcoholic, too, but Wade lived with him because he had no place else to go. He found work on a ranch near Dallas working with horses." She smiled. "That's where we met. I took a summer job at the ranch when we were both in our twenties." Angela smiled wistfully. "He had the prettiest green eyes, and I fell for him like a rock hitting rock."

Ciana had fallen under such a spell herself over Jon.

"We lived with Roy for a while, but Roy didn't like me and I didn't like Roy. Wade was caught between us. I felt sorry about that, but Roy was a mean old cuss and after Jon was born, I didn't want Jon around the old man.

"Once we moved out, Roy went back to working in the fields. He died in an explosion when Jon was seven, but you know that part." Angela pushed her thick hair away from her neck in the rising morning heat, quietly said, "Wade would have been far better off growing up here. Roy was bitter and hateful, not fit to raise a son. He hung on to a grudge like a tick to a dog. Good thing he never had another child."

Ciana's topsy-turvy world became a nightmare landscape. Olivia's handwritten words sprang to life: *This is my punishment. This is divine retribution. Oh God, what have I done?* Olivia's nights spent with Roy and a pregnancy now overshadowed two generations of Beauchamp women born years apart, her mother and herself. On a summer night the past and the present had collided when Ciana had met a man she called cowboy, and fallen in love with him. Fate had made a full circle.

Just hang on, she told herself. Right now, in this moment, composure meant everything. *Breathe in, breathe out.* "How sad for Jon," she managed to say.

"My papa was there for Jon growing up. A good man." Angela beamed Ciana a smile, oblivious to the wreckage her story had brought. "I think Jon's turned out pretty good in spite of Wade and Roy. And you're willing to marry him, so you must think so too."

"You know I do," Ciana whispered, unable to keep her voice from cracking.

Angela squeezed Ciana's hand. "You and Jon are different people from me and Wade, so don't think bad stuff is going to happen to the two of you. The two of you are going to make a good life for yourselves."

She forced herself to return Angela's smile, knowing there was no way to tell Angela Mercer that "bad stuff" had already happened many years before, long before Ciana and Jon were ever born.

Ciana kept her silence for days after Angela was gone, but the weight of the discovery was suffocating. Sooner or later she had to tell Jon and her mother what she knew. Once the genie was out of the bottle, once she shared the information and Olivia's speculation, there would be no turning back. And as for her and Jon, decisions would have to be made. Still, for just a while she could shield them from what was going to hurt them far worse than any violent storm had.

During her time of silence, she watched Jon, freed from the odious cast, again ride his horse, practice turning and cutting and roping, all the things he'd once done with ease. The doctor had warned Jon to resume normal activity slowly, rebuild the muscle with care. It had been like asking water to flow uphill. He wasn't careful, and only Alice Faye's badgering slowed him down. But he was happy. Ciana grieved, knowing she was going to be the person that shattered his happiness, and her mother's peace.

She poured herself into hard work, but late one sweltering

afternoon as Ciana left the shed housing her farm equipment, Eden stood with crossed arms barring her path to the trailer.

"Talk to me," Eden said, without preamble. "Something's wrong. Something's going on with you. I can see it in your eyes. Tell me."

Ciana was hot, sweaty, and tired, but seeing the determined look on Eden's face, she realized that Eden wouldn't be put off. She needed to tell someone. Why not Eden, who'd helped her read the diaries? "After I clean up," she said. "Meet me in the loft."

"If you try and run, I'll send the dog after you."

Eden waited patiently for Ciana, riffling through a laundry list of what the problem might be. Crop blight? Broken equipment that she had no money to repair? A break between her and Jon? Eden discarded the last one quickly. They'd acted so happy the night of the party. It was just lately that Ciana had fallen prey to some dark power.

Ciana climbed the ladder and found Eden waiting for her on the quilt with a bottle of wine. A fan had been brought up weeks before, but the loft was hot and the fan's work futile. Eden held up the bottle, but Ciana shook her head. "This must be serious if wine won't help," Eden said. "You're scaring me." She set the bottle aside.

Ciana wrapped her arms around her scrunched-up knees. "Just listen," she said. "Don't interrupt. I have to get it out in one piece."

Eden listened with escalating shock to what Angela had told Ciana in all innocence. "Holy crap," was all she said when the story was over.

Ciana cried helplessly. "I've been over this in my head a hundred times, Eden. If Roy fathered Mom, then she and Wade are half siblings. And that makes Jon and me"—she swiped the back of her hand across her eyes—"cousins, I think. So I have to tell them. They need to know that we may all be related by blood."

Eden had been the one who'd urged Ciana to keep Olivia's secret suspicion about her baby's father quiet. Now there was no way that it could be held back. *"May be."* Eden stressed the words. "But even if it's true, yes, it will hurt your mother, but I don't think it will matter to Jon. Question is, does it matter to *you* if you marry one of your kin?"

Ciana straightened. Just like that, Eden had fingered the one thing Ciana had not verbalized, even to herself. Did it matter to her? She bit her lower lip hard. She'd thought out every implication, every ramification of marrying Jon. "If we're related, then getting married would be unnatural, Eden. You know what I mean."

"If he's kin. We don't know if Olivia was right. She never knew for certain either, and it colored her whole life." An-other sickening thought slammed Eden. . . . Marrying each other might even be illegal, but she wouldn't say that aloud. Ciana was broken enough.

Ciana's chin trembled, and a tear trickled down one cheek. "Why is this happening to us, Eden? I love Jon so much. It isn't fair."

Eden scooted closer, put her arms around her friend, her own heart ripped in half. "You'll get through this just like you got through all the bad things that have happened. You're a Beauchamp, remember?"

Ciana hung her head. She felt worn down, not one bit like her Beauchamp forerunners, women who overcame all obstacles. "I need to go for a ride and clear my head." She stood, her knees the consistency of jelly. "Will you keep my secret? Just until I figure out what to say to Jon and Mom?"

"I may not be able to keep it from Garret. He'll know something's wrong the second he looks at me. I'm sorry, but that's the truth."

Ciana cringed, but she understood. She didn't want to drive a wedge between Eden and Garret. Life was full of too many wedges as it stood. "If you must," she whispered.

"Garret will help," Eden called as Ciana clambered down the ladder. Eden stayed put in the loft listening to Ciana's movements as she readied her horse, but once they rode off, Eden dragged the incriminating diaries out of the trunk to reread. Every entry about Olivia's nights with Roy and the aftermath made perfect sense. Every passage about a baby she refused to love was clarion clear.

If only Ciana had never found the old journals. If only the tornado winds had blown these books with their shattering confessions to smithereens. If only those long-ago nights between Olivia and Roy had never happened. If only.

R ain fell in hard and unrelenting streams from a lead
   gray sky during the next two days. Fields and pastures
became soggy pools of mud, bringing work at Bellmeade to
a standstill. Ciana wondered if perhaps the rains were sympathetic tears from heaven shed on her behalf. The tornado
had left destruction and devastation in its wake, but time and
nature would heal the land. The devastation inside her heart,
within her soul, was permanent.

By noon of the second day, tempers were short and patience worn thin. Garret whisked Eden off to Nashville with
no promise of a quick return, Alice Faye baked batches of
cookies between hands of solitaire and TV game shows, and
while the horses fretted in their stalls from confinement,
Ciana asked Jon to climb up into the loft with her.

Arriving early, she spread out the quilt from the old
trunk away from the open window area and any blowing
rain. She stuck Post-it notes inside selected pages of the
diaries and stacked the old books in a pile. She turned on

the fan to circulate the air and lit an old hurricane lamp to chase the gloom. She was ready, yet tensed when she heard Jon's boots on the ladder. She thought of the last time they'd been up there together. It had been raining that day, too, the day he'd asked her to marry him before the winds of spring had wrecked her home. Today she would unleash another kind of wind that could wreck their lives and happiness.

"Hey," he said, coming over the edge, his smile big and happy. It stabbed her like a knife. "Glad you thought of this." He eased beside her on the quilt. "I don't think I could have polished leather saddles one more time." When she didn't smile, he dipped his head and frowned. "You don't look happy. What's up?"

She managed a smile. "I'm happy to see you. But I need to talk to you."

"About what?"

"Remember when I told you about my grandmother's diaries? The storm destroyed the ones in the house, but not these." She pointed at the short stack, took a breath. "I need for you to read a few entries. Then we'll talk." She handed him the first book where she'd marked a passage about teenaged Olivia's infatuation with Roy. She watched his eyes skim the page, her heart hammering. When his gaze stopped dead still, she knew he'd realized who Roy had been.

He looked up. "Soder! This guy's name was Roy Soder? Like my grandfather?"

"It is, or was, your grandfather, Jon. Your mother told me some of your family background before she left. And of how you both changed your last name after her divorce."

He shrugged. "Okay. A weird coincidence. Are you mad because I didn't tell you?"

"No. But . . . well, read these entries." She handed him the most damning of the diaries.

He read, recoiled. "Is this for real? They had an affair and she got pregnant?"

"It's for real."

He reread the words, lingered over Olivia's speculations about the father of her daughter, named Alice Faye. Ciana knew the passages by heart. He set the book aside, stared out at the rain for quite a while, and Ciana gave him plenty of time to absorb the implications of Olivia's fears.

Finally he turned to Ciana. "So if she's right, we're related?"

"Looks that way. Some sort of cousin." Her voice quavered.

"Who have you told?"

"Eden."

"Your mother?"

"Not yet."

He swore, raised himself up to his knees, raked a hand through his hair. "I hardly remember that crazy old man. He ruined my dad preaching his hate about something that happened long before I was born. Dad once told me that the Soders had been screwed out of their inheritance by someone." Jon shrugged. "I was a kid. I lived in Texas and I didn't care."

"It was my grandmother who took the Soder farm over and rolled it over into Bellmeade. Remember the day we visited him in the Murfreesboro nursing home, and the reaction he had when he heard I was a Beauchamp? Now it makes sense."

Ciana rested her hand on his arm. "It would have been your land, Jon. And your mother's." She watched his face as he weighed her words. "You could have built your horse-training business on that land."

"I can build my business back in Texas, Ciana. I wanted to

build it here to be near you." He studied her. "I know what I want. Question is, what do you want?"

"You." Her voice shook with the single word. "But . . . if we're really kin . . ." She was scared and felt sick.

"You have me. Always have."

She couldn't look him in the eye. "I just never thought us falling in love could become the punch line for a redneck joke."

"I'm not laughing."

Emotion filled her throat. She wiped her eyes. "I have to tell Mom."

"So tell her. We can't let some long-dead man and woman and what they did together destroy us. If you don't want to marry me, you tell me. You dump me because you don't love me, not because of this. I don't give a damn where either of us came from. Or *who* we came from. This mess is not our fault."

But blame wasn't an issue. If they shared bloodlines their marriage could be considered incestuous. The very word made her shudder. The fury in Jon's voice made her pull back.

When she didn't respond, he asked, "Is this being-related business going to matter to you, Ciana? To us? You need to tell me now."

But words stuck in her throat. She felt like she was drowning, like she couldn't find the surface. The depths of the problem transcended the two of them. It reached to the unborn.

When she didn't answer, he stood, stared down at her. She desperately wanted to speak to him, say something, but no words made it through her throat. "I guess you're already telling me how you feel."

"No, Jon! Wait." She struggled to her feet.

But he was already down the ladder, and minutes later, she

heard the barn door open and the truck start and drive away. She began to cry, shivering and alone, shell-shocked. A future without Jon was no future at all. She bent, gathered up the books with shaking hands. The nightmare wasn't over. She still had to face Alice Faye Beauchamp.

Eden sat in the coffee shop with Garret, staring out the window and watching the rain turn a sidewalk into a mini-stream. Together they'd gone to a movie and walked a busy mall, but neither had improved her mood.

"You going to tell me what's got you snarled up?" Garret asked, following a sip of his coffee.

"It shows, huh?"

"The tornado was more subtle, love."

Eden sighed. "Trouble for Ciana and Jon."

"How so? Jon's happy."

"He won't be after today."

"Talk to me. Hard to be sympathetic when we're talking in riddles. Besides, my editor's getting a bit bothered that I've been here for months and still haven't delivered one story about traveling round America with my girl. We need to get on the road. Is this wedding of Ciana's ever going to happen?"

Eden sighed. "Don't know." He looked confused. "It's a long story."

He glanced out at the pouring rain. "Looks like we have all afternoon. I'll buy more coffee."

When he resettled with the fresh cups of coffee and a pastry, Eden launched into the story of what was now facing Ciana and Jon. She started in the past, with Olivia, Charles, and Roy and finished with her and Ciana's discussion about telling Jon and Alice Faye. Garret listened, never interrupted, his features changing from curious interest to a frown to disbelief and shake of his head when she wound down the narrative.

Silence fell between them at the end, held, until Garret said, "I'm gobsmacked!"

Eden hadn't heard the word before, but its meaning was obvious. "It's put Ciana in a tailspin too."

"It's a pisser, all right. What now?"

"Don't know. I don't think Jon will care, but Alice Faye . . . well, that's the tough one. She and Olivia were always at odds. Now it makes sense."

"Poor Mum Alice."

Eden struggled to hold back tears. "They're my family, Garret. Ciana and Arie were like sisters. When I was younger, I wanted Olivia to adopt me. Yes, Alice Faye drank, but never in public. She was never hateful to us girls. It was the family's little secret, hard for Ciana growing up, but in spite of it they were a tight family. I wanted to belong to them. Arie's family was too big and noisy, but the Beauchamps—well, that was where I wanted to be. After we came home from Italy and my mother left town, when I didn't have anyone, Ciana took me in and Alice Faye 'adopted' me. She's made me feel I'm as good as her own. Ciana didn't mind one bit. I think it took some of that being-a-Beauchamp pressure off her. Alice Faye has taught me about planting and gardening and preserving food and baking . . . all the things Gwen couldn't manage with her bipolar devils. Mum Alice's life is simple and now that she's sober, she talks all the time about being happy. This stuff about Olivia and Roy . . ." She looked into Garret's eyes. "What if it destroys her?"

Garret reached over, engulfed Eden's hand in his. "Don't like seeing the ones I care about hurt. Especially you."

"I don't matter in this."

"You matter to me." He scooted his chair around, butted it up to hers, and put his arms around her. "In Australia there are laws about intermarriage. Some relationships among family members can get away with it. Others can't. All wound up in genetics, with passing on recessive genes."

"Don't know what the laws are here." She leaned into his shoulder.

"I think we should give Ciana and Jon and Mum Alice some space tonight. Don't you?"

Reluctantly, she nodded, knowing that all the space in the world wasn't going to change the circumstances if Alice Faye was the child of Olivia and Roy Soder.

45

Ciana came into the trailer, saw her mother sitting at the small bench table and staring at a bottle of gin. All the air left Ciana's lungs. "Mama? What are you doing?"

"Thinking hard about how much I want a drink." Alice Faye looked like a rag doll with hollow eyes.

"Where did you get it? I thought you'd dumped it all."

"I'd hid it in the barn a year ago. Remembered it just this morning after I read the diaries. Image of the hiding place just popped into my mind." She snapped her fingers.

Fear clutched Ciana. The gin bottle stood on the table like an accusatory finger. Her mother had been sober for so long, and now it would be Ciana's fault if she picked up the bottle again. Ciana inched forward, slipped into the folding chair always set up across the table's bench seat. "Have you—?"

"No. Not yet."

"Have you called your sponsor?" Ciana reached for her cell. "I can call her."

"Stop."

Ciana swallowed bile. She was a child again, scared and afraid, seeing her mother slumped over, drunk. Tears filled her eyes. "Mom, please . . ."

"Please what? Back off." Her mother offered a withering stare, making Ciana flinch.

Ciana had brought Alice Faye the diaries right after Jon had driven off, told her mother the marked pages were a "must read." Self-loathing filled Ciana. "I should have never given the diaries to you."

"Course you should have. Now I know *the truth*. Isn't truth supposed to set a person free? I don't feel free, I feel betrayed. My whole life could be a lie." Unshed tears gleamed in Alice Faye's eyes. "How does she keep doing it? How does that old woman keep hurting me? Even from her grave!"

"Your life's not a lie, Mom."

"The hell it isn't! I was a Beauchamp, daughter of—who, Ciana? Who am I the daughter of?" She held out her hands as if balancing a scale. "Am I Roy Soder's daughter? Am I Charles's daughter? And who in hell was Roy Soder to make such a mess of things?"

"Mom . . . don't . . ." Ciana pushed the heels of her palms into her eyes. "She—she never meant for things to go the way they did. It was a bad time for her . . . those nights he came and stayed. The two of them were a time bomb waiting to go off. There were other diaries. Before the storm—You would see . . ."

"Well, ain't that a shame." Venom filled Alice Faye's words. "Two people who couldn't keep their hands off each other."

"She got even with him," Ciana offered desperately. "She bought his farm for back taxes. She took his land. He never forgave her for that."

"Not surprised about that either. Olivia's way. Don't get

mad, get even." Silence fell between them. The window AC units hummed in the background, worked to cool the muggy interior.

Ciana searched for a way to build a bridge between herself and her mother. "Roy poisoned Wade against the Beauchamp name too. Jon—" She couldn't finish.

Alice Faye looked stricken. "She poisoned all of us, didn't she? Me and you and Jon. I'm sorry, baby girl. You were the only thing I ever did right for her. For me too."

"I—I can't help what happened way back then, and how things turned out. Neither can you, Mom."

Alice Faye leaned back into the vinyl upholstery. "What did Jon say when you told him? He does know, doesn't he?"

"I told him. He says he loves me, no matter what."

"This is a real mess." Alice Faye eyed the bottle, making Ciana's stomach lurch. "I need some time to think."

"I . . . I don't know if . . ."

"If you should leave me alone? Afraid I'll go on a bender?" She touched the bottle. "Guess that's why I hid it. Insurance against a bad time that might come on me. Turns out, the sky has fallen in."

"You made it through the tornado. To getting Bellmeade up and going again. You take care of us, Mom. I—I don't want to lose you."

Alice Faye studied Ciana. "The tornado didn't hurt near this bad, little girl."

Ciana's chin trembled. Her mother made a dismissal motion with her fingers. "Go on now. Taking this drink is on me. Nothing you can do to stop me."

The rest of the day, Ciana kept herself busy. She went for a long ride. She mucked stalls, groomed horses, was relieved when none of the boarders came to ride. She knew she could never have stood around making small talk with them. She texted Eden, asked her and Garret to come back. They did, but Alice Faye locked everyone out of the trailer. Garret went to town for food that none of them ate. They sat on the ground under the stars by the fire pit and Ciana told them everything that had happened. Garret kept the fire going, but late into the night, Jon had not returned. Garret stood and stretched. "We'll bed in the camper. You have the loft to yourself."

Eden stood next to him, dragged Ciana up, too, hugged her friend. "Just holler if you need me. He'll come back," she told Ciana.

"Course he will. His horse is still here."

Garret gave her shoulders a brotherly squeeze. "No . . . his heart is still here."

Ciana took one last walk around the yard, Soldier by her side, then climbed into the loft. The sleeping bag had been replaced by a large air mattress and was made up like a bed. She crawled under the covers, lay awake in the dark, waiting for the sound of Jon's truck. It never came.

Early the next morning, Ciana went to the trailer. Her heart sank. No smells of cooking breakfast came from inside. She thought back to the hundreds of mornings throughout her childhood she'd been lured into the kitchen by the aromas of coffee and her mother's baking biscuits. She blew out a breath, went inside. All was dark and the back bedroom door was closed. She turned on lights, went to the fridge, stared inside, realized she'd gag if she ate anything.

Minutes later Eden and Garret came inside to see her sitting at the table and staring into space. "Mom not up?" Eden asked.

"Doesn't seem like it."

Eden crossed her arms. "I think I can whip us up something. I've watched her make biscuits a hundred times."

"Have at it."

"I'll do the coffee," Garret said.

No one mentioned that Jon's truck was still missing.

Eden did a passable job of the biscuits along with a serving bowl filled with scrambled eggs. They were almost finished when they heard the click of the locked bedroom turn. Alice Faye shuffled down the hall. Ciana peered at her anxiously. Her mother's face looked puffy.

"Coffee?" Garret asked as she slid into a seat at the tiny table.

"Okay." Tension hung like crepe paper. "Stop staring at me," she said. "I'm not a time bomb."

"Are you . . . ?" Ciana said.

"All right? No. Yesterday I wanted to go far away. But where would I go? Town's still tore up. Bellmeade is all I've ever known. Jackson was right when he said we should have moved away after we were married." She shook her head. "Olivia wouldn't hear of it."

"Mom—"

She held up her hand. "Need to work the garden today. Weeds grow no matter what's going on."

"I'll help," Eden said, more eagerly than necessary.

"You make good biscuits?"

"Great," Garret said, placing one on a fresh plate for Alice Faye.

"I had a good teacher," Eden said.

299

"I'll try one."

Ciana stood awkwardly, at loose ends, but knowing she had the day's chores ahead of her. "Horses need tending."

"Get to it, then." Alice Faye dribbled honey on her biscuit. "I'll fix chili for supper."

Ciana wanted to touch her mother, but held back. Her mother might be hurting, but she understood that farm life went on no matter what. They were all hurting. And where in the hell was Jon?

Hours later she had cleaned the stalls and put the horses out to the pasture, and was returning from a hard ride on Firecracker with Soldier at her side. Gratefully, Garret had taken Caramel for a workout at the track. She rode up just as a horse trailer pulled into her driveway and stopped alongside the barn. The dog took off barking furiously at the truck's cab and the man inside. She didn't recognize the truck or trailer. She groaned, not wanting to face any visitors, wondered if it might be another of her boarders come to remove a horse along with another hit to her bottom line. Ciana called off the dog, cantered up to the cab. She dipped downward, saw the driver, was taken aback. "You!"

Enzo's man, the one who worked for him in Italy, smiled up at her. "It is I, Alberto."

She quickly dismounted. "Well, hey! Welcome. Is . . . is Enzo back in Nashville?"

"No, *signorina*. Mr. Bertinalli has sent me to make a delivery."

"To Bellmeade?"

He hopped out of the cab, ignoring the dog, and walked

to the back of the trailer. He opened the gate, went inside, and moments later emerged with a beautiful colt. The horse was jet-black, and she could tell he was young. Alberto took the halter rope, held it out to her. "*Per te*. From the Bertinalli stables to yours. A gift."

46

"A gift? Why?" Ciana stared at Alberto in disbelief, refusing to take the rope.

The man looked confused. "Signore Bertinalli heard about your misfortune with the tornado. He also has told me you will be starting a new business training horses. He wishes you to have this yearling."

"This horse must be worth thousands. I—I can't simply take him."

"But of course you can. He is a gift."

"You came all the way from Italy to give me this horse?"

Alberto laughed. "I was sent to deliver another horse to a gentleman in Nashville, too, but this horse is for you. He has been through the quarantine period."

Mallory's father, Ciana thought.

Alberto patted the horse's muscled neck. "He is a fine horse."

"I can see that." The horse had locked his attention onto Firecracker.

"Signore Bertinalli said that he does not know from the wild mustangs you plan to bring in, but that this horse is of old and noble blood—Calabrese, Andalusian, and Arabian—the product of many years of careful breeding. We call him *Notte Vento*, Night Wind, but you may name him as you see fit."

Still she hesitated. "His name is beautiful. Enzo is too kind."

"Signore Bertinalli is a generous man. He is able to do as he pleases, and it will please him for you to receive his gift."

Again he handed the halter rope to Ciana. This time she took it. "I don't know what to say." She couldn't take her eyes off the sculpted animal.

Alberto reached through the window of the truck, picked up a large, flat envelope. "These are his papers and a note from Signore Bertinalli. Shall I tell him you are pleased?"

"Very pleased. Very honored." She stroked the animal's sleek back. "I will write Enzo, tell him of my joy. Thank you."

Alberto smiled, bowed his head slightly. "I will leave you then."

"But . . . but I should give you some tea . . ." She fumbled with words, felt her face redden. She had nothing to offer him in return. The Lincoln was gone so her mother and Eden must have gone into town.

Alberto shook his head. "No, no. I must return quickly. My plane is scheduled for later tonight." He opened the door of the truck and got inside. "Oh, one thing. I hope your Italian is good. Notte understands only Italian." He grinned mischievously. "But he learns quickly. Like Alberto." He saluted her and backed the truck and trailer up, made a wide arc, and followed the driveway to the frontage road.

Ciana's heart thudded and brimmed with gratitude watching him go. Finally she turned to the horse. *"Venire."* Come.

She led the colt to a stall in the barn, poured some oats into the feeding bin, and hoped that Eden remembered way more Italian than she did.

After supper Ciana, her mother, and friends came to the barn to marvel at the colt. "Don't know much about horses," Garret said, "but even I can see this one is fine!"

Eden spoke to Notte in Italian, and the animal pricked up its ears. "Got to brush up. I just told Notte he's beautiful and to sleep well. Don't know any horse language."

Jon did, but he was still missing—two full days and a night. After Eden and Garret left, Alice Faye lingered. "He'll come back."

"Don't know if I care," Ciana said, angry and anxious. "*We* didn't run off."

"Would have if I could have." Alice Faye studied her daughter. "What do you want to do with the diaries?"

Ciana wanted to burn them. "Nothing just now."

"Any ideas how to fix this mess?"

"Not just yet."

"Let me know when you do."

Before her mother could leave, Ciana blurted, "Do you think Roy knew? Ever wondered about Olivia's baby?"

Alice Faye took her time answering. "The diary says the man left for Texas that spring. Growing a baby takes nine months, and it's a fact that after a man lies with a woman, he can't count, so, no, I don't think he ever knew."

"She must have lived in fear that he might one day meet up with you and wonder."

"My mother feared nothing, except maybe losing you." Alice Faye turned and left the barn, leaving Ciana alone in the gloom to wonder over the war between these two women for her allegiance.

That night Ciana again slept fitfully, dreamed of Italy and of riding Enzo's property that morphed into hers. Just before dawn, she woke with a start, saw a figure sitting cross-legged beside her mattress. She gasped, drew backward.

"It's me. Don't be scared." Jon's voice came softly from the dark.

She raised up, fully awake. She now saw him silhouetted against the loft's open area, etched against a graying sky. "You okay?"

"Better than I was when I left."

Anger boiled up. "You left me alone. You told me before that you'd never leave me and you did!"

"For that I'm sorry."

"Where did you go?"

"Just drove west on autopilot. I was in Memphis before I realized it. Drove on over to Arkansas. Got a room and a bar tab. Slept it off, started back late yesterday and drove all night."

"You. Left. Me." Her chin quivered.

He rose up on his knees. "Let me hold you."

She swatted at him. He caught her hands, gently laid her down on her side, wrapped her in his arms, spooned his body behind hers. She struggled, but not hard, nor for long. He felt so good pressed against her, his warm breath on the nape of her neck. She wanted to cry, but held off.

"Do you know the first thing I remembered when I came out of that coma?" He didn't wait for an answer. "You. It was like you were in my bloodstream, and firing off so much information I could hardly handle it. I knew what your skin felt like under my hands. What your hair smelled like. You were

305

my link to my past, a key. Other stuff came real slow, but not you, Ciana. You were fully there."

She wept quietly.

"I'll never leave again. I swear. I don't know how all this is going to turn out. I just know I love you and need to be with you, no matter what."

Her need for him was just as strong. "Morning's coming soon."

"Then just let me lie here with you until it does."

They came down from the loft when the sky streaked gold and pink. The day was promising to be hot and humid. In the barn, the horses shuffled, neighed with Jon's scent. He held Ciana's hand, glanced over at the stalls, drew up short. "Whoa. What have we here?" He crossed to the stall that held the new colt.

"He's a yearling named Notte. A gift from Enzo."

Jon pulled back from Ciana, then his gaze swept the horse. "Any strings?"

She arched an eyebrow at Jon. "Tornado booty," she said coolly. "He's being thoughtful and nice and thought Notte might eventually add quality to your breeding and training business."

Jon's eyes narrowed, then relaxed. "A few years before we can begin breeding him. In the meantime, he eats."

Testily she said, "I'll plant more alfalfa and corn. Beauty of owning a farm."

Jon looked contrite, gave Ciana a nod. "Beautiful horses. Beautiful women. The man has a good eye for both."

They went into the trailer together, faced the others. Jon

apologized for leaving. "Back now," Garret said. "Good thing. Someone's bringing a horse out for you to look over and maybe board here."

Jon poured himself a cup of coffee, squeezed in at the table. The atmosphere was subdued. Finally Alice Faye set out a plate of pastries, and said, "We all know what's happened, so maybe we should talk about it. Problem's not going away."

Jon's arm slid around Ciana's shoulders. "Suggestions?"

Garret and Eden exchanged looks. "Spent some time surfing the Web and learned some things," he told them.

"What things?" Ciana asked.

"You three"—he looked from Ciana to Jon and to Alice Faye—"have something at the ready that your grandmother never had. One of the perks of living in the twenty-first century. We have DNA testing. You can be tested and find out if you're related."

"You mean like on the *CSI* shows?" Alice Faye asked.

"That's right." Eden jumped in, as Garret had shown her the Web information and she'd read every word of it. "The test can establish any genetic links between Jon and Ciana. But it's best if you get tested, too, Alice. That'll settle everything once and for all." When there was no response, Eden hurtled ahead. "It can be done at a clinic in Nashville. It's painless. They'll just swab the inside of your mouth, send it off, and you'll get the results in the mail."

For a minute Ciana wasn't sure what was scarier—knowing, or not knowing. But not knowing had turned Olivia into a vengeful woman with a secret that had shaken three future lives.

"I'm in," Jon said, gripping her hand.

"Me too," Ciana said.

Alice Faye sat at rigid attention.

"The results are private, but there are home test kits," Garret added helpfully. "But a lab seems more trustworthy to me."

Ciana said, "You don't have to if you don't want to, Mom."

"But it'd be more conclusive if I do it too."

"Better," Garret said. "It's about you too."

Alice Faye gave a look that spoke only of pain, deep and thorough. She buried her face in her hands. The AC units kept humming. The noisy stove clock ground out a faint buzz. After awhile, Alice Faye straightened. "I reckon it makes sense for me to be tested. Find out once and for all who my daddy was."

Knowing once and for all. Would this solve a problem? Or open the lid on a box of more? Ciana hoped that knowing was better than not knowing. The test would be conclusive. The future was not.

Jon drove to the clinic in Nashville with Ciana and Alice Faye sandwiched in the front seat of his truck. He turned on the radio, let it blare out country music, making conversation on the ride impossible. It didn't matter because no one felt like talking. What was left to be said? Ciana had made an appointment, was told they'd first meet with a counselor, then samples of their DNA would be taken that would determine their genetic relationships.

Before driving off, Eden pulled Ciana aside. "Need to tell you something."

Eden looked nervous and on edge. "Couldn't bring it up at the table yesterday, but there's something else that I learned from the Internet." She wiped sweaty palms down her jeans. Ciana waited expectantly. Eden said, "Just to put your minds at rest, there's no law against related people getting married in Tennessee. It's one of nine states that allow even first cousins to marry."

If the remarks were meant to give Ciana comfort, they

didn't. "Didn't know that. What about having children? That all right too?"

The genetics of inbreeding. "I think genetics matter more if you're brother and sister."

That idea didn't free Ciana at all. Marrying kin held a taint that made her squirmy.

"No need to even think about that until you know for sure about your grandfather," Eden said hurriedly.

It was like looking down a dark well and being unable to see the bottom. "I'll keep it in mind," Ciana said, heading toward the truck.

Once the truck left, Eden told Garret, "Hope this works out for them."

"I do too."

Eden slipped her hand into Garret's. "Come with me. There's something I need to do, and I want you with me."

She led him to the barn, where they climbed up into the loft, and she opened the old trunk. She dug in one corner and pulled out a gray rectangular box wrapped in an old towel.

"Your mum's ashes?"

"Time to scatter them. I should have done it sooner."

"Don't you want the others here when you do it?"

Eden thought about it, had even planned it that way. But now seemed like the perfect time. "I don't think they need any more sad moments. Do you?"

Garret took the box and went down the ladder, Eden following him.

They went to the garden, with Soldier at their heels. The large garden had been blessed by sun and rain and was now lush with blooms and budding produce. Because it was early, there was a coolness in the air and a fragrance that Eden always associated with that time of the morning—fresh earth perfumed with growing things. She stopped in the middle of the acre-sized garden. Tomatoes grew on one side, pole beans on the other. Red and green. Balance. "Here," she said.

Garret opened the box and extracted a plastic bag, handed it to Eden. She cupped it in both hands, peered at the gray mass inside, knowing that this had once been her mother and that this tangible matter was all that remained. She had told herself she wouldn't cry, so she bit her lip hard in order to keep the promise. She also realized that she had nothing to say. She looked at Garret. "I—I don't have any words."

He touched her hair. "They're in your heart. You just have to dig them out."

"What do the Aborigines do when someone dies?"

"Sometimes they cut themselves."

The idea caused Eden to smile. "Already did that."

"Then just let go."

She carefully turned the bag, let the gray dust filter out. It was light, and an unexpected breeze caught it and sailed the powder away. She kept pouring a little at a time until the bag was empty and the blue sky and bright sun had turned the air brilliant and crystal clear once more. "Goodbye, Mother. I hope you're at peace." A lump clogged Eden's throat.

Garret took the bag, stuffed it into the box, and hiked it up under his arm. His other arm went around Eden. They turned and trudged back toward the trailer, the dog close on their heels.

The clinic was located between a hospital and a courthouse, a dour beige building without personality. Inside, the place held no charm, just a front desk, a few chairs. The main business of the place was paternity testing to determine if any given man had fathered a particular child. Ciana felt a pang for any kid who could be so easily classified to either receive or be rejected for child support, while the question, "Who's your daddy?" could be answered conclusively in a few days' time. One person would be happy, another not. DNA paternity testing, a double-edged sword.

The counselor who met with them in a tiny cubbyhole of an office was a man in his forties. He wore a lab coat, but the sleeves were too short and came off looking silly instead of professional. He explained about avuncular DNA testing, of how three potentially related people could be scientifically matched for comparison of genealogy. The three of them would have the inside of their cheeks swabbed, and the sample would be sent off to be tested for genetic markers. A forty-one marker test would be the most accurate, so that's the one they paid to have.

A tech rolled a long cotton-tipped swab on the inside of Ciana's cheek and popped it into a plastic tube and sealed it. Jon's cheek swab was also quick. Ciana's heart went out to her mother, who shut her eyes and held her breath for the tech when her turn came.

When the process was over, Jon asked, "How long before we know something?"

"Usually only takes a few days," the counselor said. "But these results might take a few weeks because we're going for a forty-one marker comparison. Takes a little longer."

A few weeks, Ciana thought. Until then their lives were on hold.

The three of them returned to the truck. Heat had been building, so Jon turned on the engine and the AC and rolled down the windows. Heat waves shimmered off the asphalt parking lot. Mesmerized, Ciana watched them dance like puppets on strings.

"Now what?" Alice Faye asked.

Jon shoved the gear handle into reverse. "Now we wait."

At Bellmeade there was plenty to do while they waited. Two people showed up wanting Jon to help them work with new saddle horses, and he took on the jobs. Ciana was busy cutting and putting up early alfalfa hay and tending cornfields. Eden and Garret took over the garden, left Alice Faye to the trailer where she kept laundry and food prep going. And in a walk that became a ritual, Ciana went to the mailbox at the end of every day. After three days, Jon stepped beside her, took her hand. "Want some company?"

"Yes," she said. And the two of them strolled down the long driveway, hand in hand, between the newly planted oak trees painstakingly mixed with the old growth to fetch whatever the postman brought. One letter came that totally took Ciana by surprise. It was postmarked Chicago and bore the address of Hastings Incorporated. She opened it on the spot while Jon waited. She skimmed it, smiled with satisfaction. "Gerald Hastings wants to build us a house. Imagine that."

Jon tipped his head to salute her. "Good. You'll need a house either way."

Either way. She wanted to live in the house with Jon. She slipped the letter back into the envelope, and at the road's edge put her arms around the man she loved, where they stood for a long, long time.

313

G arret liked sleeping under the stars at Bellmeade. Eden preferred a bed, even the camper, but the camper was closed in and hot in these early summer months, so sleeping bags under the stars did make sense. "We'll be sleeping outside a lot once we get on the road," he told her.

"What about crawly things? And wild animals?"

"I'll fight them off for you," he joked, adding, "plus we have Soldier with us." He ruffled the dog's fur.

The shepherd slept out with them, and that did make Eden feel better.

They each held their electronic tablets, Garret reading over the article he'd written and was getting ready to send off, and Eden with an ebook, when he said, "Want to head to Yosemite Park soon as we can get Jon and Ciana married off?"

"Okay," she said absently. The wait for the DNA results was taking forever, and like Garret, she was anxious to be on their journey too. The weather was good now, so travel and camping would be good also.

"Amazing what science can do with a dab of spit these days." He rolled up on his elbow, gazed down on Eden. "My family comes from a line of convicts. You aware of that?"

"You trying to frighten me off?"

He lowered his voice to a conspiratorial whisper. "Well, if we marry and have children, you might want to know who you're related to. Could be some wild-eyed pirate."

She put the tablet down, unable to concentrate when he kept interrupting. "Is that a proposal?"

He grinned. "I'll plan a better proposal for later."

She blew him a kiss, raised the tablet. "And don't worry about children. I'll never have any." Garret went silent. Too silent. Eden glanced over at him staring down at her. "What?"

"No children? No wee people who look like us?"

"No." She studied his face, which looked as if she'd slapped him. Suddenly the conversation took on a whole new dimension. "Garret, I'm not being difficult here. It's a fact that bipolar passes genetically. It hit Mom when she was a teen. Ruined her life. So far it's passed me by, but it can happen to me too. I've told you that. I won't bring a baby into the world knowing this is hanging over its head."

"I—I just never thought I wouldn't have kids. I'm the last of my family."

She grasped the dynamic for him. With Phillip gone, Garret was the only Locklin son. "I thought you had an uncle."

"Three daughters."

"Maybe they'll take up the Beauchamp tradition of keeping their family name."

"They're on my mother's side. Not my dad's."

She could see that she'd rocked him with her announcement. She felt bad about it, but she knew she'd feel worse if any kid of theirs was saddled with bipolar disorder. She

315

reached up, touched his cheek. "I had a horrible childhood, Garret. I know what bipolarism is like. I know the unhappiness it can bring." His expression was still troubled. She raised up, gave him a kiss. "Let's not talk about this now. Let's talk about something fun and happy." She snuggled closer to him. "Show me on your tablet the trip we'll be taking."

He moved slowly, but finally lay back down, his head touching hers, and raised his tablet, aglow with a map. "Thought we'd start here." He touched Yosemite, traced a meandering path through the upper plains and into the northwest.

She made appropriate sounds of enthusiasm, but felt his subtle disappointment and withdrawal. Later Eden lay awake watching the stars travel across the sky, and wondered if something had broken between them.

The results of the DNA tests took three and a half weeks getting to Bellmeade, and although she'd been waiting for it to arrive, when Ciana removed the oversized envelope from the mailbox, her heartbeat jumped into overdrive. In her hand she held her future, determined by sins from the past. Jon asked, "What is it?"

"The answers."

As they walked back to the trailer, she held it gingerly, like a bomb that might explode any second. The others were setting up for dinner on a folding table close to the trailer, which was just too hot and small to be crammed into for the meal. "You got it." Eden was the first to realize what Ciana held. All other movement stopped.

"I haven't opened it."

Alice Faye squared her shoulders. "Come. Sit. We'll read it together."

316

Ciana wasn't sure they should, but her mother was.

Garret and Jon quickly set folding chairs in a circle and they all took a seat, attention glued on Ciana. She stared down at the envelope, decided she shouldn't be the one to open it. She handed it to her mother. "You open it. Jon and I have made up our minds what we'll do no matter what it says."

Jon nodded, leaving no doubt as to their choice—they would marry.

Alice Faye recoiled from the envelope, but she took it, fanned the air with it, then thrust it at Eden. "I think my other daughter should open it."

"Me? I—I—"

"Do it," Ciana said.

Eden tore open the envelope and extracted several sheets of paper. "Top paper is a cover letter with results spelled out."

"Tell us!" Ciana growled.

Eden's eyes went wide as she read silently. She looked up, her face absolutely blank. "It does appear that the three of you do have something in common."

Ciana's heart fell with a sickening thud.

Impishly Eden said, "Belly buttons. You all have belly buttons."

Garret was the first to catch on. He roared out a laugh. "Good one, love!"

Seconds later Ciana and Jon caught on too. Only Alice Faye sat with her brow puckered. Eden leaned over. "No shared genes between Ciana and Jon. Although there is proof positive that you and Ciana are related."

Alice Faye snatched the letter, began to weep. "She got it wrong. Olivia was wrong. Charles is my father."

Jon pulled Ciana to her feet, buried his hands in her thick cinnamon-colored hair. "You get a preacher. And if he has to

317

marry us out here in an open field, let's get it done before some other disaster comes along."

"I'm on it," Ciana said, raising on her toes and kissing him to Eden and Garret's applause.

Much later, after glasses of wine and beer, and water for Alice Faye, Ciana found her mother sitting alone outside and gazing up at the moon. She dragged a chair over and joined her. "You all right?"

"First time I've been at peace since this whole thing started. Amazing world we live in. Just the swish of a swab and we know who we came from. I feel a little sorry for my mother."

"She and Roy were on a collision course, Mom. Eden and I saw it all through the diaries. They had this fatal attraction for each other, and when opportunity came along, they took it. The pregnancy was a coincidence."

"But she never knew that," Alice Faye said. "In her mind, I was punishment for sleeping with Roy while she was married. 'A punishment' . . . isn't that what she called me?"

The hurt in her mother's eyes made Ciana wince. She slogged ahead with her explanation. "Great Grandpa Jacob hated Roy, so he and Olivia could have never married. She was a Beauchamp. Her path was predestined. And in those days girls like her didn't go against her family's wishes."

"I'd like to forgive her, but oh, the pain she caused me." Her mother sighed heavily, covered Ciana's hand with hers. "You are the best of the Beauchamps. You and Jon will make this place great again. I'm only sorry your daddy couldn't be here to give you away at your wedding."

"That's for *you* to do, Mom."

"Me?"

"And Eden my maid of honor. My family. Forever."

Ciana located a small chapel in Nashville and a minister willing to do the ceremony on short notice. The chapel was booked solid on weekends, but in the middle of the week, if they were willing to come in the late afternoon, Ciana and Jon could marry there. They invited no one except Angela, who flew up immediately. "We'll have a big reception at the Baptist church downtown later," Alice Faye announced. "Don't want Mama's only grandchild not having a reception befitting a Beauchamp." She and Ciana laughed over the inside joke.

Since the DNA results, Alice Faye had been a new person. Gone was her unhappiness, along with much of her anger. The change made Ciana happy. She was sorry Olivia had suffered all the years she did, but all was in the past now. She and Alice Faye and Eden held a diary-burning ceremony in the yard's fire pit late one evening. The flames blazed and danced and sent ashes of the distant past into the night sky. Eden called it a final sacrifice to the gods of unhappiness.

Ciana never did find a dress to her liking, not that she shopped much for one. On her wedding day she wore white denim jeans, a white cowgirl shirt with pearl buttons, and white leather western boots, no veil. For her bouquet she picked purple and yellow wild flowers and Alice Faye wound the stems with white ribbon and tulle. Garret pronounced her "gorgeous!"

Eden chose a flattering red dress for herself because she liked the way she looked in red. Jon wore jeans and a black, western-style dinner jacket. Alice Faye, wearing a pale blue dress, gave her daughter away while Angela wore lavender.

When Ciana stood at her mother's side in the chapel's narthex, she saw that the late afternoon sun streamed through high prism-cut windows, sending fractured slices of pure light downward. When she came down the chapel aisle, the look on Jon's face reflected what was in her heart. Joy. The ceremony was brief, and when Jon slipped Isabella's hand-forged and resized golden band on her finger, she told him with her eyes it was a perfect fit in every way.

They held a small dinner in a private dining room within the hotel where Jon had booked a honeymoon suite. The room glowed with candlelight and resonated with soft music. The next day, all would go their separate ways—Garret and Eden would hit the road in their camper and Alice Faye and Angela would return to Bellmeade to "keep the place running" until Jon and Ciana returned from a six-day honeymoon in Montana. Two weeks afterward, Ciana and Jon had booked a meeting with Hastings about the rebuild of their house.

The dinner broke up when Jon announced that he and his bride were going upstairs *without* the guests. Everyone laughed, and gathered their things. At the door Ciana hugged everyone, with her goodbye to Garret and Eden especially bittersweet. "You take care of her, you big Aussie."

"Always been my plan," Garret said with a flash of his infectious smile.

She wrapped her arms around Eden. Tears swam in her eyes. "You have a ball, little sister. And you stay in touch."

Little sister. Their birthdays were only a few months apart, but their sisterhood transcended genetics. "We won't be gone forever."

"Better not be." Ciana leaned closer. "I'm having Hastings build a special place for you at Bellmeade. Your own house."

Eden's mouth dropped open. "Ciana!"

Ciana shushed her. "*Your* home, Eden. No expiration date." She stepped away before they both broke down sobbing.

Upstairs Jon pushed open the door of the suite, insisted on carrying Ciana into the room. She protested. "I can walk."

"I can either pick you up or do the fireman's carry. You decide."

He was determined, so she relented, and he scooped her up into his arms and crossed the threshold. When he set her on the floor, she took in the suite. Impressive. On a linen-covered cart a champagne bucket held a fine vintage bottle with two crystal glasses beside it. Jon popped the cork and poured each of them a glass. Their gazes held as they sipped the sparkling wine together. The tiny bubbles tickled her nose. Beyond the cart and sitting area, she saw a doorway and a bed turned down and strewn with rose petals. A cliché, but she loved it.

She walked to the foot of the bed with Jon. "Your idea?"

"Not me. I'd have used alfalfa hay. I know what turns you on."

She stared at the bed, felt suddenly shy and nervous. He

had touched her intimately, but now it was different somehow. A ceremony, a holy blessing, two rings. Now they belonged to each other. She brushed aside the awkwardness, handed him her glass. Then she turned, spread her arms wide and flopped backward onto the bed. She laughed, flapped her arms, and sent the fragrant petals in all directions. Jon came to the side of the bed, looked at her, his gaze traveling the length of her body. The old familiar fire heated up inside her. "You just going to stand there looking?"

A sexy smile lifted the corner of his mouth. He removed his suit coat, then his shirt. In the softness of the single bedside lamp, his bare upper body glowed golden. She connected with his green eyes, began slowly unbuttoning her shirt, and scooting out of her jeans. He sat on the bed, removed her boots, then his. In no time clothing barriers vanished. He sat, unmoving, gazing at her body, almost with reverence. She raised her arms, an invitation that beckoned him to hold her. He leaned over, braced his hands on either side of her. The scent of roses hung in the air, and the light caught the glimmer of gold on her hand. She said, "I guess we're legal now, cowboy."

"That scare you?"

Her heart was beating so hard she thought he might hear it. "What do you think?"

Jon dipped to lightly kiss her. "I think we're a perfect match, pretty lady. I love you, Ciana Beauchamp."

She traced a finger along his jawline. "Don't you mean Ciana Mercer?"

He looked surprised. "I thought it was a tradition that Beauchamp women kept their family name. I'm all right with that."

She cupped his face with both hands, let go of a childhood promise. "Not all traditions are worth keeping."

A smile flitted over Jon's lips. "Hello, wife," he whispered.

She pulled him closer. Their bodies merged. And the two became one.

AUTHOR'S NOTE

I have always lived in the South. I love its rich history and warm hospitality. I especially love small Southern towns, the ones connected by two-lane back roads that meander through the open countryside. When I created the fictional town of Windemere, I infused it with my own experience. From the ballparks, high school football games, county fairs, and country music festivals to hearty breakfasts at the local diner and gathering on weekends and holidays for a barbecue or town social to life on the family farm. I made it a place where most everybody knows everybody else and it's not uncommon to leave your front door unlocked.

The Southern way revolves around building for tomorrow from the bricks of the past. I love spinning stories about people who feel like family and with whom you, the reader, would like to stay connected. So since you may want to keep in touch with the characters you've met in this novel and its companion, *The Year of Luminous Love*, there is a good chance you will see them passing on the streets of Windemere in future novels as well. I hope you'll sit a spell, drink some sweet tea, and enjoy your time with my extended family of characters.

ACKNOWLEDGMENTS

My thanks for agricultural expertise for this novel go to John Goddard, Loudon County, Tennessee, Agricultural Extension Agent; Bart Watson, Loudon County, Tennessee, Farm Bureau Agent; and Jim Farley, a dashing young insurance man, and Martha Farley, his wonderful wife.